Taken to Sky

Xiveri Mates Book 9

Elizabeth Stephens

Contents

Glossary

Centare *(cent-are-ay)*
No in Meero, the most common trading language; primary language of the Niahhorru

Eck *(eck)*
Common Eshmiri curse

Egama *(egg-ahm-uh)*
Giant-like warrior species characterized by olive green skin and one large eye

Eshmiri *(esh-meer-ee)*
Second largest group of space pirates; known for their short, stocky builds, laughter-like language, and fighting pits on the asteroid Evernor

Evernor *(evv-err-norr)*
Eshmiri-controlled asteroid known for trading and gambling and its rotational gladiator tournament

Hiannru *(he-ann-roo)*
Spear-like spikes that protrude from a Niahhorru male's spine

Hypha *(high-fuh)*
Cross-quadrant species characterized by orange skin, large, black eyes, and four fins growing out the sides of their faces

Kor *(kohr)*
Trading city located in the grey zone between Quadrants 4 and 5; ruled by the Niahhorru species commonly

referred to as space pirates; their leader is Rhorkanterannu

Krakaw *(craah-caw)*
No, in Eshmiri

Lemoran *(lehm-oh-rahn)*
Primary and native species of Lemora; known for their blocky, rocky builds and massive, dark grey horns

Lunar *(loo-narr)*
A unit of time measurement; approximately 1-1.5 Earth nights

Mok bir *(mock brr)*
Table game played with batons in which players attempt to throw batons at each other and block incoming batons; gambling is a common function of the game, as is cheating

Mok biz *(mock bzz)*
A more popular version of mok bir played with tokens rather than batons

Niahhorru pirate *(knee-ya-hoo-roo)*
Planet-less species; they operate the trading post of Kor and patrol and control most of the Grey Zone; are known for their technological prowess; characterized by grey skin mostly covered in a thick exoskeleton of armored plates, hiannru tines that protrude from the backs of their heads and spines, and silvery skeins that drop to cover their more sensitive eyes

Ontte *(aunt-tay)*
Yes in Meero, the most common trading language; primary language of the Niahhorru

Oosa *(ooh-sah)*
Species of Quadrant Eight; ruled by Reoran; large blob-like figures that illuminate from within whenever speaking or expressing emotion; extremely difficult to kill

Rekkaru *(wreck-are-oo)*
Cross-quadrant species characterized by small bodies, two arms and two legs, with thin, translucent wings

Rotation *(row-tay-shun)*
A unit of time measurement; approximately 3.5 Earth years

Shrov *(shrohv)*
Common Meero curse

Sky *(sky)*
A constructed and roving planet known for its technological prowess as well as for producing the most feared and infamous of killers in the known Quadrants and beyond, Sky assassins

Sky Assassins *(sky assassins)*
Modified by Sky Architects to be the most efficient killers in the world, they are cyber and bio-genetically engineered from predatory species and advanced technology, often against their wills; once taken by the

Sky and reprogrammed, assassins have no memoris of their past lives

Solar *(soh-lahr)*
A unit of time measurement; approximately 1-1.5 Earth days

Span *(span)*
A unit of time measurement; approximately 1 Earth hour

Tokens *(tokens)*
Credits are the common form of currency exchanged between Quadrants; credits are carried in various devices referred to as tokens; most commonly, tokens are made from yamar and shaped like black boxes, though more sophisticated models look like discs and are made of yeeyar

Yamar *(yeam-are)*
Yamar is a precursor to yeeyar, is a static non-biological power source, and is the common communication/ translation tool of the Eshmiri Reavers

Yeeshee *(yeeh-she)*
Yes, in Eshmiri

Yeeyar *(yeeh-yare)*
Yeeyar is an advanced power-source used by the Niahhorru pirates of Kor; it is a biological organism that can be melded with other static metals and glasses to create spaceships, payment discs and Niahhorru communication tokens

To my hybrid brothers and sisters,

Even though you may drift, you are not lost, and though
you may idle in the in between, you are not alone. Know
that here, there's an open seat for you at the werro table
between Miari and Ashmara, and a cold horn of hibi
waiting.

Always.

Five rotations ago…

1

Rook

"Rook, you have to throw your stone."

I frown hard enough it hurts my cheeks. "I don't want to throw it. You're going to win." My gaze sweeps the game board in front of us. Well, it isn't so much a game board as a game we made up. Azza's so good at making up games. I like to play all of them.

He laughs and his eyes meet mine and I feel myself get all warm. I don't know why. I'm jealous of his eyes — he knows that. All the Lemorans on our ship have eyes kind of like his. White with colors in the middle. The Lemorans' eyes have lots of colors and his are only a dark brown with a black dot in the middle. But still, his eyes are better than mine. I actually like them better than the Lemorans' eyes anyway.

But my eyes are just white, except when they're colorful. Color just moves across them like smoke! It's scary. I don't like the way it looks when I catch my reflection. And I don't like when they're colorful because then Azza makes fun of me. He knows exactly what I'm feeling, even when I don't. He understands the colors better than me because he sees them in my eyes often. I wonder what he sees now and close my eyes, trying to stop him.

"Don't do that. It's not fair!" I slam my fist on my knee and Azza reaches forward. He ruffles my white hair.

Our hairs are the same color, though. I like that. Even though there's lots of different kinds of beings on Golia Shuttle Two, no one has hair like we do. Bright white. The whitest white. Mine is curly and ends at my shoulders. His is straight and falls all the way to his knees. He doesn't cut it. I like that he doesn't cut it. It's pretty. Like his eyes. They're pretty, too. The prettiest.

"Just play, Rook." He smiles and I laugh when I see the gap in his teeth. He lost his first tooth last week. It looks silly.

The ridges in the brown side of his face suddenly pop with color and I squeal. "You! You! I…" I wish I knew what the colors meant, but I don't. He doesn't get colorful as often as I do. Right now, all I see in his brown forehead above his eyes are colors, mostly bright yellow, but I can't…I can't remember what that color means. Shoot. I can never remember…

He slaps his red right hand over the brown left side of his face so I can't see the colors there. Without the colors, he's the same brown color as me — that half of him is, anyway. I don't have the red parts. There are other red beings on the shuttle, but we're the only two that are that brown color. No one knows what species we are and that's okay, because we're the same species and we have each other. And everyone on the ship is nice to us, anyways.

I glance down at the board and see the stones I need to skip in order to collect his tokens. There's no way for me to skip them, though, not unless he totally biffs his next turn. He's won and we both know it, but I toss my stone at the kintarr crystal floor anyway. It shimmers pink, reactive to the stroke, when my green stone bounces off of it. I collect the two stones of his that I can and frown as he lifts his stone and then…drops it.

He tosses it at the floor, but he lets it stray way to the side. He can bounce a stone clear across the board if he wants, so I know he's letting me win again this time. "Hey! You're cheating!"

"Cheating? You won." He laughs, his half red, half brown face splitting at the seams.

My face is all brown, but I can feel it beam equally. "You let me win!"

"Centare, I didn't."

"Ontte, you did."

He rolls his eyes and rocks back on his butt. Mineria passes by the open door and snaps at us. "Aren't you two supposed to be studying with the other kits right now?" She shakes her head, her large black eyes blinking at us from the side. She is Niahhorru and really pretty, especially with all her arms. I wish I had four arms, too.

I get all hot and clutch Azza's stones in my hand. I look at him to answer.

"We uhh…" He smiles and doesn't say more.

Mineria huffs. "If you two would…" But before she can finish the sirens go off. Her eyes get all big. Her lower arms gesture at us. "Come!"

Azza grabs my hand at the same time that I reach for his. I forget about our game until I step on the rock that he threw. It hurts my foot because I'm not wearing shoes. "Are you okay?" he asks as we go out into the hall. There's so much going on out here. Everyone's out of their chambers. The colors in my eyes are so bright, they reflect off of his brown shoulder. Right now the light's all pink.

"I'm scared, Azza."

He nods and seeing him agree with me makes me feel better. Azza's always brave. If he's scared, that must mean being scared is okay.

"Don't be scared, kits. It'll be okay," Mineria says. She's holding each of our hands in one of hers and we're all moving down the hall until, all of a sudden, the whole ship lurches.

My scream gets like strangled in my mouth and I land on the floor, tangled up in Mineria's arms and Azza's legs. And then I see the male. At least...I think he's a male. He's got tentacles for legs and two big arms like a Voraxian would have, plus wings like a Rekkaru, only they're metal instead of the grey silky film the Rekkaru on our ship usually have. He's wearing all black and has some metal pieces on his legs and stomach. He's...doing something weird. He's holding something in his hand. Something I've never seen before. It's sharp and glittery. It's pretty.

"Rook, we should..."

"Kits, hide!" Mineria screams. She lunges to her feet and holds up her arms, but the male I don't recognize is bringing the glittery thing down against her hands...and he cuts them off. Two of them hit the ground and then so does her head when he cuts it.

Blasts fire behind us and in front of us. The ship is shaking again. Azza's hands are on mine and I'm crying when the male turns to attack someone else. It looks like Fallow — she's trying to fight him, but he cuts her, too. I think he's...I don't understand what he's doing. I don't want to understand, so I block it. I just focus on the sight of Azza's brown hand on my brown hand, our palms both a lighter color, streaked with lines. No one else has hands like ours. Not that we've met. It's the first time I've ever wondered why.

Azza's breathing hard and his long white hair is whipping in the breeze. Bodies are falling in the hall in front of us, two more creatures in the same black clothes going after them. We turn around, but we can't go back. There's more down the hall we came from.

I look at Azza and he's already looking at me. A door blasts open behind us and I see the kits like us gathered for school being grabbed by three more creatures in black. All of them have some partly silver skin. They're holding whips. They're whipping the kits. One of them looks up, but I don't know if she sees me because Azza's suddenly pulling me down the hall to the left.

There's too many bodies here, too much noise. "Here! Hide!" Azza opens up a panel in the pink-colored wall and shoves me in. I don't like that it's pink. It reminds me of fear and makes me afraid of what's about to happen, especially because it's just big enough for one. I panic when he slides the panel back into place, except he doesn't push it in all the way and I can still see out of it when he sneaks into a panel on the wall opposite from me.

Seeing him get inside the wall makes me feel better. I breathe and I don't cry. I'm proud I don't cry. He's safe. Azza's safe. Everything's going to be okay.

We've been traded to so many different species across so many different planets, but somehow, we've always managed to stay together. Azza's made sure of that. Sometimes it feels like he's a million rotations older than me. Like he's a real grown up.

But I remember when he lost his tooth. I laughed at him when he got embarrassed. And I remember that he's little. Just barely bigger than me. We're littler than the other orphans on this ship they say is a Lemoran safe haven for refugees. I don't know what that means, but I know we've always been littler than the others. I never liked that, but right now I wish we were even littler. If we were, then Azza could fit into this hole in the wall next to me. I wish he was next to me.

I can taste something bad in my mouth and I don't like it. I wipe my mouth with the back of my wrist and squeeze the stone in my hand, remembering its color. It's green. Green is for when I'm happy. I like green. Azza turns green sometimes in his brown cheek, too, and I like that. I like that. Even if he never turns green in his red cheek, he turns all the colors in his brown cheek. Because his brown cheek is the same color as my brown cheeks, except when the lights go off. I don't have lights in my cheek. I have lights in my eyes, but other than that, we're the same and as long as we're together everything will be okay…

It's quiet. Really quiet.

Azza doesn't come out though, so I don't come out… and then I hear it — them. Footsteps. They sound *strange*, those steps, but they're big and heavy, that's for sure. I can also hear the fluttering of wings. I gasp — it's the one that *killed* Mineria — and I jerk. I don't mean to, but I can't stop it. I…I let the stone drop out of my fist. It hits the ground and sounds so, so loud. Oh nob. Nob nob nob. I want to grab for the stone because it makes me feel safe, but I can't move. I can't look away from the thing in the hall that killed Mineria. It's turning, looking to kill me now.

I know it's going to find me. I don't move. I can't. I'm frozen like the bodies in the hallway. The thing with wings has blood all over it. It's so scary. I'm so scared. I've never been scared like this. It's coming closer, looking at the wall. It sees the panel I'm hiding it. Can it see me? I think it can. It reaches out a long arm that doesn't look like it fits with the rest of its body parts and…

All of a sudden, the wall where Azza's hiding bursts open. He explodes out of it like a…like a…like an explosion and hits the thing in its wing, but its wing doesn't tear, even when Azza gets it with his red hand, which has nails that are extra sharp. It turns around and grabs Azza and I move onto my knees and press my hands against the panel because it's going to take him and I'm going to go, too, because I don't want to be away from him. We'd always be together. That was our promise. Always.

"Don't, Rook!" His legs kick into the air as the male in black grabs him around the waist and carries him down the hall on strange, half metal, half tentacled legs. "Stay!"

With my hand on the panel in front of me, I don't.

With my hand on the panel in front of me, I stay.

I want to go. I'm too scared to stay here alone, but Azza said not to to. I'll always trust Azza. Always.

The ship gets loud and then gets quiet and the voices finally go away. And I still don't move. I don't do anything. I wait for Azza to come back. I hope Azza comes back soon because I'm thirsty. I'm hungry, too. I hope Azza's okay and that the guy in black gives him something to eat. I hope he takes him with the other kits and that maybe, they're not so bad and they come back and find me. I hope he comes back and finds me.

But no one comes. No one comes for a solar. Maybe more. I…pee my pants. It's so embarrassing…but Azza said to stay and I don't want to miss him when he comes back.

Darkness.

It gets cold. Another solar passes. I go to sleep.

Darkness.

I'm so cold…

I open my eyes at the sound of the panel in front of me bending and then popping free of the wall completely. "Azza?" My voice croaks. My throat works. My pants are stiff and I'm ashamed. I hope he can't smell it. I'm not a kitling. I'm a kit like him, big and strong and brave. *But not brave enough to go out and help him when they took him away…* Panic grips me and I know the creature that looks down at me can see it in my eyes when I look up at him. He isn't Azza. He isn't in black, either.

"You're not Azza," I whisper and I push myself onto my hands and knees and back into the corner. There isn't anywhere for me to go. I'm a small kit, but this hole in the wall is smaller.

I blink at the light from the glowing ball that floats behind him. I have to blink a lot in order to see him clearly. I…don't recognize him and that makes me scared. I can see pink lights from my eyes shimmering in the dark between us.

The creature isn't one I've seen before and I've seen a lot of creatures with Azza when we were traded on Kor. But this one is new. He's not really tall, but he's got a lot of muscles and he's got a blaster on his belt and another bigger one on the strap on his shoulder. His head is small and his eyes are real big. His mouth is scary because he's got sharp teeth and he's smiling at me. I think he's gonna eat me and I start to cry.

"You're not Azza…"

He starts to laugh at me and that makes me cry harder. Another one that looks just like him comes up to him and his ear flaps twitch. Then there's two more. They're gonna eat me for sure…

They're all laughing when the one in front reaches out his hand. I wince, but he doesn't grab me. He just smiles and laughs again and I don't understand why. "Azza?" I say.

He shakes his head and gestures at his friends. "Eshmiri."

"Eshmiri?" I try to repeat, but my tongue doesn't work right. I can't breathe good. I'm tired and I feel sick. I want to go to bed. But I've never slept in a room without Azza in it.

They giggle together some more and one of them says, "Ashamari?" He points at me. I'm confused.

"Eshmiri?" Maybe I'm saying it wrong. "Eshmiri," I try again, but they just giggle. Except…maybe it's *words*. I wonder if they're talking to each other in giggles when one of the creatures nods at the other. What a funny language.

Finally, he repeats, "Ashmara." And points at me.

I point at my chest. "Me? Ashmara?" I'm confused.

He nods. They all nod. They all laugh and giggle. "Ashmara." The one in front points at his chest. "Tintin." He holds his hand out lower, right in front of my nose.

I glance into the hall around him, but there's no more creatures in black. There's just…bodies. The smell makes me close my eyes. I focus on Tintin's hand. It's brown, not like mine though. *Only Azza's hand was brown like mine.* And they took him. *I let them take him.*

Tintin's hand is lighter brown and kinda hairy. There's long golden-brown hairs all along the back of his hand and knuckles. He's got four fingers on his right hand and a different number on his left. His fingers are bigger than mine and very fat. They look silly. He doesn't seem to notice I smell like my own pee. He's just smiling. Maybe, his teeth aren't so bad.

"Rook," I tell him, pointing at my chest as I take his hand and slowly try to stand up on my own, but I can't.

My knees hurt and I start to cry, but Tintin and his friends gather around me and hold onto my arms. They pat my head and my shoulders as they prop me up between them.

"Ashmara," Tintin says and I sniffle deep and look up into his black eyes. He doesn't have the white parts like Azza does or like Lemorans do, but his eyes…they still look kind. "Ashmara *safe*," he says in Meero, the pirate language, but he doesn't seem to speak it so good.

"Azza safe?" I ask him.

He just pats my head again and says, in Meero, "Come. Ashmara safe with us."

Now…

2

Jerrock

"More."

The Architect before me responds not in gestures or in words but in sensations. All of them are *pain*. Pain is good, but it is not enough to erase my failure.

As the burning fades from my limbs and my stalyx-infused bones settle, I say, "More."

They repeat the process.

"More."

The Architect and I continue this excruciating loop until my vision begins to fade in my remaining biological eye — a nuisance. I would have it removed, but its organic quality has come in handy in disguising myself. Some can see through the matter displacement shield and those that can always look first to the eyes. *She always looks first into my eyes. No matter how skillfully I shield my appearance, she always sees me. At least, she has ever since that first time.* I do not think of that.

"More." My voice comes out scratched, charged, a roar. The Architect is unconcerned by the change in my tone, likely interpreting it as pain — or rather, misinterpreting it. It is not pain. Pain is inconsequential. However, what I feel now is feeling itself. To feel is to be

vulnerable. And among the emotions that can derail even the most sage and skilled, rage is among the most dangerous. Rage causes mistakes. I am fortunate only that the Architects know nothing of those that I have made again and again and again.

"More."

As ionic pulses flare through my body, causing the sinuous muscle to seize and my thoughts to scatter just as rapidly as the yeeyar that contains them, the Architect flits to the door. Its hand, if you can call it that, disappears into the black yeeyar wall, registering something in the yeeyar controls I cannot sense as the next charged wave pulls through me. Though I may be able to lock and unlock yeeyar manacles and open and close doors, the Architects would be fools to grant full yeeyar permissions to all of their assassins. *They are fools to have made me an assassin in the first place.* I have failed time and time again. Pain lances my next treacherous thought and I lose vision in my biological eye entirely.

The Architect releases me and I slump forward against my chest restraints. The door before the Architect opens and they disappear through it soundlessly. The only sounds to be heard at all are my breath and the wind as it crashes against the outside of the tower. It is so constant, it sounds like waves.

I focus on the sound of the wind until the pain fades enough for me to be able to move my arms. I use my stalyx and yeeyar-reinforced arm to release the chest restraint. I stand, irritated at how quickly the sensations of pain fade. Pain is the only thing that feels grounding and, for too long now, I've been unstable.

But the Architects created an assassin with endlessly terrible abilities, even some that they themselves perhaps do not know. Because even though we speak with our thoughts, there are thoughts that I have managed to keep from them. *Hesitation. Failure. Treason.* They do not know, the Architects. They cannot. If they knew of my treason, I would be decommissioned.

I should decommission myself. I *would*, except for the fact that I continue to hold one outstanding contract. All of the others I have completed and I have declined to take on any more. Not until this is finished. I refuse to allow her to live. She *cannot* live. She is too powerful. There is something about her. I don't understand it. She is my greatest failing, my only failing, and I do. Not. Fail. I am Sky's most feared assassin. I am their greatest creation, a gift from the Architects to Death itself, and still...

She lives.

I killed an assassin for her. The hesitation in my next step brings me to the door, but not through it. I think about what I am up against, this...pathetic excuse for an opponent that has become my greatest enemy yet.

I draw up her specifications in my yeeyar sight and read over her strengths and weaknesses again, for the thousandth time. Where it says weaknesses, the list is long. Where strengths are listed, there is only one word: None.

And yet this creature with no notable strengths finds herself in the rare position of being my nemesis. The only one I've ever had, as all other creatures to challenge me have fallen like waves. The fall is inevitable. And yet...I remain uncertain of my ability to kill this one. So, I have safeguards in place. Safeguards that will ensure that should she defeat me and somehow manage to introduce me to Death, there will not be an assassin who does not know of it. I will send the full force of the Sky for her so that even if I am not the one to kill her, I will ensure her death, nonetheless.

I take a deep, fortifying breath and will the door to open.

A brutal wind crashes against my body. It is violent, so much so that I have seen it take lesser beings from the platform to crash into the world far below. I remain standing through it, however, white hair whipping around my face as I look out over the other Sky towers rising up into the pale purple sky. The black towers look like the jagged shards of screa cliffs against such brightness. It hurts my biological eye.

As I watch, sweeping gales of orange wind climb through the purple and wrap around the tallest towers' tips. I am not on one of the tallest towers now. Those are reserved for the experiments. As I was, once.

Now, I am perfect.

Almost.

My ship sits on the edge of the platform. There are no railings, only black yeeyar shifting beneath my feet. Below, all the way at the bottom, are the slums of Sky where wretches native to this planet scavenge for the few resources that are left.

So far below I cannot even see them from here, but my hearing is excellent. I can just make out the sounds of screaming and lesser beings succumbing to pain. They attempt to rebel, these creatures, upon occasion. But they are no match for the Architects and their assassins. I do not understand it, their will to defy Death. Death is king. You either exist on his right hand, as I do, or you bend the knee to him. There is nothing else.

But her. She bends to nothing. Only that isn't true, is it? She bends to muuir. And I cannot even manage to catch her when she's addicted to the vile, mind-addling substance.

The thought of muuir makes me restless. *Angry.* I fail to comprehend my feelings towards the substance. I *should* think favorably of muuir. It slows her down, makes her easier to entrap. She has to make many stops at ports and pleasure planets in the Grey Zone to acquire more of the illicit drug. I wonder which of them she has chosen now.

On board my ship, I power on the locator, fingers moving deftly over the yeeyar panel before me. The pain I invited at the hands of the Architects has made the fingers of my red hand stiff. I flex them and watch grey yeeyar rise from the control panel up to eye level where it turns and twists, dancing with reds and yellows and blues.

To anyone else, it would appear as if the yeeyar was simply moving in random patterns, rising up and falling from the control panel. But in my yeeyar eye, I see everything, the full span of the Quadrants and, among them, a single beacon that's illuminated, even though it shouldn't be.

My arms lurch and I grab hold of the edges of the table. Her shields are down. The Eshmiri are known for their shield technology and the last time she lowered her shields, it was to lure me into a trap. It was only partly successful. I was entrapped, but not for long, and now that I know her ploy, I do not believe she would attempt the same ruse twice. She would not be so careless. Perhaps, under the influence of muuir she might be, but members of her crew wouldn't. They are Eshmiri and none of them are as careless as she is. No one in the cosmos is so careless.

So why is her tracking beacon on and why are her shields off?

Perhaps she believes me to be as careless as she. Or worse, not careless, but arrogant. Hm. Would I willingly walk into her trap twice? I should not. I should wait for her to move. Now that I have located her ship's beacon, it will not be hard to track, even with her shields, particularly as she is currently in the remote reaches of the Grey Zone where few other trading ports will be available to her to source more muuir. Where is she…

I study the star chart in closer detail and my toes curl in my boots. She's on the Tiringdam pleasure planet. My mind flashes. Memories revisit me that I have fought to bury in my subconscious where light and shame cannot find them. My ship separates from the platform under directions I did not consciously give. My subconscious mind is active and it should not be. It should not even exist. Yet…

My ship takes off and I do not redirect it.

3

Jerrock

Her screeching, slurred voice does not bother me. It does not bother me at all. "And when the ship…docks…at the port of Pianzaaaaa…all of the sinners sayyyy…."

"Grab the hibi! Hide your tokens! You're here in Tiringdam where legs and bars are always open!" The crowd's shouted-sung response doesn't bother me. It doesn't bother me in the slightest.

I have Ashmara the Eshmiri's ankle trapped in my red hand. In my red hand. I should be holding her with my stalyx hand, but I'm not. I should be…but I'm not.

Her skin is warm — I'd go so far as to call it hot — against my rough palm. Her skin isn't soft, either, her leg hairs prickle my hand. While not necessarily soft, she's still smooth. Tender. Easy to tear through. I recall how easily my blaster fire tore through her hand when she reached for the muuir on board the Sky ship. It was there that I'd detained her, where she should have met Death, but didn't. Instead, I offered him another in her place. *Failure.* And she lived. I will not make the same mistake.

It took me just under a Sky solar to arrive on the Tiringdam pleasure planet and, once here, I discovered her location right away. She'd been singing loudly as I approached her, reclined on a floating divan, drinking amidst a disorderly cluster of species all equally intoxicated.

She is wildly inebriated, her consumption of whatever liquids only the start. She's got a muuir patch behind her right ear and her eyes glow a hazy yellow-grey-brown that, in Voraxian ridges, reflects illness, only her eyes fill with spots of other colors, mostly blues and greens. Contentment and amusement. The occasional dash of violet lust. Her eyes flare more frequently with purple when she looks up at me. I am disgusted by it.

She's on drugs.

My fingers twitch around her ankle and she kicks her other leg into the air as she begins another refrain of the same song. She's been singing it over and over again, changing the words each time, unable to remember them. Her body drags on the filthy ground, white hair catching colorful and sticky substances and becoming stained by them. Mostly black, a little red, a glob of orange, green, blue. The blue is definitely Oosa and I do not think she'd appreciate knowing what it is. Disgusting. *She* is disgusting.

"...can't be found on the map, but once you find it, it's a trap..."

"The pleasures of Pianzaaaaaa..." comes the chorus, shouted by beings who line the gang planks.

Water thrashes below the synthetic platforms, an endless maze of waterfalls whose gravity cause water to rush up the stones near the center of the island before crashing back down the outer island. Nothing lives within the water. Nothing natural exists on this planet besides the water. The only life exists on the platforms that we walk now. And all of it is foul.

Not one of the beings here is sane or sober enough to care that I am here, an assassin in their midst. Not even Ashmara seems to care, even though she's a token's throw from her inevitable doom. She never does. It's as if she knows something I do not. It's as if she trusts me. Perhaps, she is friends with Death.

The thoughts ravage my mind and I focus on the sound of water falling below so as not to kill everyone on this platform when their collective singing picks back up. A Voraxian pair hails their horns at Ashmara as I drag her past their low, nest-like seats and she laughs wildly, deep and from her belly. Her eyes dance with blue-green mirth as she stretches her fingers towards the Voraxian female. The female bends down from her nest to hand Ashmara her cup and Ashmara drinks from it — *tries* to drink from it, but ends up spilling most of the liquid on her face, neck and chest.

"Whoo!" She tosses her cup aside. It hits a Rekkaru in the wings and they turn and toss a mok biz token down at her. It's aimed fairly accurately at her face. I twitch, watching the token sail through the air in slow motion. My hand. My perfect hand. My perfect hand behaves imperfectly. It launches a small ion blast without my telling it to — no, with me telling it expressly *not* to — and collides with the token, dissolving it midair.

Ashmara doesn't seem to notice. She laughs and shouts up at the Rekkaru, "Is that the best you got, heelee?" She uses a term of endearment that makes the Rekkaru smile.

"You look like you have your hands full, reaver," the Rekkaru replies, flashing an uncertain gaze to me.

"What are you talking about? I'm having the time of my life." She laughs as I drag her all the way through the

Pianza Pleasure Port of Tiringdam, down the ramp leading to the lower pleasure rooms where mostly aquatic creatures are serviced, across the rickety wooden bridge that leads to the docks, all the way to the largest hangar where ships remain parked in no discernable order. Chaos is the only constant outside of the known Quadrants. Chaos is what I have come to expect from those on my list. But right now, as I look around, I do not expect this.

My ship is not where I left it.

What has she done?

With my yeeyar eye, I search for its signature, finding traces of it in between two gold ships from Quadrant One — where I left it. I go to the spot, dragging Ashmara with me. I can scent the presence of several other species, Eshmiri most strongly. I glance over my shoulder at Ashmara, lying on the ground, ignoring me entirely in favor of whatever high has dragged her down.

Does she truly think she can trap me again?

The urge to ask her is strong, though I don't know why. She isn't coherent enough to give me a reply, let alone entrap me, and I have no intention of torturing information out of her. I have only one intent. To decommission her. In private.

I follow the scent trail the Eshmiri left to the edge of the platform. The flimsy metal barrier has been broken. I step up to the edge and look down into waters that shine an iridescent white and a cutting blue. There, scattered across yellow rocks, are traces of yeeyar, but traces only. The water rushes too hard and too fast to identify any larger pieces of what was once my ship.

I turn and follow the Eshmiri scent trail to the center of the hangar, and then right. I continue to follow it easily — it's been laid on thick — until I reach what I know to be Ashmara's ship. The putrid thing is larger than many of the others crowded beside it and looks thirty rotations older. Made of rusted metal, the thing emits steam from a right exhaust valve. The fact that it even has such valves is deplorable. It smells like oil. Ancient oil. And it's leaking. Did her Eshmiri horde think to discard my ship and take to the skies? Did their ship break before they could? Or is that what they want me to believe? This trap is so clumsy as to almost give me pause, if it is even a trap at all.

That I am not certain guts me.

I glance back at Ashmara to find her white eyes focused on mine. My entire chest ripples beneath the slick black fibers that cover it. She smiles. Her teeth are white. The bottom row of her teeth are crooked, the front two right teeth slightly overlapping.

She's wearing Eshmiri rags and, because of how I've been dragging her, they've lifted to show her stomach. Her skin is a dark brown color whose closest comparison can be made to the skin tone of a Rekkaru's grey or a Lemoran's brown hue. The color pulls at something in my subconscious, but I cannot access it and that, more than anything, makes her dangerous. I have corrupted my own yeeyar to be able to keep information from the Architects, yet I did not discard the information for myself. The memories…

I pull back from them and, at the same time, pull back from the feeling that there is something inside of me, even deeper than that corrupted yeeyar, still shielding itself. I cannot see…and I do not feel.

Facts are superior to feelings in every possible way, so I tell her one truth, "I will kill you this solar."

The sound of my voice is odd. I have not spoken to anyone in this form in rotations. With the Architects, I communicate solely through the yeeyar that binds us. Otherwise, my matter displacement shields allow me to speak in other tones resembling the creatures whose likenesses I wear. The sound of my voice now is…

It does not bother me. Neither does her response.

"Did you like my singing?" She blinks slowly and tries to prop herself up on her elbows. I yank her forward by the ankles and she slumps back, boneless. She is barely living. How has it been so difficult to kill one already so close to Death?

The ramp of her ship has been lifted shut, but I go to the metal block guarding the control panel and quickly flick it free. I extend my stalyx wrist towards the black and copper-colored cables and a series of needles appear where veins should be. I stab them into the center of the control box and allow the yeeyar to work. It takes less than the span of a heartbeat to break into her ship. Her heartbeat, not mine. Her heart beats so slowly. An effect of the drugs? Or does she truly not have any fear of me or Death?

As the metal monstrosity screams its way open, I find my lips forming an unfamiliar frown. Steam wafts from the darkness and smells of sweat and spoiled food as I make my way on board, dragging Ashmara behind me. I leave the door open as I glance around, the scent of Eshmiri thick yet the sight of Eshmiri distinctly absent.

I kick aside odd objects and metal boxes, bins full of discarded equipment and weapons that look like they haven't worked in eons, as well as too many empty bottles of fermented hibi, as I make my way to the control room. It sits at the front of the ship behind a large and murky bay portal window in a defunct style. Most modern ships take after the Niahhorru and Lemoran styles, where controls are located in the center of the control room and there are no windows as the ships themselves are either partly or wholly translucent.

Yet, this is not a modern ship. Six seats occupy the control room. They were organized once — I can see it in the scorched and charred markings on the floor where the control seats were once placed, but they've been moved. Now, they sit scattered in what looks like random order, four facing forward, one facing right, another facing left. One is tilted at an angle. Another is missing its left arm.

I stand in the center of the cluster and drop Ashmara's legs. She doesn't bother to move, but lies there with her white teeth shining up at me and her white eyes swirling with indecisive emotion that causes me a small measure of distraction. In the color wheel, I catch a flash of tan, a color that I know to Voraxians means pain, which is unusual as I haven't touched her.

I open my mouth. She parts her lips. "Azza," she whispers and my mind fires with confusion, my subconscious rising like the tides of the waters far below before crashing down with just as much violence. What *is* this word? Why does she call me by it? Wait — what did she just say?

"Azza!" She shouts this word again, but this time she shouts it as if it were a fist, where before she spoke it as a caress.

A latch opens in the floor that an Eshmiri reaver pops his head through. He stabs me in my biological leg through my black pant leg, a fact only made possible by the needle he uses. It's sturdy but remarkably thin.

I point my stalyx arm at the creature but Ashmara, in a feat of swiftness that I had not thought possible with how intoxicated she is, rolls her body on top of his. I fire, tearing a wound across her right ribs. I've grazed her, the majority of the ion blast from my wrist tearing a hole through the floor beneath her rather than through her spine, where I'd been aiming. I'd been aiming at her spine, just like on the Sky ship I'd been aiming at her head. In the end, I shot my own fellow assassin, instead. I missed. I failed. I can't seem to hit her beyond delivering superficial wounds.

Frustration that I have only felt in front of this pathetic adversary, my inebriated nemesis, rises like a swelling tide in my chest. It causes me to hesitate. I shouldn't have.

A panel opens in the wall before me and I fire into it, but it's empty. Several other panels open, each with the same intent to distract. Combined with my previous hesitation, their efforts are met with success and when a panel opens above my head, I do not expect an Eshmiri to fall out of it on top of me and stab me in the side of the neck.

I fling him off of my body to the screech of a whistle blowing. I look down and find Ashmara rolled onto her back, a crude whistle that was dangling from a string around her neck now in her mouth. It must have been tucked into her Eshmiri rags — robes. I hadn't seen it. If I had, I would have thought little of it. And that would have been my mistake. Another of so many I've made with her.

She blows air into it madly. The high-pitched sound has no effect on my ears, but I am nonetheless destabilized. How did she...

Fury grips me. Crude, pathetic technology. Weak, disorganized Eshmiri. A drunk hybrid of unknown origin. And yet, their inventiveness has unseated me. Whatever device was inserted into my neck is connected to the other that was inserted into my leg and, when Ashmara blows on her rusted little whistle — the kind a kitling might use — charged vibrations run between the two points and cause the stalyx in my body to vibrate uncontrollably. I lose mobility in the silver, stalyx half of my body, but I refuse to be undone by this band of fools and the muuir addict leading them.

I lunge for her on my biological leg and grab her throat with my red arm. I lift her from the ground and it is effortful in ways I do not like, now that my stalyx limbs have been deadened, leaving my left arm and leg to drag just as she once did on the metal and wooden planks of Tiringdam. I fight through the agony of the devices at work and I squeeze Ashmara's skinny neck until the sound of her whistle cuts off. The stalyx side of my body regains sensation. My yeeyar muscles ease.

"Azza," Ashmara whimpers, blinking at me with nothing but tan and blue in her eyes. Pleasure. Pleasure and pain. She reaches out and touches my jaw. Her fingers are rough and electrifying. What…what technology is this?

I grab her hand, turning it over as I search for the source of the electricity between us. I find none.

"Azza, look at me."

I do. My thoughts are destabilized. I feel my mission sliding off the edge of a shelf just as a second needle pricks me in the side of my neck. I see the rush of excitement reflected in Ashmara's eyes in shades of silver light and I know…

I drop her. She lands in a crouch, looking lithe and lethal, her silver eyes never leaving mine.

I know…

I fall against one of the command chairs — the one with the broken arm. I crash through the other, wood and metal and wire shattering beneath my weight. The yeeyar in my mind fights for control against the blackness invading it. That swell of subconsciousness surges up and up, higher and higher, pressing against its cage.

I don't break the line of her gaze, but watch her rise to stand above me as I hit the floor and I know…

As the drunk, drug-addicted Eshmiri reaver hybrid slinks towards me with a look of concern in her eyes… I know that I have lost.

4

Ashmara

"It worked." Tintin looks at me like he can't believe it.

"It worked." Gibli claps his hands.

Hunhun bounces on the balls of his feet. "It worked!"

I shout, "It worked!"

"It worked! It worked! It worked!" Retro starts to jump up and down.

Luzu bursts into laughter. "It worked."

And lastly, there's Uuni, who stares around at the rest of us, aghast. "Wow. I can't believe it."

I can't believe it. I give Jerrock's extended leg a good kick but he doesn't react. His foot flops to the side and his chin lolls down, tucking against his chest. White hair spreads over the right, leather-covered half of his torso, underneath which I know he's still Drakesh. They let him keep some of his own skin, but the rest...*the human bits...*

My whole body tightens, clenching at the memory, the dream, the nightmare. I scratch the muuir patch on the back of my neck and stagger a little bit, wanting to add another beneath it, but knowing I don't need it. I drank enough to calm my nerves even more than the muuir already had. It's getting less effective. I've started to have to use its crystal form, take multiple patches at once, or add harder stuff into the mix in order to settle the nightmares and the dreams and the memories. But it's all been worth it. The plan came together. It worked.

"It worked," Uuni echoes, stepping up to Jerrock's other side and poking at his stalyx arm.

The shimmery silver fingers twitch and we all pull blasters out of our robes simultaneously. I move so fast, I stagger backwards into Tintin, who shoves forward, pushing me up against Luzu, who pushes me back. I waffle between them for a while, my vision a little tricky to hold onto given the sheer staggering quantity of hibi I drank, but when I come to, everything's still and steady.

"It worked," I say on a chuckle, repeating the common refrain just for the eck of it.

Nodding picks up all around. A couple of my crew start to chuckle with me and then we're all laughing wildly as we fan out around Jerrock, then jockey for position at his limbs because nobody wants to grab his stalyx arm or his head.

Letting his head dangle, I do the noble thing and take it upon myself to heave him up by the stalyx arm. He weighs as much as an ecking hevarr and we all chuckle again, or rather, keep chuckling as we lift him until he's hovering just above the floor.

"Now what?" Gibli asks, looking at me. How should I know? I got us this far. I had exactly eck all for plans after this. *I didn't think we'd make it this far. By now, I kinda thought we'd all be dead, Jerrock by our hand — this isn't exact science — and us by his. Both. Somehow I thought it'd be both.*

"To the med bay?" Retro offers with a shrug.

Panic blitzes me, but I focus on the muuir coursing through my bones, the booze enhancing it. I smile like my heart isn't about to beat out of my chest — *maybe I did take too much muuir.* My grip is sweaty around his slick metallic wrist. I nod once and chuckle for good measure. "To the med bay."

We waddle together, carrying Jerrock's heavy as ecking eck body between all seven of us and we laugh as we trip over junk and crash between the walls. The whole experience makes me think back to our latest exploit — tearing apart the ship of a Quadrant Five warlord who'd just taken over an Eshmiri reaver ship with the intent of enslaving all those on board. We freed them and some of them even joined our crew.

Retro is one of them. He's good Eshmiri. A good reaver. Good with the maps. I'll ask him to navigate us to a safe place in the depth of space where we won't be interrupted. Last I checked, he and Hunhun had already thought of a good place, near to some dark, abandoned planet outside the Quadrants and outside the Grey Zone where we can spend the three solars it'll take to extract Azza from Jerrock.

That's how long it took for us to free Manila… I chew on my lower lip nervously. But then, we had a team. A Walrey healer, a Voraxian expert on all things Sky, and a Niahhorru female called Yeftra, an expert in yeeyar and a harvester at that. Now, it's just us. The team I paid to help extract Manila trained me and my Eshmiri family again and again. I know we *can* do this. But…will we?

We won't know until we're finished and he wakes up after the operation. I only hope that my supply takes us that far — not my supply of ionine, of course. That's the substance necessary to disentangle yeeyar from blood and flesh and nerve endings, disconnecting him from the Sky home world, and I have a ship's worth of the stuff. Literally. A ship's worth. We had to sell our last ship in order to get it. Krakaw, I'm worried about *my* supply.

I think about the weight of the muuir in my pocket as we reach the medbay doors, grateful I've got plenty with me — at least enough for us to make it through the three solars it will take to reprogram Jerrock and a few solars more, long enough for us to stop over at the nearest port after all this is done and Azza's back. *But what if it takes longer?*

Krakaw. I packed enough, I'm sure of it. I usually stash enough muuir to last me a lunar's turn. I shake my head, refusing to allow thoughts of muuir to throw me into a panic. I've been…it's been along ecking time that I've been waiting for this moment.

We slide him onto a cot in the medbay. The only cot. I feel hands on my side as I stand over Jerrock and I notice Tintin and Gibli affixing a cauterizer to my wound. Huh. I didn't even registered that I'd been hit. I can't feel it at all. I can't feel any pain in my extremities. Only bliss.

I worry a little about operating on him with so much muuir and hibi in me, then I slap another patch on. Eck it. Besides, without it, I'd have the shakes too bad to operate at all.

"I can't believe it worked," Gibli says.

"That was the easy part." I smile at him. "Now, for the fun part."

Six solars later…

5

Ashmara

"Is he awake?"

"What do you think?"

"I'm not sure…"

"Did you use the ionine gun correctly?"

"We watched the video a thousand times, but maybe…"

"I practiced a thousand times…" I hiss in response to their criticism. We're all tired. We're all drained. We've been awake for six solars and lunars, carefully injecting ionine into Jerrock's yeeyar veins. Well, I've been awake all six solars. The rest of the crew has managed to sleep in shifts. I don't need sleep, though. Who needs sleep when they've got muuir? Only problem is that this wasn't supposed to take this long… I'm gonna have to ration soon if I want to maintain my current muuir high, which I fully intend to, but I don't wanna ration.

Jerrock doesn't like the muuir. I have a feeling he doesn't, anyway. He shot the muuir out of my hand last time he and I and muuir were all in the same room. I'd been ecking furious. But that was Jerrock. This — this right here? — this is Azza. Azza always indulged me.

I smile at the thought, slap on another patch and shake my head, my mind firing with fresh waves of euphoria and concentration that help me to avoid going cross-eyed. "He had more of that gunk in him than Manila, that's all."

My crew all nod their heads in agreement. Tintin claps his hands together. They're stained in the black, expelled yeeyar that Jerrock's been vomiting up and sweating out — another grizzly part of the process that Manila went through, too. But why did hers go so much faster?

"Yeeshee, that must be it." Gibli places his hand on my shoulder and gives it a gentle squeeze. I smile at him, knowing that he, of all Eshmiri, can see straight through me. "You should sleep."

He's right. I know that. But I don't think I can. I start to shake my head when Retro shouts, "Look! He's opening his eyes — well, eye."

"Finally," I exhale in a rush. I edge around the cot, pushing past Luzu and Hunhun so that I'm standing next to Uuni — Uuni, who's got a blaster pointed at Jerrock's skull. I tut at him. "Put that down."

I lean over his body, blocking out the orange light above so that he's cast in shadow. "Azza?" I speak on a wobble, trying the name out tentatively, worried that he won't remember it.

And worried that he will…

His face twists, his black-lined lips slackening, then pursing. His nostrils flare. His red eyelid twitches and lifts to reveal a brown pool inside a white pool with a black pinprick in the middle. The black dot expands, becoming larger and then narrower as he focuses on my face.

His yeeyar eye is still active, but there's no more red. Just blacks and greys, no longer connected to the Sky home port. The yeeyar in his eye starts to shift and I smirk, "Azza, you in there? How's it feel to be out from under the Sky's ecking mind con..."

He lunges at me, moving fast and breaking through the iron ion chains latched around his wrists, anchoring him to the bed. A blast fires, but Jerrock chops his hand against Uuni's neck, taking him down. Manila was sluggish coming out of her assassin state, but Jerrock leaps off of the cot, landing behind me in the open doorway of the med bay, his eyes alert and wild, muscles threaded with tension, expression a grim thing.

I scramble for the activator hanging around my neck and bring it to my lips. I blow and blow and blow and Jerrock falls to the ground, half debilitated from the two yeeyar traps we plugged into his neck and ankle — thank the stars Tintin suggested we leave them in when I wanted to retract them. And even though I'm blowing as hard as I can and he should be down for the count, his red hand still claws at the floor, his black claws carving deep grooves in the metal as he drags himself forward.

His eye blazes. The yeeyar in his other eye swirls, the black ink flashing against the flat, grey socket maniacally, terrifyingly. His nostrils flare and spittle flies from his lips. *"What have you done?"* he hisses, tossing Retro and Hunhun aside as they charge at him.

"I freed you, you ungrateful ecking..." I scramble backwards, my adrenaline thumping in my veins as he reaches my foot. He grabs hold of my ankle and squeezes hard enough to break it. He's shaking. I can't catch my breath.

"I set up…a failsafe…in case I couldn't kill you…to disperse your contract to *every*…Sky assassin… They are coming for you, Rook… What did you do? You *fool!*" he groans once, long and loud, sounding like he's in pain — and that's right before Gibli steps up behind him with a huge pipe and thwacks him over the head.

His metal skull hits the metal floor with a thunk. My heart…eck…my heart. The muuir slowing down my pulse can't cope. And it's not because he just told me that every cold-blooded killer in Sky's arsenal is now out for my head, but because of what else he said.

What he called me.

He called me Rook.

We're all breathing hard. Otherwise, silence reigns in the med bay. Tintin is the first to break it. He chuckles, "So, did it work?"

They all look to me, but I've got no idea what to say, so I settle for "Eck." And then I throw another patch on to mask my excitement for him to wake up. Because when he does, he'll be Azza and Azza will be calm and loving and Azza will forgive me for everything. Everything.

6

Jerrock

Ordinarily, a brick to the skull would have little effect on me, but with the largely botched and only somewhat genius way the reavers disconnected the yeeyar from my system, I struggle to recuperate. My body and mind are fighting, ever fighting against the yeeyar molecules lingering in my nerves and in my bloodstream, desperate to find and return to the planet that commands them.

But there is no more planet. There are no commands. The contracts that existed in my mind have been, not erased, but burned. I can still see their ashes though the contents are gone. And what's worse is that I have no more anchor. The tie that bound me to the Sky planet has — poof — evaporated. I cannot feel the other assassins in orbit around me. I no longer know where they are. There is only a void left where there was once the faint yet ever present pulse of my Sky key in my stalyx arm.

I have no ship left to command, though I don't doubt the yeeyar left in my body would still be enough for that. I could even likely regain access to the Sky towers so that the Architects   might reverse whatever these foul Eshmiri have done, but they wouldn't even if I begged them and I wouldn't beg them. I wouldn't ask. I would return to Sky for only one purpose, a purpose that feels eons away in this hunk of floating metal lost *somewhere* in the Quadrants — or more likely, outside of them — piloted by the lousiest group of mercenaries I've ever come across. And the infamous reaver Ashmara is the lousiest among them.

Rook. She was called Rook, once.

My body shivers. One of the Eshmiri speaks, "Is he awake?"

"I think he's awake." Her voice. A sudden rapping against the stalyx side of my forehead. "Knock, knock. Anybody home?"

I cannot contain my growl. I hear the sound of an ion blaster powering to life and feel the press of the barrel to the biological side of my head. But...I also hear something else. Something this band of mercenaries don't seem to, merciless as they may be. And they have to be merciless, don't they? Because I can remember... *everything*.

My biological eyelid springs open. My yeeyar-powered sight fires to life — still intact, still connected to me, but no longer connected to the Sky home world filled with Architects of Death. Now, I'm no longer his right hand.

Now, I'm just the failed assassin who stands in his path.

I see the needle-thin tip of a boring tool penetrating the ceiling between the med bay and the body of the ship. The assassin, for it can only be an assassin, will drop down and close the door, sealing us inside, then jettison the entire med bay into space so that they can collect all of us and tow us back to Sky so that the Architects can do with each of us as they see fit. The

Eshmiri will be killed, I will be decommissioned, and Ashmara will be…

I growl, knowing what fate they have planned for her.

Beneath the looming threat, there is a halo of faces suspended above me — identical in their Eshmiri homogeneity but for the one. The one whose very presence is a blade sawed back and forth across my skull.

What did she do to my skull? She cleaved it apart. *What did she do to my bones?* Stripped them bare. *What did she do to my heart?* Took an axe to it.

My chest is wrapped in vines of yeeyar which squeeze at the sight of her eyes beaming down at me, all blue. She doesn't even notice the assassin removing a section of ceiling large enough to fall through, the fool.

I sit up, ignoring the dizzying sensation attempting to keep me prone, and grab a swatch of Ashmara's bright white curls. She shrieks in pain as I yank her to me and hurtle onto one foot, and then the other, leaving her sprawled over the floor where I just was.

An Eshmiri holding a sling blaster fires and misses as I bring my stalyx forearm down onto the barrel of his weapon. It's a poor excuse for a blaster, but it'll do. I take it from him and kick him in the chest to get the creature out of my way. He skids over the floor, knocking into the legs of a cot, perhaps the same cot I first woke up on, because there is only one and it covers the floor now in scattered pieces.

I shoot the metal rod out of the hand of the Eshmiri that approaches me issuing a futile battle cry that continues long after the weapon goes flying out of his eight-fingered grip. I push him aside, sweep the leg of another and punch a third so hard he slams into the wall to the right, rattling it on its frame. I leave the med bay to a chorus of discontented grunts and braying wails from all of the Eshmiri, and arrive at the opening in the ceiling in time to meet the assassin prepared to drop through it.

I jump, latching onto the edge of the perfectly carved circular opening with one hand while the other maneuvers the blaster into the darkness of the crawlspace. The assassin takes the weapon from me and I let him — I wasn't planning on using it, I wouldn't dare. Modern ships have safety blocks preventing breaches from affecting the integrity of the entire ship. But to puncture the outer hull of this decrepit beast would send all of us to our deaths.

The assassin has the Eshmiri sling blaster in one hand and a weapon of his own in the other. Occupied as he is, it leaves him a heartbeat too slow to defend himself from me. I pull myself up into the criminally dank darkness and grab onto the back of his head with both hands. He growls as he topples forward, falling through the opening after me. He crashes onto the floor at my feet and I snap my stalyx hand down at his throat, intending to remove it.

He blocks and swivels, aiming to kick out my feet. I jump over his strike, landing hard on one of his legs. It breaks beneath the screa-lined sole of my foot, encased in black fiber. He does not scream, but lurches up on his good leg. The move costs him. I kick in his knee. He collapses onto his back and I swipe my red hand across his face, drawing blood with my claws.

He hisses. I stab two fingers up his wide nostrils and rip them clean off. He bares his teeth at me. They are white and shimmering, a testament to his Niahhorru heritage — one of the few things that is, given that they've removed two of his arms and replaced them with coils of yeeyar. The old model. I sneer and wrap the yeeyar around my stalyx arm when it lashes towards me. I hold him down by the chest with my foot while I rip both yeeyar arms clean off.

He does not scream. Not even as I reach in through the empty right socket and find his biological heart beneath layers of flesh and blood, beneath organs that have been harvested from other, stronger creatures and that don't belong there. I am lucky that they found my organs satisfactory. *But not my skin.*

I wrap my fingers around his heart and squeeze. His arm darts forward with speed, one last dying attempt to kill me. I block with my forearm and, with my stalyx hand, rip his heart free.

Silence.

I stand slowly, unfurling to my full height. These Eshmiri creatures left me in my assassin's uniform, the black molded to all of my red skin. My stalyx enhancements continue to shimmer. I frown down at them.

"Holy ecking stars." Her voice is as rough as a wave and just as turbulent. When did it get so rough, so hardened?

I look up. Her eyes are huge and white, no color to be seen. But she does the damnedest thing. She smiles at me.

I drop the engorged Niahhorru heart and it lands on the corpse it once belonged to with a squishy splat. I don't move. I simply attempt to categorize my thoughts and raze all feeling, as I was trained to do.

For the first time that I can remember, it doesn't work.

"That was impressive."

I meet her gaze. It feels like falling into a fog from which there is no escape. "That was only the beginning. There are more assassins on their way."

"Excellent," she says, her voice full of cheer. "Tintin, Gibli, are we closer to Tiringdam or Evernor?"

"Neither. We're on the edge of Quadrant Eight," one of the Eshmiri replies. He is the one who once held the pipe.

He goes and recovers it now, then waves it in my direction. "You fight good, my assassin friend."

I am not his friend, but I don't tell him that. I'm too disturbed by the fact that he no longer seems to fear me. None of them seem to. Of the six Eshmiri present here, none of them watch me with the eyes of those expecting to meet Death. Instead, they begin to move around me, two Eshmiri approaching with a hover lift stretched between them. They place it beneath the hole in the ceiling and one of them rises up and calmly and jovially begins patching the hole while the other returns to help two others drag the corpse of the assassin I killed off towards what appears to be a trash chute.

Ashmara is the only one focused on me at all and she's never feared me. Not once. I take a step back as she approaches, a swagger in her step and a strange expression on her face that I don't like at all. The colors in her eyes, however, she keeps from me.

"How you doin', Azza?" She punches me in the stalyx arm too lightly to hurt, but I still react to the assault.

I grab her wrist, twist it behind her back and shove her into the nearest wall. Hard. "Oof. That good, huh?" she says on a laugh, her previously slurred Eshmiri now more comprehensible.

The heat of her body…its shape…

I…can't…fight…

It's new to me, but it isn't. I've seen it dozens of times — hundreds — but never this way. Never through the lens of a male who has the ability to feel, to *crave*. Through clenched teeth, I say, "You need to return to the known Quadrants. Seek refuge on Evernor, if you dare, though I don't imagine you'll last long there, either."

I pull away, releasing her. My biological fist flexes at the absence of her warmth. I turn my back on the Eshmiri and move through the ship, taking a ladder up to the upper deck as I seek out the control room. Each room I pass through is filthier than the last. The living quarters are a mess. There is a small separate room that betrays a foul smell that I don't dare look into. The control room, I remember.

I take a seat at one of the upright and functioning chairs and drum my fingers over the controls, maneuvering the ship around until I can spot the one the Sky assassin arrived on. I maneuver us closer to it and, when I have the breach portal of this ship just beneath the entrance of the smaller Sky craft, I command the yeeyar of my fellow assassin's ship to dock us together.

There is no reason to create unique ships for each assassin. We do not make them our own as any other creature might and we do not defect. Not until *her*. That's *twice* in the annals of history that Sky assassins have been forced to remember their previous selves and both such *liberations* were her fault. *They will never let her live.*

She has now become the Sky's prime target. It will be one of only a handful of times that the Architects assign a contract themselves. And that's on top of the contract I held of hers covering a dozen different bounties, all small but cumulatively worth not an insignificant amount of tokens, *and* the contract I took out for her in the case of my death. She is now the most wanted female in the cosmos.

"So, where're we going?"

I jump. I blink. I look to the left to see Ashmara standing at my right shoulder, a nonchalant smile on her face. She tips her head to the side and giggles like the Eshmiri do, though the sound is odd in her lower pitch. There's a beat up backpack dangling off of her arm. She cocks her head, glancing from my face to her pack and back again, then sweeps her fingers through her short curls.

"Did I sneak up on you?" She smiles more broadly.

I don't answer her. My throat works, wanting to, but I restrain myself from such a compulsion. Instead, I give her my back and start up the stairs to the breach portal. The well is rusted, but the wheel still moves. I turn it with one hand while, behind me, I can hear Ashmara chattering to one of her reaver friends.

"Yeeshee… Krakaw. Not sure yet. I'll let you know when we get there, Gibli."

The reaver doesn't sound impressed. Louder and louder, as he approaches, I can hear his high pitch. "He's not nearly as much fun as you said he'd be."

She talked to him about me? The yeeyar vines around my heart grow thorns and my hand slips from the wheel. My yeeyar hand. Not my weaker one. "He's plenty fun! What are you talking about? He ripped the heart out of that guy who put a hole in our ceiling, huh? That was fun."

"I guess that was kind of fun…"

"Already, we have so much to tell everyone. We found the recipe for liberating Sky assassins. You should start broadcasting it. Actually, on second thought, make our Lemoran friends pay for it, first. Then give it away for free to everyone." *What?* The insanity of her suggestion has me hesitating. *Kra-krakaw,* my thoughts stumble suddenly into the Eshmiri tongue. Krakaw. I will not be distracted by her, no matter how foolish her actions become.

I continue spinning the wheel until it stops. Then I push the door open. White light and a sweet, almost sickening smell spiral down, clashing with the odor of Ashmara's filthy ship. I shouldn't find the smell of sweat and alcohol more alluring than that of yeeyar and Sky enhancements, but…

"That's a great idea. You think we could get a few pouches of kintarr for the information?"

"Try *tuns.*"

The Eshmiri giggles. "I'll contact them now. Have fun on your trip with Jerrock!"

My foot slips on the rung at the sound of my name. *She talked to him about me.*

"Don't take less than one tun! Then tell everyone. Start with Herannathon. He'll get a kick out of it. And make sure Deena knows. You know how much she loves to talk. She'll make sure everyone in the known Quadrants knows by…"

I kick my foot down, fully intending to dislodge Ashmara from the bars — I can *feel* her weight shaking the ladder as she crawls up after me, spewing madness as she climbs. "Hey!" she shouts as her grip slips, but she doesn't fall. Instead, she grabs my pant leg. Her grip is firm and unafraid, but I don't focus on her strength. Does she know that she has subtle tremors in her palm? How much muuir does she regularly take?

The smallest anger causes me to jerk. I kick harder to dislodge her hold, but she grips tighter before releasing the ladder and catching my ankle with both hands. I shake her hard enough it looks like her neck might snap, her Eshmiri friend giggling maniacally beneath her the entire time.

This isn't working. I jump. She shouts as she falls with me, landing hard on her side on the grated metal floor. She moans in pain, cursing me to the cosmos as she rubs her hip and rolls out her shoulder. She struggles up into a seat. As she moves, my gaze moves over her body.

She's outfitted as she always is, like an Eshmiri because that's what she is, with a black robe thrown over the whole ensemble. Like most Eshmiri, the rags covering her shoulders and chest end before reaching her stomach, leaving it visible before her tattered hide and cloth pants begin at her hips. She has a small depression in the center of her stomach. Many species do, but I find myself focused on it, on the small bones of her hips that shape her, on the waist that slims up from them before reaching her rib cage. It's narrow, her rib cage, like something I could fit both hands around. Her abdomen is sculpted between them, glittering brown. I tell myself to look away from the exposed flesh of her body, but my gaze...it lingers.

She shifts onto her back and color flashes in her eyes too rapidly for me to catch. The only thing in this universe that can claim that. "You aren't coming," I finally say, voice granite and hollow at the same time.

"Hmm, funny you should say that, because I am coming," she says from her prone position beneath me. She gives me an odd gesture — lifting up one thumb — then she closes one eye in a blink. I'm familiar with hundreds of different languages, spoken and unspoken, but not this one. It annoys me that I don't know what it means.

"There are hundreds of assassins after you as it is. If you announce that there is a recipe for ruining them — "

"— freeing them —"

"— there will be thousands." I lord over her, but she looks unintimidated.

She drops her gaze to half-mast and smirks. "You think that scares me?"

"It should."

"What scares me is the fact that you haven't showered in about a dozen solars."

"I have," I say foolishly for the simple reason of correcting her.

"Doesn't smell like it."

The Eshmiri standing with us in the corridor laughs. I see that there is now another behind him. He laughs too before jerking one of seven fingers over his shoulder and saying, "There's another ship incoming. Should we blast it?"

"Your blasts will be ineffective." It's a true statement, one that Ashmara surprises me by agreeing with.

"Go ahead and leave it," she says, taking the hand of her Eshmiri friend — this one's called Gibli, I believe she said — and letting him help her to her feet. "Let the assassin come to us. We can kill it on board with our yeeyar destabilizers." She hoists her pack higher onto her shoulder and I refuse to betray my surprise. Destabilizers, she said. More than one. More than just the one they used on me.

I want to know what the weapon is, how it works, why it requires an ancient tool — a *whistle* — to activate and why they simply could not use their yeeyar tokens or more ancient yamar boxes to replicate the necessary frequency to activate the tool. I've never seen a weapon like this before. Crude yet remarkably useful. If the Architects know of such a weapon they have not shared its existence with us assassins, and they would have. They would have also hunted down every whistle in the Quadrants and eradicated them all, along with anyone who had ever touched or carried one. Their assassins cannot be so easily taken down. Then again…

I was.

I am frowning slightly and, in an uncommon display for me, I allow Ashmara the luxury of seeing the displeasure on my face. She smiles brightly and blinks at me again with one eye. "You're not the only one with tricks, hey."

I sneer. "Save your weapon," I tell her reaver brethren. "You'll need it."

"Save them?" Them. There it is again, the plural that astounds me. "If we save them then we won't get a chance to use them." Her and the other reavers' laughter grates on my last nerve.

I return to the ladder. "I will handle it. And then I will hunt down the others hunting you, giving you time to get to Evernor. Use it wisely. Don't spend it broadcasting information from your precious ship that will make my task even more difficult."

"Was that sarcasm?"

"Every moment you waste that keeps me from returning to the Sky planet and killing the Architects will cost lives. Mine and yours."

"Sky? Did he just say he's going to Sky?"

The Eshmiri reavers voice their dissent. It may sound like laughter to most, but I now know better. These Eshmiri can be cunning creatures when it suits them.

"How you planning to get to Sky, my friend?"

"I'm not your friend. And with my Sky key..." My voice trails off. I pause in my ascent, halting in the very same place that I previously did.

Frustration makes me seethe. I turn and jump, landing on the metal grate with a rickety bang. I advance on Ashmara, backing her up until she stumbles into the arms of her friends. They hold her up, supporting her by the back, the elbows. One thick, three-fingered Eshmiri hand is curled around the curve of her waist in a way that bothers me, but shouldn't. These males don't breed with females, but among themselves.

She lifts her twitching hands. Her backpack slumps down her arm, getting caught on her elbow. I reach for it, but she jerks it away in a move that wouldn't have prevented me from taking it had she not simultaneously said my name.

Krakaw. *A* name.

"Azza, you really think I'd keep it in my backpack? Seriously? I managed to trick you, trap you and crack you open like a nut and you still think I'm that dumb? This is my go bag. I hid the Sky key on our ship."

I move away from the stairs and shift to move past her, fully intent on rooting out the key she stole from me, but she just clicks her tongue against the backs of her teeth in a way I don't like. "Tintin, how long do we have before the Sky reach us?"

The Eshmiri standing slightly further back looks down at his outdated yamar box. He speaks into it, forwarding along the request for information, and responds in an echo. "Not long."

What a response. It's uttered with the same degree of nonchalance displayed when he and the others placed a dead assassin in the trash.

Ashmara shows the same degree of carelessness with her own life. The desire to strangle her... "You really gonna waste the *not long* time you have left trying to find your missing key, or are you going to go kill your buddy who's closing in? I don't think you'll have time to do both."

"He's not my buddy." I hesitate for a moment longer than I should — longer than she can spare — before ignoring the temptation she presents and returning to the ladder. It is only because my back is turned to her that I allow my nostrils to flare in irritation.

I'm halfway up, back to the place I have now twice abandoned, when Ashmara calls out. "You're giving up on your key that easily?"

I'll come back for it. It's as simple as that.

"You could come back for it, but you still won't find it. You might, but have you seen how big our ship is? Plus, it's uhh...kind of a mess. You'll eventually find it, sure, but it'll take you solars and solars and solars and solars..." A hollow threat. "Or you could save yourself the trouble of looking and I'll just tell you where it is." I pause, gripping the warm, rough metal hard enough I am surprised the rung doesn't shatter beneath my stalyx grip. The infernal female. She knows what to say to me. She always does, because I believe her though I shouldn't. She may be a fool, but then what does that make me?

"You would *give* it to me?" I uncertainly repeat.

"Sure." She shrugs as if I'm asking to use her wrench, rather than the rarest artifact in the cosmos.

"You know its worth." It's a question, but I state it as fact.

"Duh."

"Why?"

"You really wanna stand here and try to figure me out or are you ready to accept my terms? I'll give you the Sky key if you let me fly with you."

"Just this once." I'm bartering. I've never...

"Sure." There's mischief in her gaze, but even though I can read her every emotion, I cannot see what she has planned. I don't like her plans, her traps. They're so stupid, I fall into them.

A growl. I feel it build in my chest. It is not a sound I've made often before, but when I have made it, she's always been present. *In the best and worst of ways.* My mind jerks at a memory so distant as to nearly be forgotten, before slingshotting back to the present. *I do not have time for memories. Not even* that *one.*

"Come," I bark. "Stay out of the way."

I can feel the ladder vibrate beneath me as she follows. "Sure thing."

Sure. I hate this word. "I won't be responsible for your life."

"Yeeshee, yeeshee."

"And I will return for the key and to deposit you back onto your ship."

"Sure," she says, even more emphatically. *Sure.*

"You will not deceive me."

"Yeeshee, of course." Her tone is fully patronizing and carries not a hint of believability, but I climb the ladder into the control chamber of the Sky ship regardless.

It is larger than the one I am accustomed to and features a second chamber as well as a detached void room and sleeping pod. It's a sleeping pod for one. A shiver runs through me as the memory comes traipsing back into the forefront of my thoughts.

Krakaw, we will not be sleeping here, so it doesn't matter. This is a simple task. Eliminate the incoming Sky ship, return to the Eshmiri's floating hovel, recover my key and deposit Ashmara back into the dump she came from. *A dump filled with muuir.* I frown. If I bring her with me, she'll only serve as a distraction. *But she'll be free of muuir.*

As soon as she boards behind me, she utters an ominous goodbye to her fellow Eshmiri before slamming her ship's portal shut with a loud clang. She also says something else as she speaks to them.

"See you later! See you back at the rendezvous point at Evernor. Love you!"

Love you.

Love you.

Love you.

She loves them.

My eyelashes flutter over my biological eye while my yeeyar sight draws up thousands of definitions for the term, *love*, in millions of languages. Because in all the cultures in all the cosmos, the concept of *love* exists in every one.

"So, Azza." She then slides her hand along the seam of the Sky ship's opening until she finds the manual release for the door. It whispers closed, the yeeyar utterly silent as it works.

Ashmara's voice jerks me into the Sky ship and I reprimand myself mentally for once more getting lost.

"So," she says, standing up. I realize I'm still watching her as she brushes off the legs of her pants. Dust and dirt falls from them and sprinkles the starch-white floor. The soles of her boots also leave footprints.

She tosses her backpack against the wall and it slinks down until it meets the floor. Something clinks inside her pack. Bottles would be my guess. In addition to muuir, I saw plenty of fermented drink bottles littering her ship. My biological eye twitches. I wonder if there is no substance this female is not addicted to.

"We got some killing to do?" She moves toward the hifelai control board dominating the space, but I cut her off.

"Sit down and stay out of my way. This ship is meant to be piloted by one."

She shrugs, not getting riled as I expected she might. Very little seems to rile her. I fight an unusual urge — to try.

"Sure thing." She gives me a funny smile that I don't like while I turn to the controls and let my fingers work.

The panel comes to life under my palm and, as soon as it registers the yeeyar in my system, becomes mine. I'm grateful that it does. I…I wasn't certain it would. But it seems that whatever Ashmara did to me may have severed my connection to Sky, but did not destroy the yeeyar within me itself. I can still feel the ship around me as I could before, as easily as I can my own skin. *As easily as I can her presence.*

I turn my face away from the murky shadow she makes on the pristine white floor and try not to think of anything other than the tasks before me. This is how I have been led to operate. Trained. *Forced.* But errant and troubling thoughts continue to breach my concentration and slice at me and every time, they draw blood. *So much blood.*

"Woah there. Haven't you ever flown a ship before?" She chuckles as the ship takes flight, moving away from her hunk of metal rapidly enough to cause both of us to sway. I don't reply to her jeers and continue to ignore her watching me with her arms crossed over her chest, and I most definitely don't attempt to analyze the colorlessness of her gaze and what her expressions might convey.

I focus on the hifelai as it rises up in front of me like black shards of glass and sand forming shapes and spheres in shades of grey and the occasional pinprick of color. More sophisticated than a holoscreen, yet a thousand times more difficult to interpret, it allows me to determine where the ships within blast range are located and how quickly they're moving. The Sky ship is easy to spot given its speed, and Ashmara's ship even easier given its lack.

I redirect twelve degrees and dive. Meanwhile, I can feel Ashmara's stare. It's brutal, beating into me like no amount of pain delivered by the Architects ever could.

She clears her throat. Her voice is gravel. "You *do* remember me, don't you?"

The ship dives harder and Ashmara reaches out to grab onto something but there isn't anything there but the wall, so she grabs hold of that. I move to the left area of the flat, seemingly static hifelai and open up the ship's arsenal. The arsenal powers on, panels on the control board shining a darker, shinier black than the grey tones beside them.

"I think you might remember me," she says more smugly.

I don't answer, but drum my fingers over the keys. Liquid ion iron ionyx'ix fires from the blast portals. I waste no time in attacking the incoming ship, which hovers like a blot of ink-blackened sand in the air before me. It shimmers pink in the hifelai as it activates its shields and continues to close in on the much larger misshapen blue point with speed. It moves so quickly it makes the reaver ship appear completely inert. Knowing their penchant for danger, it likely is. The concept of self-preservation doesn't seem to exist within the reaver community. Her Eshmiri friends likely haven't even begun to take off yet. *Maybe, they're waiting for her. Maybe, they love her back.*

My pulse accelerates only a hair, but it's enough that I can feel the tension begin to thrum throughout my entire body. I hate it and yet that hatred does nothing to deter me. I will not allow the assassin to board that ship. Right now, I have only the element of surprise to my advantage. Otherwise, all Sky ships are built equal to one another. It will take some effort to bring it down.

I have not stopped firing, though the blasts have done little to penetrate the ship's shields. That is not the point, however. The point is to get the Sky ship to turn away from Ashmara's, which it does. The assassin on board does not attempt communication. It cannot. Our ships contain no such ability. What would be the point? Anyone who saw a Sky ship incoming, should they see it, would know its purpose.

Their life for a contract.

"So, since it seems that you *do* remember me, I uh…" She stutters, voice coming out scratchier than it was before. "Azza, I... Eck." She crouches down on one knee as I bring the ship up abruptly, intending to draw the Sky ship out further into the Grey Zone. We are, as is, too detectable within the area of Quadrant Eight and I have no desire to be detained in an Oosa jail where inmates are kept in isolated cells located so deep beneath the ocean's surface escapees are immediately crushed should they attempt a jailbreak.

She starts to rifle through her bag, pausing a couple times and shaking her head before jerking upright. "Aha. Here it is." She withdraws and begins futzing with her small yamar box, then clears her throat. "Azza, I am Ashmara. You may remember me as Rook. It is fine if you call me Rook, by the way." She's reading in a stilted and robotic way from the small projection made by her yamar box. The holo projection fizzles in and out and I wonder, not for the first time, why she and her reavers don't use the infinitely more sophisticated yeeyar versions. Such irrelevant details, and I'm hung up on them. About her, I notice everything. "My first memories are of you."

My ship takes incoming fire. I can feel it blast the hull in small pulses, but the shields are fully operational and will not crack. Not like I'm about to crack.

"You were different, then. Your skin was red, but also brown, like mine." Her voice gets louder and she opens her mouth, about to say more. *I want her silent.* I tilt the ship to blast the opposing ship with the droherion canons, a necessary move. *Necessary to shut her up.*

She slams into the wall, but it does not have the desired effect. "Augh-ow-oy-ouh! Okay, where was I? Azza, you and I used to play games together on board the refugee ship. We were refugees of Lemora. The female who took care of us told me once that we had been purchased by Sky Architects, but that the Drakesh ship responsible for brokering the deal was intercepted. We'd been kitlings.

"Then we became older kits. They kept us together. We grew up on that ship. I am not sure how much you remember, or if you remember me, or what you did…" Her voice does something truly damning then. It breaks. "Oops," she says on a laugh, attempting to cough in order to mask her mistake, and yet what an ecking mistake. I can't take it…

I arrive in front of her before she can take her next breath. I slam my palm over her mouth and slam her back against the white wall, which is the same white as her hair. My gaze is lost in her curls. I refuse to look into her eyes and acknowledge the strip of yellow that flares there. The Voraxian color for shame. What has she to be ashamed of? She wasn't the one turned into this wretched beast, living a borrowed half-life.

Our ship rocks on its axis, the jolt surprising and infuriating. I'm too distracted by her. I slap the yamar box out of her hand and turn back to the controls only to see something…alarming. Knowing that their blasts won't penetrate our shields, the assassin has fired a containment pod at us. It is bold, and dramatic, especially since the Sky ship attacking us only carries one pod and no backup. I know this because it's a smaller model than the ship Ashmara and I are on now. *It's the same ship I used to fly, back in another life.*

The sleek white tube thuds off of the side of my ship dully, but I quickly activate a gravitational wand to reel it back in. I use the wand to maneuver the holding pod into position in front of the blasters, intent to blast it back to the ship it came from.

I open the canon portal.

The pod explodes, tearing the canon apart.

I grind my teeth together as the ship spirals off of its intended flight path. We fly out of the orbit of the Ooso constellation, Oosmo, expelled further into the Grey Zone…and the assassin keeps coming. Clever.

"Ow wow. Okay, anyway," Ashmara says, evidently recovering her yamar box. Next time I'm going to blow the thing to pieces. "Where…was I?" Ashmara plasters her back to and splays her arm against the wall for support, but her gaze never strays from her flickering holo projection after she powers it back on. "Yeeshee, yeeshee. Here we go. Azza, I don't know if you remember what you did for me, but I remember. The Lemoran ship we were on was attacked by Sky…"

My hands are flying over the controls, attempting to stabilize the ship, but the exhaust valve for the canon ports connects directly to the hifelai, which operates the thrusters. The ship is no longer level and, as it takes hit after hit, we're pushed further and further towards the orbit of the next closest planet, whose gravitational pull slowly begins to reel us in.

I activate the thrusters, but the hifelai has already begun to short, surges of light and color blinking into and out of existence in tiny explosions of dying yeeyar.

"…we were attacked…by a Sky ship. They boarded and killed everyone except for us. Because we hid. It was your idea. You were always so smart. But I…" Her voice snags. It ecking snags, and that snag is like a Niahhorru hiannru tine hooking straight through my skull, tearing my attention away from anything it *should* be focused on and giving it all to her. "The area where I hid was too small..."

We're going down and she's still reading from her projection like she's delivering an ecking sermon. "So we couldn't hide together..."

Eck. Eck her for distracting me. Ecking *Rook*. I can feel the ship begin to spiral out, the next blast slinging us into the orbit of a small green planet. I don't know what planet this is, if it's hospitable or if we'll even survive the impact.

Quickly, I open the panel in my stalyx arm and download all of the information I can from the ship's larger database before even that is lost. The planet is unnamed, with a rock exterior and a gaseous core. Good. Better this way than a gaseous planet with a rock core. At least this way, we stand a chance — even if the planet is inhabited by higher life forms, which it is, and even if those life forms are categorized as violent and dangerous, which they are.

I don't allow Ashmara to say another word. I grab her around the waist, throw her over my shoulder and run to the back of the ship. I throw her into one of the ship's holding pods and I'm well aware of the grip she has on my suit as I do...

She tries to pull me in after her, but I pull back even harder. Her fingernails break off against my suit with how violently she clutches me. Her eyes are red and murderous as she stares at me. They blaze like raw flame.

"Don't you dare," she says. "Not again."

I cut my forearm down and break the hold she has on my jacket — along with her arm. My nostrils flare at the pain that streaks across her expression. It's a mild break. A mild one, that's all.

I toss the healing wand into the compartment with her, seal it shut and expel the holding pods into space. It'll hit the planet's surface before I do, so I'll have to do my best to track it.

At the controls, black yeeyar spills out of the hifelai control board and bleeds onto the white floor. It lashes at everything, live wires glittering at the tips with dying sparks. I avoid its touch. I take a moment to survey the damage, survey my options. I could take another holding pod — there are three — but I need to ensure that Ashmara has the best odds.

The ship is hit again and this time, I can feel the gravity within the central pod begin to drop. This ship won't survive the impact and neither will I, if I remain here. Yet, if I take another of the two holding pods, which in this case will double as escape pods, the assassin may assume…

Yeeshee. An idea comes to me and I release the remaining two pods into space, then return fire with the weak, ineffective blasters still mounted to the front of the ship. The incoming ship avoids the projectiles easily, if I'm even aiming in the right direction — without the hifelai, I'm relatively lost. It returns fire and as I feel the ship begin to disintegrate around me, I head to the single sleeping cell and seal myself inside of it. It is strange…

I feel so uncomfortable in this small white cell even though it is familiar to me. It should feel familiar. I have slept in cells such as these many, many times before. Hundreds. All my life…

Before, I slept wrapped around Rook, two cubs afraid of the dark.

An explosion in the side of the cabin causes my heart to jump as I watch bits and pieces of the ship tear free and catch fire as I enter the atmosphere. My only chance is if this ship lands in a body of water, and if the automatic thrusters respond as they're supposed to — releasing the remainder of their reserves right before impact. If not, I won't have the chance to hear the rest of Ashmara's speech.

I exhale.

It's for the best.

I close my eyes.

I really don't want to hear it.

7

Ashmara

It happened again. I waited five rotations for my shot at redemption and I failed the test.

Sitting flat on my ass next to the ruins of the containment cell Jerrock cleverly used to help me escape in, I finish using the healing wand on my swollen arm before I dig jerkily into my pack. My fingers close around the silver pouch and I exchange it for the wand in my hand. Withdrawing it, I pull the ties and unfurl the rubber across my lap. Muuir shines up at me in little vials, organized by intensity. It's the only thing on my ship — in my life — that was ever organized.

My fingers dance over the powder and leaves, the crystals and patches until I reach the vials glimmering with clear liquid. It could be water, it's so clear, tinged by only the faintest pink and blue shimmers when the light hits it just right. Muuir is beautiful in its liquified form, but as a liquid is also my *least* favorite way to take the crap. Right now, though, I feel like the hurt. *I deserve it.*

I take the first vial and lift it up to my eye. I flip the mini lid free and keep my eye open as I stare blindly up at the bright orange sky, marred occasionally by random bursts of red. Red curls and twirls, feathers against the horizon, lithe dancers on the wind. I wonder what it is.

"Maybe the blood of other unlucky bastards who landed here." I chuckle as the muuir drips from the vial and, in a moment of burning intensity, causes my vision to blur. It takes a moment to set in and when it does, my entire body buzzes pleasantly. Pleasant though it is, it isn't enough. I look down at the few vials remaining. There are only four more after this. I should save them. After I use the vials, which are stronger than the powder and the patches and the leaves and the crystals, I'll be left to the rest and I run through that crap like the wind.

But on the other hand, I just got my best friend killed.

Again.

I lift a second vial to my other eye and let it burn the ecking comets out of me, the pain tunneling back through the nerves and chewing its way through the nape of my neck before moving on to my spine. The pain fizzles out about halfway down my back, but doesn't compare at all to the ache in my belly. Way down deep. *Deeper.* Krakaw, deeper than that.

Because when I close my eyes, I picture a little tiny Ashmara digging a grave for Rook, ready to lay her down for one final sleep. Yeeshee, that lifts my spirits. I wonder if the amount of muuir I have will be enough to do it. I snort. Even if I only apply the patches, the amount of muuir I have could kill an Egama if taken all at once.

"It'll do." I nod down at my muuir as I repack it carefully, grabbing a leaf or two and popping them into my mouth before I do.

I smile, spirits lifted by the muuir and the thought. I've overdosed before, but the others always brought me back. Gibli was pissed at me the first time. He never found out about the second. Not that I blamed him back then. I was pissed at me, too. Overdosing then would have meant that I would never get to liberate Azza from the shackles of Jerrock. Rook may have killed Jerrock, but now Ashmara's killed Azza for good.

I exhale roughly and wobble as I rise. "Now, all that's left is to find the *body*." My voice cracks over the word, but I don't want him to die alone. I want him to know, even in death, that he was loved. That he's been loved since I first came to understand what love was.

I've been watching the sky for as long as I've been on this planet without finding any answers in the shifting red. I didn't see the ship crash. I don't know why or what it means — if the ship was blown out of the sky and never even made it to this planet, or if Azza was able to patch whatever was broken and took off, leaving me here. He'd have had every right. But somehow, I don't think he did. *He wouldn't. Because no matter what, he always looks out for me. Even when I don't deserve it. And I never deserve it.*

The only other option is that, in the time it took for my pod to reach this planet's surface, he already landed and is looking for me. Yeeshee, maybe he is. Maybe, he's already busy engineering a way for himself off of this planet.

Whatever the case may be, I hope he left me, or that he will. I hope he's out there in the stars rediscovering himself, sampling all the delights all of the pleasure planets have to offer. I'll keep looking for him, though. Looking for him until I starve to death and finally take that last muuir trip. Muuir is my friend. It's been my closest friend, in his absence. And with it in my system, at least I won't die alone.

Hoisting my pack higher on my shoulders, I take a step. My high takes over, making my feet feel like they're sinking into Oroshi goo. The moss is purple under my toes. Pale lavender and dry as a bone, layered over pale yellow sand. A few more steps later and the universe settles. Pleasure radiates up my legs and brings a smile to my face. The sun — wait, where did the sun come from? — shines very pleasantly on my skin. I shed my outer layers as I walk and walk and walk until I eventually find a river.

The river leads me out of the sparse forest decorated with white bark trees to a wide, barren stretch of land. I can't call it a plain, because there is no grass and plains need to have grass, don't they? I'm not sure. I'm not sure what to call it. Studded infrequently by short trees, whose leaves are all pale blue and whose thin boughs and trunks are all white as bones, *like a graveyard*, the plain of moss and sand stretches all the way out to the horizon, all the way to…

Is that the slight hint of a smoke trail disappearing over distant yellow hills?

I grin and start to walk faster. "Azza, here I come. You can be pissed at me, but you've got to live."

8

Ashmara

It's been three solars and three lunars since I started walking and I haven't reached the hills yet. Not that much time has passed, either. It's just the ecking planet. It's small and the solars and lunars pass by at intervals frequent enough to make a female nauseous. I'm feeling nauseous. Am I going to get my period in like two breaths just standing here? I hope not.

I stop and drink from the river a few times, even though I hate how much it slows me down. I need to find Azza, in whatever state he's in. Treacherous thoughts have started to creep into my mind, too. Thoughts that *maybe* he really is still alive, fine, healthy, even. Maybe, just *maybe*, I didn't kill him. It wouldn't be the first time he's avoided death, despite my best efforts.

I fiddle with the strap on my bag, my fingers twitching while the muuir throttles my system, attempting to force me to slow down and chill. *Just be cool, Ashmara, be cool...* I always am. Usually. Not now, though. Now, my heart is pounding *hard* and I'm sweating like a block of ice in a violent desert. I'm used to the sensation, but not like this. This time, I'm nervous.

The fifth solar has come and gone before I finally pass beneath the shadow of the mountain. It's not a little yellow hill, as it appeared to be from so far away, but in truth, jagged and soaring cliffs, spears and stony turrets. It looks nothing like the picture of serenity it did in the distance.

"It looks ecking creepy," I tell no one.

Sandy slots made of jagged stone mark the way forward. I hesitate, eyeing the sand and moss paths that weave between them. I don't have many other options. The mountain doesn't stand alone here, but is one of many forming a range that arcs beautifully and unhelpfully over the horizon. I sigh, tension in my shoulders deflating. I go into my pack and grab the last of the muuir leaves, toss them into my mouth and start feverishly chewing as I stalk forward through the slots.

The slots rise high overhead, flat stone blades slicing at the lunar sky. The sky is dark but not black, constantly illuminated by flashes of red. I thought it was creepy before, but now I'm grateful for the color, no matter how sinister it is. I don't have a hand light in my pack, only a few Eshmiri torches. I don't have much in my pack besides muuir and if I get lost in the dark I likely won't find my way out again.

I tear off pieces of my clothing, wet them with saliva and paste them on the rocks every once in a while and definitely whenever I'm forced to change direction. I hope they stick.

One of my pant legs tears all the way up to the crease of my thigh when the slots start to get closer and closer together and I'm forced to climb. Frustrated, I tear it off completely and make some shreds out of it, then stuff the rest in my pack. I end up making it halfway up the mountain without crossing any of my markers. I consider it a success because it *feels* like I'm traveling in circles.

It also feels like I'm being watched.

There aren't any footsteps in the sand, but the path I take up over and between and through rough, rocky passages seems worn. Creepy.

"Or maybe it's just the muuir ecking with me." I chuckle, to lighten the mood, but in here, my voice doesn't echo. Yeesheee, definitely creepy.

Solar light comes again, hazel at first, then lavender, then blue. The changing colors have no bearing on the red that streaks through them. The red becomes my only constant. The muuir starts to wear off. That means three meal slots have passed and I haven't eaten in any of them. It's the solar-lunar eckery of this planet. I can't keep my head on straight. I start to get dizzy. Wait. Is that a piece of pant leg?

I've been wandering the mountaintop for a solar and a lunar and another solar again. Finding my way up was easy, but I can't seem to find my way down. Maybe, I should just go back.

Krakaw. Azza needs me.

I forge ahead, passing by the same or maybe a different scrap of clothing. With the muuir rattling my brain, I can't tell the difference. On the second pass around, I pick up the scraps and rearrange them. The muuir is now fully out of my system and my bottom jaw is trembling — the first signs of withdrawal. I grab the powder and rub it in my armpits — my second least favorite way to take muuir — and keep going. I pass the scraps a third time and then a fourth and then suddenly the mountain opens up before me

"Over my dead body," I say down into the hole.

A big, black cave appears, though I don't know how. It wasn't there before and I'm *sure* I've taken this path. Pure black, I can't see into it at all. All I can see is a pinprick of light coming from the far end. So, it's a tunnel. It's not a natural formation, either. A creature made this tunnel. Creatures. Beings. Likely sentient and intelligent. The hole is jagged around the edges, but the floor is smooth. Well-trodden. Creatures pass through the mountain using this tunnel. It doesn't make me feel better. It's creepy as eck.

"Nah." I shake my head and backpedal. "There's another way. There's got to be." Shivers rack my body that have nothing to do with the muuir quietly anesthetizing me from the brutality of my fear and the reality of my situation. The sky shifts lazily from blue to pink overhead. The red flares sharply, turning fuchsia against the pink. I wonder what color my eyes are right now? Pink like the sky? Shining bright with dread?

"Nah." I take another step back and then another and then a third and then I turn and smack straight into a wall.

My chin takes a beating, skin scraped straight off of it as I canter back. I find my footing and shake my head. "Comets," I curse. "How much muuir did I take?"

I'm boxed in. It's just not possible. I blink and rub my face roughly. Nothing's changed. I'm surrounded by rock on all sides. One of the rocks even has a piece of fabric slapped onto it, but it's just not possible. The rock is surrounded by other rock. I *couldn't* have passed through it. I can't walk through stone. Muuir may make me fly but not even muuir can do that.

"Krakaw, it just...can't ecking be."

I dig into my pack for a knife and, finding it, whip it out in front of me. It's a dull thing with a worn wooden handle, mostly used for looking intimidating. I haven't stabbed anyone in a long time. Well, Sky assassins excluded. My hand still stings at the memory of Jerrock shooting me through the palm on board that ship with Nalia and Manila. The scar's still there. I refused to let Tintin remove all of it.

I stab my knife into one of the rock walls, though I don't know what I expect to happen. It really is rock.

"Alright." I swallow hard, rubbing my eyes with the heels of my hands.

I tongue the wet wad of muuir leaf in my cheek, hating it and needing it desperately. It's all I've got right now, yet it might also be the reason I'm clearly going insane. These rocks weren't here a heartbeat ago. They *can't* be *moving,* can they?

Rocks don't move.

Mountains don't rearrange themselves.

I laugh out loud, not because this is funny, but just to hear another sound besides my nervously shifting feet and my labored breath. This planet is quiet. Eerily quiet. There aren't enough trees for the wind to whistle through. There's just moss crinkling and sand spraying and wind making a hollow whistle as it passes through the slots and around the high turrets of the mountain.

Through the mountain tunnel especially.

The rocks that have me boxed in are too high to climb. Flat faces, every one of them. There are seams at two edges, but they're too thin to whittle a knife through, let alone squeeze past, and they're too far apart to be able to leverage against and shimmy up. Not that I've got the strength for that.

I turn back around and face off against the mouth of the tunnel. I stare into its depths until I start to imagine things inside. Shadows shifting that look like monsters. Shadows shifting that look like flowers. Nothing looks inviting. Nothing feels right. But there's no other way forward. There's no way back at all.

"For Azza," I whisper to myself as I take a steeling breath. I edge forward into the dark, one step and then another.

I keep my gaze focused on my destination — the light at the tunnel's far end. I try not to think about how all this feels creepily metaphorical. I try not to think about how I'm walking to my death. I just focus on Azza's face as I remember it from my kithood. I just focus on Jerrock's face, as I've fallen in love with it as a female hunted. I just focus on the muuir running through me making me feel like this might all be alright — not on the bit of the muuir that makes me feel like this might not be alright, urging me to take more and more of it.

I'll take more as soon as I exit the tunnel. That will be my reward for making it that far.

The thought spurs me forward faster. Faster and faster. Faster and faster and faster. I'm almost there, the light source nearly on me. The exit. I can see low yellow mountains on the other side, then what looks like forested hills after that. I'm almost there…

And then it hits me.

Literally.

I run straight into a flat wall. My nose takes a beating and I taste blood as my face smashes against a wall that I *thought* was the open end of the tunnel. I rear back in shock and see the world on the other side of the tunnel through a red film. My blood.

"That's my blood," I say aloud, reaching a finger forward to touch it. I leave a clear streak through the smear and stare at the world through it, then I widen my stare. The entire hilly and forested world on the other side of the tunnel is still there, but…but I can't get to it…

I reach forward again and press my palm flat against what looks like open air, but isn't. It's warm and clear, thick and only slightly murky when the light hits it at certain angles. It's glass. "Of course, it's glass." I pad around the glass with both hands, looking for exits, searching for seams and finding none. The glass folds straight into the rock, rocks built around it in such a way that I can't find the edges. "Ow." I nick my finger on a rough, rocky shard and laugh only so that I don't scream.

"There has to be an exit somewhere in this tunnel." There has to be. "Because there was wind." I can still hear it, that eerie, chilling whistle, a haunting refrain. "Maybe, there's an offshoot somewhere…" Not that I'd want to take it. I shudder, scratch the back of my neck, spit out the muuir in my mouth as it's entirely lost its effect, and start to turn.

I scream when I see the creature before me.

Then I laugh and slap a hand over my chest when I register who, or rather what, it is. It's a kit. A small kitling. I can tell that much even though they're a species I don't recognize. They're a pale green color with two eyes and shallow yellow nostrils carved out of a reptilian face. They have a yellow-green underbelly and darker green scales covering the rest of them. They walk on two short back legs and when they scuttle back, looking afraid of me, they drops onto all fours. Their many-fingered hands are tipped in short claws that, given their stature and demeanor, don't manage to look particularly threatening. I take a step forward.

"Hey, friend. Any chance you know a way out of here? I'm Ashmara, by the way." I offer them a smile as I dig in my pack for my yamar box to translate, but I never get a chance to extract it.

The kit attacks, blitzing me savagely. They're weaponless and half my height and I've got my knife and muuir in my system keeping my adrenaline pumping but it doesn't ecking matter. None of it matters. They're quicker than lightning and out for blood.

Their cute, dainty little claws swipe my stomach and as I canter back, they strike again. They land cuts on my neck, over my cheek, and score both of my legs. I try to lift my arms to block, but they flay the skin off my forearms and screech loud enough to make my thoughts spiral and my body sway. The sound is deafening, defeating. I fall to the ground. They grab my leg and as they start to tow me away, I cling to consciousness with everything I've got left. Krakaw, not with everything. Because clinging to my pack is more important. Not because I've got a healing wand inside, but because of…

My head thuds against a rock as they suddenly turn into an offshoot halfway down the tunnel that I hadn't seen, or that maybe hadn't been there. Did the rock move again? I ask them the question out loud on a chuckle, but they don't answer me.

They just drag me down, down, down, the sound of their claws scraping getting louder until it becomes the sound of many claws scraping. A low rattle. When I blink again I see faces illuminated by fire. Reptilian faces covered in scars and chipped scales. Faces much larger than that of the small savage's stacked on top of bodies twice as tall as Jerrock. Claws that look mean when they cut.

Together, they beat the crap out of me. I don't see their faces, because I black out pretty quick. But they seem to be enjoying themselves, so much so that one of them kills another when they move to take the other's place in line to punch me around the circle. Huh. Funny.

They don't kill me though, they don't seem to want my body, either, for breeding or for eating. That's lucky, I guess. They don't even try to take my pack, which is odd, as I'm left with very little understanding of what they *do* want me for when they drag me out into the light.

How'd we get out of the mountain? Every cut hurts as they drag me through the sand. *What is happening? Where are we going?* We're not in the mountain anymore and, when I tentatively try to blink, I see the world through a sheen of blood. We're back in the slots, megalithic flat rock panels towering above us. *Where is Azza?*

They start to pull me off of my back and into a vertical position where they then string me up by the wrists. They hang me between two towering boulders by ropes that are the same purple shade as the moss of this planet. My head lolls. My feet are left to drag on the sand below. My armpits strain painfully, even through the muuir I rubbed all over them. I shouldn't have spit out that muuir leaf. At least it would've given me something to work on.

"Eck," I croak, blinking up at the red dancing sky. "This isn't good…"

The reptile beings of this planet that, after having been mauled by them, I've reduced to angry lizards, are all making these terrible cawing sounds. More battles rage near me, a few lizards die. I feel their bodies hit the ground through vibrations in the rock before suddenly the others disappear, leaving me alone in a world of rocks and corpses.

Hanging there, I feel true fear for the very first time in rotations. With my hands bound, my pack out of reach and my blood flowing so freely, the muuir will soon be entirely out of my system.

What a pity.

9

Jerrock

I hover over the site of the wrecked ship for less than the full length of one of their short solars before the creatures of this planet come out to ravage it. I hide among the moss to observe my enemy at a distance, using the scope of my yeeyar sight to track their activity.

There are many of them, whatever they are. These creatures have tough outer hides that will be difficult to penetrate. To kill them, I will have to pry scales off.

I watch the way they operate, the way they move as individual creatures, the way they move as a pack. Violent and unintentional, I watch as two creatures fight over a droherion blaster until one of the smaller creatures comes by and kills them both. It doesn't even take the blaster with it, but feasts on the flesh of the fallen.

The smaller ones are more dangerous.

They don't wear clothing and their anatomy doesn't betray genders to the layman. I don't care. I only care that they move like carrion insects as they sniff, hunting by scent. They have found mine and are moving in my direction.

There is nothing out here with which to mask my scent, so I will have to fight. Even armed as I am with the blasters and knives I could salvage from the ship, it isn't something I look forward to. I am deadly, but they are many.

As the assassin Jerrock, I recognize that my odds of surviving the battle against their pack are slim and that I'm likely to end up as the next feast for the few of them that manage to overwhelm me. As the assassin Jerrock, I know this plainly and this knowledge, fact that it is, does not affect me. *But as the Jerrock that I am now, whoever he may be, I am…*

I clear my throat. Flex my hand. Feel the dry brush of the moss against my fingertips, those that still feel sensation and haven't been replaced by a synthetic superior. The air that smells like dry wind and sand and a little like the smoke from my wrecked ship fills my lungs. I hold it there.

…unsettled. I do not want to die.

Movement tickles the periphery of my gaze. I glance up at the sky and might have laughed had I a sense of humor. The Sky assassin that blew me out of the sky has located the wreckage of my ship and is closing in. Why they continued to chase instead of returning to Ashmara's ship for the Sky key, which was ripe for the taking, is unclear to me. But it is appreciated.

The assassin's ship decelerates near to where I lie half-hidden by thick clumps of moss and positions itself, perhaps unknowingly, halfway between me and the creatures. They become frenzied at the sight of the invader. Their screeches penetrate the solar like shrapnel and cause the moss to vibrate around my feet. It feels like insects and I remain wary of it the first few moments, especially when I notice that the vibrations cause several sinkholes to appear. Hm. I will need to tread carefully.

I use the distraction of the incoming Sky ship to my advantage and take off, moving away from it at speed. I have the locator beacon for the holding cell in the hidden pocket over my breast and I withdraw it at periodic intervals, changing course and moving towards the very distant trees that appear over the flat horizon. There are few landmarks on this planet and few hills. There is almost nothing as far as the eye can see. Only endless fields of sand-covered moss and the occasional tree.

I arrive at the holding pod that once contained Ashmara and find it empty but undisturbed. There is a loosening in my chest knowing that the creatures of this world have not been here, followed by a retightening of that same cord. She did not wait for me.

I pluck out her footsteps easily among crushed moss and follow them as they move towards the river. She doesn't walk straight, but lurches and swerves. Her path is painted in all the signs of her stupidity. On muuir, no attempt to cover her tracks, no foreseeable destination. She makes it to the river, but neither wades up it nor crosses it to hide her trail, both of which I do, but what's the point? I'm following Ashmara and she's painted a path in glowing signs marking every place she went. Every stupid, stumbling step.

The river cuts across an immense stretch of dry, arid land. Situated at the far end of this wasteland is a stack of stone cliffs, undoubtedly the lair of these creatures, their central hive, the one place I have no desire to go and the place that Ashmara has set as her ultimate and undoubtedly final destination. *Is she trying to kill herself or is she simply stupid?* The fact that I hesitate to arrive at an answer vexes me.

Huffing under my breath, I take off at a jog while another lunar passes overhead. There is no moon, so the lack of light makes the world look sinister, though it brightens again into something more docile as solar light touches it. The red aurora slashes across the sky no matter the time of solar or lunar, painting it in brush strokes that remind me of the stroke of a blade across the throat of a Voraxian *or a human* — any number of creatures who bleed in copper or scarlet shades. The sky surrounding it shifts into various other colors, pink and blue, orange at a point, without any pattern. It reminds me, quite acutely, of Ashmara. It simply does whatever it wants.

My journey across the flats feels long, though only a solar and lunar pass before I arrive at my destination. There are no gradually rolling foothills here, just spears of stone that jut up out of the flat landscape. From what I can see beneath the mountain's eye, the lower tiers of the mountain range are made of vertical tranches of stone through which paths of sand weave. The river must have worn it down over time. Perhaps it continues to — from what little I read of the planet, it has a brutal and destructive rainy season. And yet there is something not quite…

Aware that this is a path forward with few outcomes that don't lead to death, I approach the first stone monolith and quickly ascend its flat face. It's a climb made easier by my claws and I'm aware as I reach the top that Ashmara isn't just an idiot to have walked the sandy paths below, she's an ill-equipped idiot with no claws or biological defense mechanisms of her own. *But she's a survivor. She's still alive. And what need has she of defense mechanisms has she when she has…*

Krakaw. I refuse to think on it. Instead, I study the trap spread out before me, made so abundantly clear from an aerial view. It's clever, yet archaic and so simple as to be stupid. Again, it makes me think of Ashmara and her wily entrapments. Is there anything that won't make me think of Ashmara?

Grunting, I return my gaze more critically to the present, to the trap laid by the inhabitants of this place. Mirrors. They use mirrors strategically placed between the stone passages to stage their ruse. Rough to the touch and thick, the mirrored panels are crude but effective in directing unknowing travelers along a specific path, one that leads to the mountain.

I follow the path from above, leaping from rocky ledge to rocky ledge. The rocks that form the path are clustered more densely and, in a few places, gaps between the mirrors and the rocks reveal worn steps in the face of the mountain that lead to cracks or caves. Easy entrances and exits for creatures much smaller than I am. Ashmara wouldn't have taken one of those paths. She couldn't have. She'd have had to press on, moving forward. Then, they would have at some point closed in on her from behind.

There is a new scent on the wind. Blood. Coppery and metallic, but also musky and salty. I cannot identify if the blood is of one of the creatures or if it is Ashmaras or perhaps both. I hope it is not both. I move faster, tracing the scent paths to their origin, following the labyrinthine trap until I find its lure, the bait that's been set out just for me. It's a bait that I take and a trap that I will fall into willingly because I have already been entrapped. There is no escape. And even if there were an escape from Ashmara, I would not search for it.

I pause, dropping to my haunches on the next stone pillar, the one that gives me the best view of her. A sensation I have not felt before, therefore can place no name to, rolls over me as my focus narrows on Ashmara.

She hangs there, dangling between two stones, dripping red blood onto the darkening sands below. She has shallow cuts all over her body. Covering her every inch. Intended to bleed her, but not to kill. I wonder what purpose they have in keeping her alive at all, and then I decide that I don't really care. I'll send them all to Death. Their souls are already his.

Metallic blood mingles with a saltier scent. Three of the larger creatures lie dead on the ground around her feet. I'm not sure why they were killed, but I suspect their deaths were simply a reinforcement of hierarchy among these beings. So far, hierarchy tends to be the only trend among them that I see.

Smaller creatures at the top. Larger at the bottom. The corpses are two large creatures, twice my size, and one as long as I am high. I glance around, wondering how long ago they were killed. How long Ashmara has been hanging there. No more than a short solar, of that I'm sure. I glance up at the sky as it drips from orange to purple. The sun is setting again for this solar. It feels appropriate. It feels like a sun is setting within me, too. A darker tide rises.

I hold still, though it is…

My fingers twitch as I crouch atop that boulder, watching Ashmara slowly die. I stroke the fingers of my right hand over the rough stone, feeling the vibrations running through it. Creatures rustle in abundance in the stone tunnels beneath these, yeeshee, but those are not the movements I'm counting on. Waiting for.

The sky switches from purple to pink. Red continues to slice and spray across its oscillating face. Ashmara's blood continues to drip, drip, drip onto the sand. She will survive this, though. She will suffer, but she will live.

I wait, holding, refusing to drop fully into their lure. Not until I can ensure her extraction. It seems to take an eternity, even though it takes less than the rest of the solar to pass before I feel the heavy beat of a pair of feet moving closer, a sound entirely distinct from that of the creatures below. Two feet. No tail. Much larger and heavier than these reptilian beings, I wonder what manner of assassin has come for me. The species matters little. The arrival of a proficient killer is my only hope.

Purple to pink to a dark silver, the colors of the sky thrash as the lunar sets in quickly. I know that the coming solar will be right on its heels. The vibrations in the stone below intensify. The assassin is closing in. Not quite yet at the mountain, judging by the even pace, but close. I continue to hold still, waiting, but…

My hand engages, the stalyx arm moving without my express command to do so. My wrist opens up and a dagger appears in my hand. A radium dagger, inspired by the Va'Rakukanna of Voraxia's original design, only this one doesn't just burn as it cuts but throws electrical impulses to incapacitate its prey before the cut ever occurs. Though I did not intend to draw this weapon forth quite yet, I plan to use it now. Soon. Just a few more…

"Azza?"

Ashmara jerks on her chains and I jolt where I kneel. My gaze travels up from the blood pooling beneath her boots, up her thighs, over her exposed stomach, her chest, her chin, which had drooped against her chest but is now lifted. Her head lolls against one of her splayed arms, her cheek coming to rest against it. She looks brutalized yet utterly magnificent. Have I ever thought her otherwise? She is the most brutal perfection.

Her eyes swirl with blue and then with straight shots of pink that send blasts exploding through me. To say that I don't understand my body's own reaction to that color would be a lie so bold as to border on criminal. I hate her fear. *Hate* it. I always have…

"Azza, krakaw! Krakaw, get away!" she shouts, body jerking to life. Blood coats her lips in a thin sheen. The pink glaze to her eyes sharpens, but there is blue at its very center. Just one final shard. It hurts me just as much as the pink, causing my fist to tighten even further around the blade I hadn't meant to withdraw. "It's a trap, Azza! They're hiding in the mountain. Stupid ecking lizard things. Gah, they're ugly," she groans, head lolling back before she finds the strength again to lift it. "Ugly and annoying. They cut me all up. Lost all my muuir…" I growl, reminded again why I will free her, but cannot keep her. "There're too many of them. Like… hundreds. Thousands. Get out of here! Run!"

The assassin has arrived and the creatures have gone from excited to frantic. I drop down to the sand and instantly feel the world come alive around me. The dark sensation rippling through my skin comes alive to match it and is spectacular in its vivacity. I have never felt like this prior to a kill. I have never felt like this…because assassins do not feel.

Her cheeks are grey, drained of all color, but her eyes are kaleidoscopes as she stares at me pleadingly. "Azza, run! Can't you hear them, you big idiot?" She starts to jerk on her bindings, but the material is made of something like rope dipped in something like glass. Perhaps, shards of their tough carapaces ground to powder and spread over moss woven into rope. That would be my guess. It's slicing into her wrists and, if she keeps at it with the violence she is, will take her hands. She cares nothing for her own skin, for her own life, begging me to flee instead of save her. Hatred flashes through me. Krakaw, not hatred. It is…

I extend my stalyx arm and fire two blasts. The ropes fall apart and Ashmara falls to the ground in a puddle of limbs. I watch her curse up at the moonless sky while red illuminates her skin. She remains still, steadily cursing, as the Sky assassin arrives.

He is an old model. Older than I am, with fewer upgrades. His original form is difficult to decipher, though I imagine some of him may at some point have been Mormora. Instead of stalyx parts, however, he's been retrofitted with an Oosa carapace. Bright and glowing blue electrifies his back and one half of his mottled green face. He has an Egama eye, which will make his sight sharper perhaps than even mine, even with my yeeyar retrofit, but only in the light.

So, I will have to kill him in the dark.

But first…

He and I turn so that we are back to back. Hm. His back has been fitted with Niahhorru tines. This makes him more formidable. They are already stained in bright orange blood. It glitters and smells of the moss growing so ubiquitously over this planet, musk and salt. He had no trouble with the roving horde of creatures earlier, it seems…nearly no trouble. He limps on his right leg and his left arm is missing a finger. Based on the shredded skin surrounding it, it seems like it might have been bitten off.

Good that he has a weakness that will slow him down slightly. So do I.

I hear the sound of her rustling through her pack even louder than the scraping of claws over sand and stone as the first battalion closes in around the other assassin and me. She's cursing, muttering to herself about muuir. I would shoot the pack out of her hand if I weren't concerned about her existing blood loss, and if I didn't have need of it. I need her to keep herself out of the way. It shouldn't be hard. The creatures are focused on us and move past her like she's not worthy of their concern. She's not.

Wavering on her feet as she stands, she holds a dagger and stumbles as she tries to stab the large creature who lumbers past her. The thing slashes at her with its claws. I throw my radium dagger, severing the creature's wrist and knocking it out cold. It falls. The yeeyar-laced dagger spirals through the air and returns to me.

Behind me, I hear the assassin grunt as he engages his first opponent. Another large creature, I notice. We are besieged by the larger members of the species. They are attempting to soften the battlefield. I thought they were primitive. Perhaps, they'll make for a more challenging adversary, after all. I wonder if this is not why my Sky brother aligned himself so quickly to me. He hasn't tried to kill me once, so far.

Instead, he uses a weapon not entirely dissimilar to mine to attack the incoming beasts. He strikes for their throats and I mimic his efforts, trusting his instincts after having fought a small contingent and lived.

I slice the throats of three large beasts. The next that comes for me is slightly smaller. He moves quickly, though not so quickly as I do. He kicks me in the right leg, drawing blood. I decapitate him with my Drakesh claws.

They come in waves, hard and fast. Their willingness to sacrifice themselves is their greatest strength. My energy has not begun to flag, but I can feel the assassin at my back begin to wane. He takes a claw to the stomach while a smaller creature leaps onto his back and buries all four of its limbs in his blue Oosa flesh. As a distraction, it is effective, but it is a mistake for the creature, who is burned alive from the electricity that the enhanced Oosa flesh generates.

It crumbles to the ground, but two clawed hands are still stuck in the Oosa flesh. Another creature attacks and meets the same fate.

The smallest of the creatures are on us now. Two engage me at once and they are the quickest I've seen. I take three cuts to the abdomen, my stalyx skin screeching beneath the touch of their claws, my synthetic armor shredded. I block the next attack with my stalyx arm while wielding my radium dagger but…a slight "oomph" pulls my attention away from them.

I throw my dagger at the small creature Ashmara is attempting to attack. She staggers to the side, righting herself like a clever drunk as her flimsy blade clinks uselessly off of the creature's thick scales. The creature turns around to face her and seems bored at the sight of her. Casually, it lifts its hand, capable of delivering to Death so glibly and I'm sure it will.

That dark surge of violence within me eclipses every ounce of my reason. I fire two blasts at the creature and though they ricochet off of the creature's too-thick hide, it's still a successful distraction. As it turns, I fling my radium dagger into its throat. The dagger gets stuck and does not return to me. That's fine. I withdraw an extendable helos staff with a serrated blade edge. It'll be slow going, killing with this, but it at least keeps me from having to get within striking distance of their claws. I spin, dancing with my new weapon as I kill another creature and then another, a third and then a fourth and then a tenth.

The waves of their onslaught have begun to slow and the incoming creatures have begun to look nervous. The next creature does not advance. It tucks tail and runs. The battle changes.

The moment the first of the creatures flees, my tail lashes out at the assassin behind me. He reacts a split instant after I do, turning to block the strike of my weaponized tail with his own, an enhanced addition as Mormoras are naturally tailless. Our tails meet and pain reverberates through mine, but it is not enough to slow me. I turn. He fires a blast. I block it with the blade of my staff. It refracts, grazing his left cheek. Sensing he'll be too slow with blaster fire, he unhooks a weapon from his belt and extends it into a staff just in time to meet the downstroke of my own.

We battle across the sands for so long, the solar unfurls from the lunar's bleak gaze. He moves with more precision beneath the orange light, but he's still too slow to defeat me. His death is inevitable.

"Woohoo! Get him, Jer!" Jer. I hate this name and growl.

The assassin's gaze strays. He lunges and fires a blast, aiming not for me — but past me. I jump and spin to block it and take a blast to the right shoulder. It sears my red skin as I land in a crouch. The assassin is ready for me. He is also learning. He releases a continuous stream of blasts over my shoulder, forcing me to fight on my weaker side.

He kicks and his boots are lined in blades. They shred the remainder of my armor and I skid back, landing on one knee. He dives straight past me, heading straight for Ashmara, who's staring at him with rounded eyes. I do not know why she doesn't run…even as he grabs her by the throat.

He turns to face me and I go from a full-out sprint to stone in a moment. I lower to a crouch and place both of my palms flat on the sand, my staff beneath them. He smiles and it's an ugly thing. It's a *strange* expression. It doesn't look in any way like it belongs to a being of these cosmos. Even the creatures of this planet look more sympathetic. There is life in their eyes, a hint of intelligence. In this being's great gobbling eye, there is nothing. Just the absence of everything. *Is that what I looked like? Not like a living being, but like a being's shell?*

My hand twitches. I shake my head, trying to recenter myself, but the assassin thinks the gesture is for him.

His grin spreads. "The rumors are true."

I do not reply.

He laughs and the sound echoes between the glittering orange rocks and similarly bloodstained sands beneath our feet, loudly now that we've been left alone. "You've been corrupted. Sky's greatest failure. And because of a weak *hybrid*." He whispers the word as if it's a virus, bound to corrupt his immutable programming. I thought mine was immutable. Then again, perhaps it was. Perhaps, the true failing was that of the Architects, who should have known that I'd already been programmed from the start.

Ashmara gives me a little wave, then balls her hand into a fist and lifts only her thumb. I believe her intention to be positive, though I do not know how it could be given that she's one stroke away from death and I am uncertain I will have the time to get to her to prevent it. *If she dies, I will never forgive her.*

She smiles to show all of her teeth and blinks at me again with just one eye while her other hand peeks up over the assassin's shoulder. In it, she holds her dull blade.

I keep my focus trained on her using my yeeyar sight while my biological eye remains trained on the assassin's face. I hold. Her plan is risky, foolish, stupid and clumsy, and yet…I do not have a better plan to act out in its place. So, I simply continue to kneel there without reacting to the sight of the blade flashing in her grip.

"The Architects will be happy to have you back, Jerrock." He reaches into his pocket and withdraws a set of shackles. These are made of conix, a material native to the Sky planet and found only there. If I put them on, I will not be able to break them.

The green-grey shackles sit dully before me, looking thin and unassuming and breakable. I hesitate. I cannot. If I put them on and Ashmara… I can't…

"Hey, big guy," Ashmara says, voice sharp and clear.

His large head swivels to towards her face. His clawed hand swipes down to hurt her. I hurtle up into a sprint, but I'm not fast enough to stop whatever will happen next. All manner of eventualities play out before my eyes and in all of them, Ashmara ends up gutted on the yellow sands while I stand above her, too slow to save her this time. *Never.*

But Ashmara doesn't aim for his throat or his heart, well hidden beneath layers of electrified Oosa flubber, or even his approaching hand. She aims for his eye.

Mossy green spurts back at her face and she sputters and chokes as it lands in her mouth. He screeches his rage, but doesn't release her neck. He prepares to snap the thin line of her throat, an easy feat for most creatures in the cosmos, but I lift my stalyx wrist and fire a dozen small blast rounds into his extended arm, just enough to sever the joints at his elbows and prevent him from killing her as he squeezes.

Leaving my helos staff behind, I vault from the ground. I don't need a weapon to finish this. I reach into his mouth and grab his tongue. I rip it out. He falls, landing on his back, and I sink my boot through the Mormora side of his chest before stabbing my staff through it and cleaving him apart in an effort to find his Sky key.

But I am too late.

The creature emits a light groan and before I know it, his eyes roll back and become covered in black yeeyar. He chokes it up, black spittle flying out of his mouth, smearing my stalyx arm as it hits me. He's finished himself off for good and the Sky key has died with him, leaving me no closer to discovering the location of the planet I need to reach. *That I need to incinerate.*

I stand above him, frustrated, a common sensation for me in recent solars. In past solars, too. I think of

Ashmara, as I once saw her. *The* memory I try to fight, but cannot.

"You really know how to show a girl a good time, don't ya, Azza?"

The spell of the memory breaks as she laughs and I tip my chin down to watch her roll up onto her knees. She squints against the sun as she looks up at me and lifts a hand to shade her eyes. She wavers on her feet. Her breathing is ragged and shallow and yet, her chest isn't the only part of her that's trembling. I don't understand it at first, the movement of her lower lip. She's trying to draw it up into a smile, and all I can think is that her smile looks nothing like the assassin's did. Hers is pure life in all of its angry confusion and misguided conviction. Her smile, right now, is the sun of this planet, ephemeral and elusive, but present. It makes everything glow. I take a step, caught in its gravitational pull.

"You shouldn't have done that."

I stop, one foot still sunken into the assassin's shattered chest. I tilt my head and narrow my eyes. My biological eye. "That's three times now." She stares into it with sincerity that frightens me. "And this was a trap. It was so obviously a trap, you must have known that..." Her voice trails off in a way it's not often apt to. "You're a Sky assassin, Jer..."

I *hate* it when she calls me that. I advance on her, grab her beneath the arm and by the back of her head. I lift her off her feet and prop her up against the nearest blood-glazed stone, wishing to slam her against it, but I can't.

"Stop this," I hiss into her ear in a low voice, one that usually brooks neither response nor argument.

I remember things being predictable with Rook.

Nothing is predictable with Ashmara. "It was a trap."

"You think that mattered? That I wouldn't come for you?" I snarl against her bloodied lips. "I've been coming for you before I even remembered you existed. I've been searching for you my entire life."

I comb my fingers through her white hair and shudder wildly. Her hair is just as soft as I remember it being. And it is, like the smoothness of her skin, exquisitely familiar to me.

"I missed you, Azza. I missed you so ecking much." She bursts into tears. It's awkward seeing *Ashmara,* reaver of all reavers, cry.

"Ashmara," I growl in warning. "Stop this."

She doesn't listen. She continues to weep. "I love…"

"Don't." I slam my stalyx fist into the stone beside her head. *"Don't.* Don't. I barely have a heart left. Don't try to break it."

She sniffles and blinks and whatever hold she had on the emotions shining in her gaze releases, if she ever even possessed such a hold at all. Her gaze beams with color, with every color of the universe all at once. "It is true, though. I do love you. I've loved you ever since we were kits…"

I slam the narrow edge of my Drakesh hand against the side of her neck. I'm not quick enough to avoid the calamity of her initial words but I am quick enough to stop her from saying anything else. She slumps into my grip, her full weight falling into my hands. I catch her and throw her over my shoulder and retreat from the mountain and from her words beneath the setting solar, knowing that she is a little lost thing using words that she does not understand. Because there can be no such thing as love in the realms of Death.

10

Ashmara

My head feels fuzzy. Did I take too much muuir again? It wouldn't be the first time, though the last time I made that mistake I promised myself it would be *the* last time. Guess it wouldn't be the first time I've broken promises, either.

I sit up and pat the space around me, searching for my bag before I bother to open my eyes. Whatever's under my palm is flat and dry. I move my fingers over it carefully. The textured surface feels vaguely familiar. Where am I?

I push myself up into a seat and blink. Everything's dark. Like, really dark. Too dark to see far, but I don't need to see. "Aha!" My pack had been shoved underneath my cheek. I open and close my mouth, shifting my jaw around. It's a little sore and so is the rest of me, but I'm not one great big open wound anymore. I rub my hand over my stomach and feel what I know is dried blood flake off onto the stone below and…

Stone. Rocks. Blood.

I remember now. I also remember that I lost enough blood to drain the muuir out of my system. Eck. My hand dives into my pack. I know where the hidden compartment is by memory. I could find it in any light, or none at all. I push past the spare clothes, my yamar box, a few rations of nutrition supplement, a few more bottles of Eshmiri booze. The bottles clink together as I find the hidden compartment, undo the latch and reach for the packet of muuir, but…

Krakaw. My fingers fumble in the empty place where the pouch should be, but isn't. Oh krakaw. Krakaw, krakaw, krakaw.

I sit up and try to lurch all the way up to standing, but don't make it farther than rolling onto my hip. My chest sears with adrenaline and panic. I'm gonna have to go back… Back where? I shake my head, trying to remember the rest. Trying to think.

Tunnels of stone. A bright solar. A dark path. I'm going to have to go back into the tunnel…down…down into the lizard pit. *ECK!* I'm gonna have to fight a pack of lizards to get it back and that's only if they haven't used it all yet. There were a lot of the bastards.

I slide both hands beneath me and move onto my knees at the same time that a slight shuffling alerts me to something I should have probably noticed before. I'm not alone.

I thunk back onto my ass and shove my hand into my pack, finding my light because it *is* where it's supposed to be. I toss the miniature Eshmiri torches into the air. All three of them power on. One yellow, one orange, one white. They hover a few feet above my head and throw a typically warm glow over the space that manages to look sinister now when refracted off of the hard stalyx planes of the male's face. The assassin's. And he's never looked more deadly than he does now.

"Eck." The word chokes out of me. I rub my hand roughly up and down my face, unsure if this is a hallucination produced by muuir withdrawals or my current reality. I give my arm a little pinch and it hurts, but not that much. Inconclusive. And then I see the beat-up packet shining dully against his silver skin. He's holding it. Crushing it in his stalyx fist.

"Ohmyeckingstars! Are you real? Is this real? Are you here? I thought you were dead!" I slam the heel of my hand against my right temple, trying to shake the rest of the memories free.

Jerrock standing up on top of a boulder, silhouetted by red flashes in the sky, looking down at me. The terrible sound of lizard beings coming to claw and cut him to shreds. My own ragged breathing and the rich and tangy scent of my own metallic blood filling my lungs on each of my short, staccato breaths. And then a new ally coming to join the fray... Krakaw, an enemy...wait...

"What do you remember?" Jerrock's voice is low and freaks the shit out of me because it seems to cement the fact that Azza lived. Jerrock or Azza, whoever he currently is.

The fact that my eyes don't explode out of my head as the words storm out of my chest is a miracle. "You're alive! How? I didn't see a ship fall out of the sky and there's no way you landed before I did."

"What do you remember after reaching the mountains?"

A little kit. I shake my head and snort and roughly ruffle my hair. *A little kit with claws.* I try not to focus too hard on the pouch in his hand, but he seems to tighten his grip on it every time I glance at it and his angry hold is causing me to panic. I don't want him to ruin it.

"I got *got*," I blurt out, my voice low and breathy. "I… I walked down a tunnel I shouldn't have gone down, then a lizard kid sliced me up real good." I slide my hand across my stomach. My clothes are shredded and crusty. I make a disgusted face down at them and vow to change as soon as I get my pouch back. As soon as I'm sure he'll give it to me. *What if he doesn't?* I was prepared to fight an entire planet's worth of lizards, but am I willing to fight Azza for it? Krakaw, not really.

Maybe.

As my stomach pitches and a familiar nausea creeps up on me like an assassin, I know the truth. I'm going to have to fight. Muuir is only a fair-weather friend to me. It won't give me a choice.

"What happened next?"

"Jer, I'll tell you everything, but could you please give me my stuff back?"

He tilts his head in a way that I imagine he does before he murders most victims and says, "Krakaw."

"Jer…"

"Krakaw," he snaps, voice like a whip, making me jump. "Not this name. Never this."

I nod once, his tone brooking no argument. Not that that ordinarily would have stopped me, but right now, I'd do anything he commanded. Almost anything. Krakaw, anything. I wince, hating myself a little bit at that realization. He must see, because when I open my eyes, he has his bio eye narrowed.

"Okay, Azza," I tell him. I clench my teeth and lean forward onto my hands and knees. I worry I won't be able to stand right if I try and I don't want him to see how much I ecking need the stuff in his hand.

He says nothing with words, but speaks volumes with his silence.

"What?"

"Azza," he hisses.

I start, a little weirded out by him saying his own name. "What?"

"You called me Jerrock a moment ago, but since Tiringdam, you haven't called me Jerrock. Not once." His voice jerks. "Not once."

I cringe and I clench my fist and I drop it to the stone by his shin. I drop my head, too, feeling all kindsa ways. Terrible, mostly. My stomach takes a dive. *Krakaw, krakaw. Just tell him what he wants. Tell him anything!* I blurt, "Because Jerrock might give me that pouch and I don't think Azza will." I feel like shit. I'm so pathetic. I'd be embarrassed if I weren't so desperate. "Jerrock, *please.*"

He clenches his jaw and the yeeyar in his eye shifts rapidly from right to left. I wonder if he's looking me over. I can't tell. I know his other eye is brown, but in the darkness it looks black. His red lips twitch like he's going to flay me alive. He looks ecking furious. Well, more furious than usual. But staring at him in this low light with the little food I've eaten and the ecking buckets of blood that I've lost *and my lack of muuir* it's hard to concentrate on what might be his potential retaliation against whatever wrong I've committed against him. It's gotten so hard to even see straight.

The next wave of nausea rolls up from my hips to the back of my neck, causing my spine to bow. I retch into my elbow, the dry heave painful as nothing comes up. Spots fill my vision, but clear quickly.

This wasn't so bad. It wasn't so bad. I know that it can get much worse. The one time I detoxed, I didn't think I was going to survive it. I got robbed on Kor and ended up without. The folks at the pleasure house had to go out and get me more before I could even leave the establishment. It was so embarrassing, making things even worse given what I'd done there. I wince. That memory has no place here in front of him.

I open my eyes at the light sound of scraping and see a muuir patch on the ground by my right hand. Oh eck! Yeeshee, yeeshee. I grab the small beige-colored rectangle, peel off the thin film with shaking hands and slap it on the back of my neck.

I exhale in one great big sigh, "Aaahhhh."

The muuir floods my system, filling me with euphoria. I remember now. There was the other assassin. I killed him. Well, I tried. Is that green blood on my hands? Or are the spots in my vision still fading? I laugh as I rock back onto my heels.

"Thanks, Azza…"

"Don't ecking thank me. Not for this. And don't call me Azza, either."

My chest pulls. My stomach pushes. One last breath of nausea passes and I feel like myself again. "I…"

"Passed out. You asked me only for more muuir even though you had this with you." He holds up the healing wand, a small cylindrical device, white, just like everything else on the Sky ship was. "Why didn't you ask for it? You did not forget you had it with you. You healed your arm…"

I cut him off. "Look, Azza. I was out of it." I try a laugh, try to regain control of the situation.

"Don't talk to me like I'm one of your reaver friends. I don't even know you. Tell me the truth."

There is a truth, just not one he'd understand. I barely understand it myself. My jaw works stupidly. I have no control here.

His gaze narrows further. "You were in pain. Either you didn't feel your pain because of the muuir and you're just a simple addict, wanting more at any cost, even your life. Or..." He swallows, gathers his knees and drapes his arms over their tops. "You were in pain and felt you deserved it."

It's my turn not to answer because he asked me for the truth. The truth is that he's right. He's also wrong. He thinks it's an *or*. It's not. I feel those things. I feel them all.

He sneers and it's the most emotion I've ever seen play out on his face. "I don't know which explanation I like less."

"The first one," I lie to him. "I just like the stuff."

I like the idea of him thinking it's the muuir. It's a simpler explanation. Makes me seem simpler. Seeming simple to the creatures around me who don't understand me has been my greatest strength. Jerrock always thought I was simple. That's how he allowed himself to be lured onto my ship.

The idea that I'm just a simple muuir addict isn't the worst thing in the world. If I squint hard enough and tilt my head, being addicted to muuir is kind of like being in love, even though the object of my affections will never know I exist or love me back.

Wait a moment, I think on a grunt, that sounds kind of like...

My eyes widen while Azza's squint. "Tell me the truth."

Was I Jerrock's addiction? When he was incapable of love, incapable of remembering, yet bound to hunt for me mercilessly. Living with me like a ghost on his shoulder that he could never quite see.

That's what muuir feels like to me. And it's a funny thing, because the only thing separating love and addiction is that I don't *want* to be addicted to muuir. Does Jerrock wish he, too, could be free of me?

"*Rook,*" he barks, his voice a slap in the face with a rock.

I gasp, struggle to breathe and all but shout, "It was all that I had after they took you." My voice echoes, making me wonder where we are. "It was my only friend."

His lips thin. "*This* is not your friend. And neither am I." He stands and shoots my muuir pack a look of pure revulsion. I slide it over the ground towards me so quickly that the empty vials clank inside. "I did not get carved into pieces and turned into a monster to find you like this." My gut sinks like a stone in still water. In just a few words, my universe is set ablaze. The forest of my soul is burning.

And he's still talking.

"Once we get off of this planet, I'll drop you at your ship and then we're done. I'm done. I'm done chasing you. Azza and Rook will be left where they died, where they should have always remained — on that Lemoran refugee ship six rotations ago. I'm not interested in watching you rot from the inside, so don't come looking for me either. If you do catch up to me, I won't know you. Because I don't know you."

The knife just keeps coming.

"Get up. Take one of your nutrition supplements, or don't. The solar is nearly on us and we have ground to cover."

He moves to the mouth of the cave and I watch his back — the silver, the black suit he wears to cover most of the red. It's shredded now. Just another rescue mission that got him hurt. *I* got him hurt. And he's right. I'm not worth rescuing. The universe would be better without me — krakaw, I don't believe that. But *he* would.

I bowl over, a slicing, sickening sensation filling my stomach with hot coals. I can't...I can't... I squeeze my eyes shut as violently as I can, but wetness still comes to cover my eyelashes. *Krakaw.* Don't. Don't...I can't...

I reach with both hands for the pouch of muuir and I grab a handful of patches until I can feel it. Pure bliss. Total enlightenment. What Azza said...he didn't mean it. It's not so bad. I can get off of muuir. I can show him he's wrong. Yeeshee, no problem.

On muuir, everything feels so easy.

I leave a few dozen patches — I won't take them, of course not. I mean, not unless...

Krakaw, I'll get off muuir. It'll be easy, no problem. I'll just save this for... *If it's so easy, why are you saving it?* I take one more patch and hate myself as I slap it on over the rest. Okay, that's it.

My fingers fumble as I gather what's left of the patches, shove them in the pouch, shove the pouch in my pack and take off after him. He's already so far away. I have to run to catch up. It seems to take forever. The moss is crunchy underneath my feet and the breeze feels incredible as it sweeps my skin. Like being wrapped in layers and layers of the softest fabric and cradled against the sun.

I am warm. I touch his arm. His red arm. It's beautiful and the texture is amazing. "Azza, wait, I can…"

He rips his arm out of my grip, recoiling from me and turning my entire world out, making me cold. So, so cold. Red flashes in the jade sky above him, jerking like a dagger forming a crooked wound across the face of my soul.

He looks down his nose at me, his words icy as he speaks one final declaration, in which he's wrapped and brutalized all my hopes and dreams. "My name is Jerrock."

11

Jerrock

I don't look back at her as I walk, but I do slow my steps. I can hear her thrashing through the river. She falls every few paces and is slower and slower to get up afterwards. She sighs. The sound is...euphoric. It makes my abdomen clench. My lower abdomen. Teasing me as I remember what...

The sound of scrambling on the horizon increases, concerning me. The creatures of this planet did not chase us after the battle. They retreated. A few of the larger creatures came later, when I found a cave to hole up in during the lunar, a place among scattered hills in the moss flats safe and seemingly remote enough for me to let Ashmara rest and pass the healing wand over her many wounds. There were so many. The thought makes me...displeased. Even more so than the wounds I sustained, also easily healed by the wand. Allowing Ashmara her rest was a decision that vexed me, but I was willing to face off against the few *lizards* who came for us.

But the larger creatures didn't come to harm us. Instead, they dragged several dismembered stumps of flesh in front of the entrance to the cave. Two of the stumps were clearly reptilian while the other belonged to the former Sky assassin. It was unusual behavior, demonstrating typical patterns of beta pack members to a greater alpha. That, I might have been able to understand, had I not heard the sounds of crunching moss and claws tearing through sand chasing us now.

Faster.

Our destination isn't far. Another three lunars and two solars more. I can see the rise in the distance where we need to go but for a creature on muuir, it's a difficult trek. For a creature on *this* amount of muuir, potentially impossible.

I remember the words that I told her and cement them in my mind as vows. Vows of separation. To separate myself from Ashmara in a way that Jerrock the assassin never could, and that Azza the kit never dreamed possible. I loved her, once. As a kit, she gave me great joy, great purpose…

The sound of her splashing and sighing and singing behind me grates.

…that purpose is all but ended. I cannot bind myself to one that is already bound to something else. Not even I hate myself enough to endure the slow torture of watching her kill herself.

My feet sink deeper and deeper into the wet sand. My pants are shredded around the left ankle and the water floods my suit. It's warm. I close my eyes as she splashes into the river again. *It could be different…*

Krakaw. These types of fantasies will only end with disappointment. The kind that no heart can remain intact against, and though I barely have a heart left, it does exist. And I cannot…

"Azza?" she says.

My irritation spikes and cuts. I round on her as her legs slice noisily through the water. My steps make almost no noise by comparison. To be so loud and clumsy would have resulted in great pain administered by the Architects. I'd have requested it myself for such a failing. My eyelid flickers and I remember so many things that I requested — *krakaw, things that were done to me* — and I remember them all in a new light. I don't like it. That male is not me. I may not be Azza anymore, but I certainly am not Jerrock the killer, either.

Jerrock the killer was soulless and the male that I am now very much has a soul. If he didn't, it wouldn't be so painful watching Ashmara now.

Returning for her, I grab her arm above the elbow and yank her up and drag her forward. I don't acknowledge the way my fingers warm against her skin, or the sounds she makes. They're all soft and desperate, two things I know Ashmara not to be. And I absolutely do not hear the way she slurs and stutters my name intermittently between apologies I know she doesn't mean.

"I'll stop, Azza…I mean, Jerrock, I promise, I'll stop. For you… I'd do anything for you, don't you know that? You know that… Azza, can we just slow down? The sun feels warm, doesn't it? I like this planet. I'll call it Lizardia, huh? Like Voraxia but Lizardia? Or is that dumb? Dumb…dumb, dumb, dumb… Ha. That's a funny word, dumb. You know who's dumb? Me! I thought that little lizard was a kit." She laughs again.

"You know who else was dumb? That assassin who was following you. He totally didn't see the knife I was holding, did he? Krakaw. He was just looking at you and then wham! Easy." She sputters out a little laugh, this one much lighter. "Serves him right for underestimating a human. Wouldn't be the first time."

I stumble.

Stumble.

I try to mask it as if I were taking a step up out of the river and continue on, but her words dig into my skin like my fingers do into her arm. With pressure and a dash of violence. *Human.* It is a species I've heard about only recently. One of my most recent targets was a suspected human hybrid. She's now very much free and alive and mated to a Lemoran Clan Chief while the male who'd requested her brought to him for whatever nefarious purpose has himself been repurposed back into stardust.

Ashmara interfered, yet my inability to maneuver freely in her presence was not my only failing in that mission. I knew that the Lemorans were a peaceful yet loyal people and I had pitted their desire for peace against their loyalty...and lost. I thought they would abandon the human hybrid in an effort not to incite war, but instead, to recover her they brought war with them in the form of Ashmara and her band of reavers and a whole host of Niahhorru pirates.

I had underestimated a human then, true.

Until now, I have known that Ashmara is a suspected human hybrid as well — that is why the Architects want her for the horlax, a hair-raising thought — but it has never really, truly crossed my mind that *I* could be of that species, too. It hasn't mattered. What I was, who I was, was all but irrelevant. I find the idea more interesting now.

"What do you know of humans?" I ask her, though I had vowed not to speak to her at all.

"Quite a lot, actually. Some silly little human landed in my lap in the Evernor pits and took it upon herself to give me this manual about humans. They sound like an extravagantly arrogant bunch. So many little things they need or don't need in order to accomplish the most basic tasks. Did you know that a male — a *man* — must first *woo* a female before they can couple or mate? He has to bring her little gifts or food before she'll even think about coupling with him. Isn't that crazy? Like an offering to a god."

"Goddess."

"What?"

"An offering to a goddess." Memories unbidden flood my mind's eye, but I blink them furiously away.

"What do you…"

"Do you have this human guide?"

"Yeeshee. It's in my yamar box."

I nod, intending to investigate it later on the ship. For now, we need to move faster. "You're too slow. I'll have to carry you."

I don't give her a chance to reply, but throw her over my shoulder and start to move at speed over the flats as another solar rises over the horizon's crest.

She continues to try to talk to me. It's aggravating. I continue to run and listen to the sounds of clawing in the distance. They move faster than I do, laden with my present burden, and are gaining ground.

Finally, I begin to see the tip of the Sky ship shimmering in the distance. It is a differently shaped craft than the one I arrived to this planet in, pointed at the roof, with six wings that dig into the ground at its base. All unblemished white, it refracts pink light brilliantly whenever red snakes across the sky behind it.

I feel a burning in my thighs despite their enhancements. I will need rest after this, a thought that seems unimaginable. For now, I'm almost there. "We're almost there," I say aloud, though the words startle me as they come out of my mouth. Why did I say that?

It takes me until this moment to realize that she's stopped talking. "Ashmara."

"Az...za?" she says on a bounce.

The tightness across my chest loosens somewhat. "Jerrock."

She falls silent again.

Since we departed the cave two solars ago, it has been a while since she has had rest. She hasn't drunk any water since we abandoned the river and even then she didn't drink much. She hasn't eaten either. I don't know if she even reached for a nutrition pack when I suggested she eat, or if she left it. I did suggest that it didn't matter. That her life didn't matter. But she's *Ashmara* the Eshmiri, the most wanted female in all the Quadrants, the only creature to elude the Sky assassins for as long as she has, the liberator of the enslaved, the only female Eshmiri. She's infamous and famous all in one. And she's a fighter to a fault. She's a female who is foolish bordering on suicidal. Is that what this is a case of? Or is this simply the behavior of an addict?

Has she taken what I said to heart? Has she given up?

Nearly at the ship now, I feel pressure. Yeeshee, pressure. It is unlike anything I have ever felt. But it is no worry. None at all. I'm almost there. The doors of the ship open at my approach...and thirty paces away, I come to a stop.

Standing in the shade of the open doorway is a Niahhorru pirate in droherion chains. They are broken.

Two additional pirates move to flank him. A fourth appears in their shadow. They must have been prisoners of the Sky assassin locked away in control tanks. It is impressive that they managed to escape them at all, a feat I know to be only. possible because of the death of the Sky assassin who held them. When his connection to the ship was broken, they likely had instants to fight their way free. They did not let those instants go to waste, I see.

I hesitate. A Niahhorru pirate is no adversary to scoff at. Four will be trouble with the dead weight I carry. Krakaw, not dead. Is it the muuir that makes her so quiet? The thought makes me feel too many things, all unfamiliar to me.

The first of the Niahhorru males smiles at me widely in a way that shows all of his pearly teeth. "You're not the one who put us in here, but you'll do just fine." His tines flash silver as he jumps down onto the moss below. His eyes appear matte as his shields come to cover them. He is angry and prepared for battle. I am angry, but for the first time I have ever known, I am not so prepared. She narrowly survived the last one.

"You risk much, engaging me," I say to him in Meero.

"What are you talking about?" He laughs and cracks the knuckles of his bottom two hands. "Engaging you will be fun." Pirates. Just as ridiculous as Eshmiri with their dark sense of humor.

"You'll die," I warn.

He shrugs. "Maybe. Maybe not."

"Who's your friend?" the male to his right says, jumping down after him.

I cannot help the low sound my throat emits, nor do I wish to quiet it. The look in his eyes is overly curious and has me positioning Ashmara to my other side.

"More than a friend, then, is she?" the one in the back says.

"Centare. He's an assassin. They don't have friends."

"Well, we could liberate her then."

"We should," another replies on laughter that I despise. "It would be our duty."

"You will not touch her." My tone is unfamiliar to me. I do not bother to decipher it, or marshal it into something less violent. "It is not a threat, but a certainty. If you wish to live another solar, then you will vacate the transport and keep your eyes from the female."

My ability to lie has never been so poor. The Niahhorru laugh. All four of them. The two who've descended the ship to their deaths advance towards me a few leisurely paces. One of the remaining pirates grips the door frame in his upper hands and leans out until the sunlight strikes him. His skcin is up, leaving his eyes exposed. I should take the opportunity to shoot them out, but don't. I am more concerned with the sudden tilt of his head.

"What is that?"

On cue, the scraping of feet and claws is punctuated by a shrill shriek. It sends a shiver skittering up my spine. I hazard a glance over my shoulder. "Ashmara," I say, speaking to the weight on my back finally, "we are about to be overtaken by the creatures of this planet. I will put you down to fight."

I begin to lower her to the ground, but as she passes over my shoulder and sinks into a cradle hold, she whispers, "Arc we not friends, Jerrock?"

"Krakaw."

She chuckles, but her voice is hollow. "I guess you're right. Your only friend died a long time ago." She starts to cough as soon as her back hits the moss. She rolls onto her side in a fetal position, curling around her stomach like she's in pain. But then she laughs brightly once again.

"Come on then!" she shouts in Meero, rolling onto her knees and staggering up to her feet. Her pack is strapped across her back. In her hand she holds the healing wand. I take it she thought it was the radium dagger, or perhaps the flimsier dagger of her own. Right now, she carries both

The pirates laugh.

She laughs, too. I turn to face the fifty or so creatures who are just a few moments from fully descending on us and wonder if it would not be more prudent to first kill the pirates. I'm not making clear decisions. I find myself…distracted.

"Have you heard the one about the Niahhorru pirate who walked into the arena on Evernor?"

The male closest to her pauses in his next step and reaches out his arm to block his mate from moving past him. "Centare. What happened next?"

Ashmara waves the wand around as she talks, all of them fully ignoring the horde of angry creatures charging us. I guess it leaves all of them to me. Tension threads my bones. *They are many and I'm still recovering from my injuries.* I watch the tide of creatures rising.

"The pirate walks out into the middle of the arena unarmed and the Death Hound he's up against bites off his leg."

"Would never happen," one of the pirates shouts.

"Shh! Let her finish," another says.

Ashmara continues, "The pirate looks at the Death Hound and says, 'Hey! You do that again and I'm going home!'"

Silence.

What?

And then all four pirates and Ashmara burst into raucous laughter all at once. "That's a good one..." "G o i n g   h o m e ..."   "W a l k i n g   h o m e ..." "BAHAHAHAHA!"

I find myself contemplating the alleged joke longer than I should be given the present predicament and realize that the words in Meero for walking and going are the same. Therein the joke lies.

Hm. I still fail to find the humor in it.

"Tell us another one."

"Okay, okay," Ashmara says, her words still badly slurred. She rubs the healing wand against her temple. "What do you call a Niahhorru pirate born with an extra set of hands?"

"Got me!"

"I don't know, tell us!"

"Centare, centare. Wait, I've got it. You call him *hand*some. Handsome, get it?" another pirate says to a riot of laughter.

"Centare!" Ashmara shouts, wiping tears of laughter from her own eyes. She's practically wheezing and I wonder if she won't suffocate on this thin air laughing as she is. "You call him a *hand*ful!"

They all return to laughing while the first of the lizards — creatures — springs towards me...and dodges my strike. He doesn't just dodge the fist I level towards his maw, but switches past me, circumventing me entirely. His tail flashes and gleams. He's one of the smaller ones, his scales a lighter green. I am prepared to lunge and intercept him should he choose to veer right towards Ashmara, but he doesn't. He heads directly for the pirates and releases a piercing scream.

The pirates' chuckles have died off as they move away from the ship and further out onto the mossy flat. There, they are able to stand tine to tine, in a square formation, each one only breaking formation to slaughter an incoming creature. And in they do come.

The creatures pour around me and Ashmara like we don't even exist. I don't quite understand what motivates them, but I don't attempt to question them about it. Instead, I advance on Ashmara and grab her by the upper arm. She's facing me when I grab her and stumbles back when I charge forward.

"We should help them, huh, Jer?" she muses, caught in her dream state. None of this is real. None of this can hurt her when she's this way. Nothing can. Not even me. Is that why she took so much? I snarl, not caring anything for her reasons.

"Jerrock. And krakaw," I tell her, switching back to her native Eshmiri. I haul her body up against mine and vault up onto the ship. There are already two lizard creatures inside, busy scuttling back and forth, tearing things apart. They don't seem to be searching for anything, but are tearing through the blaster control panel at random, as if it simply amuses them.

I modify my vocal box to be able to replicate the shriek I've heard from these creatures and unleash it at a high pitch.

"Ecking comets!" Ashmara shouts behind me, lifting her arms to cover her ears as I drop her on the floor.

The creatures react instantly, devolving to shrieks and scampering away. I don't hesitate, but rush to the hifelai control board, insert my wrist into the reader and attach the yeeyar flowing through my veins to the ship's yeeyar membrane.

"We should help them," Ashmara says, moving to the damaged control panel recessed into one wall. The yeeyar there is fried, but Ashmara still reaches her hand out to it and strokes it, not caring for danger, for her own life.

I want to tell her to stop it, but I bite my tongue at the last instant. What do I care if she dies now? She's going to die anyway. At least by way of electrocution will be quicker.

I won't say anything. I won't…

"Ashmara," I bark, voice loud. It echoes off of the walls as the ship powers to life and begins to lift from the sand.

I can hear the sound of claws digging into the outer shell of the ship. Several continue to cling to it and, using the control board, I lift and close several of the exterior panels in rapid succession until I finally feel the last of the creatures shake free and plummet to its death.

"What?" She turns and plunks down onto her ass, leaning against the wall where the silly, violent little monsters tore it open. She keeps her pack between her legs and her arms folded over it, like it's the most important thing in the cosmos to her. As a receptacle for her muuir, it is, isn't it? I hate it. And what I hate more is that I could never compete with it. "You didn't want to save them?"

"You think they'd have done the same for you?" I snarl, attempting to keep the rage from my tone.

Assassins don't hate. Assassins don't feel. I glance once more at her pack, noting with frustration that my feelings haven't receded.

She considers, tilts her head. "Probably."

"Yeeshee, but only to perform shekurr with you."

She snorts and laughs and digs through her pack. I fully expect her to withdraw additional packets of muuir, but instead she holds up a bottle. It's a translucent light blue, filled with a dark liquid. I don't need to know what it is to smell its potency, even from here.

"Right." She follows the line of my gaze to her hand and lifts it. "Want some?"

"Krakaw."

"Psh. You don't know how to have fun."

"That's correct."

She laughs like I've made a joke when I'm only stating fact. "So, why didn't you want to save them?"

You laughed with them. I didn't like that. I didn't like the way they looked at you. Like something to eat. Like something to treasure. "It wasn't prudent."

"Saving me isn't prudent."

"Why did you want to save them?" I snarl. There is tension thrumming through me, all the way to the bottoms of my feet. My hate has become something else. I feel *angry.* It is not an entirely unfamiliar emotion, but in this moment, I understand neither its provenance nor its target.

She shrugs. "They had a good sense of humor."

"That is not something you'll need to worry about in my company."

She laughs quietly and runs her dark brown fingers through her bright white hair. "Guess not. Though you used to find me funny. You and I used to laugh together all the time, remember that?"

Sitting with her as she watched her pranks unfold on the Lemorans who fed and clothed us, laughing more at her laughter than at the spilled hibi or cloth dyed in unfamiliar shades. Her laughter always made me laugh. It was always so reckless.

And it was mine. Making her laugh in that specific way, with a wild squeal, tears in her eyes. I've heard her laugh many times since then, always at my expense or the expense of some other thug sent to hurt, maim or kill her, but never like that. And I'll never hear it again. The female before me is not the one I knew back then and I'm not the kit that existed back then, either. Her laugh is gone forever. Like everything else.

The male she saved is corrupted. The female who saved me is ruined.

"Krakaw."

"It's true. I used to hide and jump out and try to scare you. You were always scared and you always got so mad and tried to pretend you weren't. Then you'd laugh. You were always so handsome when you laughed. You know it was my biggest fear that you didn't think I was beautiful?"

Emotion rises in me unbidden. I hold it down, like pressing a face underneath water and waiting for my victim to drown. "They can't all have a good sense of humor."

"What?"

"The creatures you save. The reason I was called out for your contract was to stop your interference in the collecting of souls for the Architects. Why would you do that? Go after the most costly cargo again and again?"

She laughs and takes another long drink from her bottle. She shivers as she sets it aside and tilts her head back until her crown rests against the wall of the ship. There is something odd about her — off. I cannot explain it.

"You really don't know?" I don't like not knowing and I don't respond.

She lifts a slender white brow and her eyes, they are surprisingly colorless for once. I find that I don't particularly like when her eyes are devoid of color. I like eliciting responses from her. They help me see into…help me see past…

I grunt, "You couldn't even resell the cargo if you wanted to. There are few slaving species and even fewer who take the typical kinds of species that the Sky are apt to recruit…" The Architects take great pleasure in breaking souls that fight back.

Her shoulders shrug with each chuckle. She lightly bangs the back of her head against the white wall, as if trying to distract herself from something, or trying to concentrate very hard. Her attention flicks to me. "I didn't steal from the Sky for tokens, Jer."

"Jerrock."

She licks her lips and stares at me very intently before looking off. "Jerrock," she breathes.

She doesn't continue, merely stares off into the distance unseeingly. Her odd expression only gets stranger, more strangled. She seems uncertain and tense as she says, "You ever considered why I go after Sky cargo pretty much *exclusively*?"

I tense. I had not considered that she was exclusively going after Sky merchandise. It did not matter to the contract. I cared only for the contract. Only that's not quite true, is it?

"Are you gonna ask me?"

"Are you going to make me ask?"

She grins and it's fuller than it was, even if she squints at me like she can't see me against the overhead lights. They aren't that bright. I lower them anyway. Her smile wobbles. I don't understand the uneven tilt to her lips or the strange tremble of her chin. It's dimpled, her chin. Has it always been dimpled?

Yeeshee. I remember now. Even as a young kit, I remember noticing that about her, wanting to poke it. Now, I'd like to trace it's shape with my finger in another way.

"Yeeshee."

My stalyx hand twitches. My lips tighten. "Why did you hunt Sky targets more than any other?"

"I wasn't *hunting* anything, Jerrock. I was searching for you." She chuckles, like she isn't simultaneously speaking and digging my heart out of my chest with a dull spoon. "Freeing the others?" She jerks her thumb over her shoulder and shakes her head. "That was just collateral damage."

She laughs and drinks more from her bottle. "Never did find you, though. After like the thirtieth raid, you found me. Do you remember that? The first time you found me?"

Yeeshee. The moment that everything changed. I saw her standing in the center of an exclusive slave auction hosted by Igmora and Tyto — now both dead, thanks to Ashmara and the Lemorans. It was there that I made my first mistake. I was supposed to shoot her in the heart, but at the last moment, I let my disguise slip just enough to be recognized by a being in the crowd. They caused a panic. Ashmara turned, saw me, our eyes connected and I…felt.

I just felt.

"Krakaw." I am proud of myself for the even, cold tenor of my voice.

"Of course not." Her laughter dies and she smiles at me more knowingly. "Anyways, I got away from you then and after I realized what you were — who they'd made you — and how dangerous it was to be around you, I came up with my plan. All I had to do was figure out how to liberate you, and if I kept doing what I was doing, you'd find me again. And again…and again. You never could kill me though, and you were trying. I never could figure that out. Why couldn't you? You've shot, burned, punched and stabbed me before, but you've never gone for the kill shot…"

Something stayed my hand. Every time. I had no control over it.

"Mistakes."

"Jerrock the Assassin of Sky doesn't make mistakes. Azza doesn't either, but you know what Azza does?"

Silence.

"He lets me win. He always has," she whispers, taking another long draught from her bottle. "*You* always have."

I say nothing and offer her nothing in return. She continues to stare and stare and stare until her stare lists to the side and soon she's staring to the spot just left of me. I swivel in my seat, but there is nothing behind me but white walls and a white floor.

She releases a loud belch and, without preamble, rolls onto one hip. She uses the bottle in her hand to help herself onto her feet. Her other hand grips her pack in a vise, so she has to use the hand holding the bottle to catch herself against the wall. She stumbles towards it, then away, then canters back into it and presses her forehead against the pure white surface, smearing it with dirt from her forehead. We are filthy, the two of us.

"There is a cleaning tube aboard the craft. You're welcome to it."

"Krakaw," she mumbles. "After."

After… I wonder what she means.

I watch her smear her dirty knuckles across the wall as she moves towards the solitary sleeping chamber and enters it. She doesn't look back at me as she walks across the small room to the murky white panel on the wall. She feels around for an eternity as I attempt to return my gaze to the scanner, where I hunt down the signature of an Eshmiri shield. They are incredibly difficult to find. I've had practice. I've found her a dozen times. But I've only found her on her ship *once* and it was only a trap to lure me to her. I've fallen for her traps so many times.

And she's only fallen for mine once.

She doesn't know it.

And I hope she never does.

I don't return my attention to the scanner. Instead, I watch her pound her fist against the wall until she forces the panel open, revealing a small, single-soul cell. It's for sleep, but I never slept in it. I don't know why. I preferred the floor, if I slept at all.

As she lowers herself down, she does something very strange. She seems to tussle with her bag against an invisible foe before eventually setting it down just outside of the sleeping pod, as close to the pod as she can get it, before climbing inside.

She thunks down onto her back and closes her eyes. She massages her forehead. Her jaw clenches and masticates convulsively. She huffs out a laugh and shakes her head at some point, then opens her eyes and stares sightlessly up at the low ceiling above her.

She never settles and it's after half a solar more, as a Voraxian flies, that I finally understand what's happening.

Shock and fear and anger and so many sensations and feelings that I am unfamiliar with come over me, but I repress them all. I am getting...excited, but I know it is folly to assume that anything she's doing is *my* doing or that it will result in anything more than her death or my heartbreak.

Yet...

I return to the controls and stare at them with every ounce of concentration that I have. I will not intervene. If she wants to do this, then it is for her. She must do this. She cannot rely on me for help. I remain at the controls for as long as sanity allows before repeating the mantra to myself as I rise from my place at the control panel and stalk into the sleeping chamber and crouch by her pack on the floor. Her startle reflex kicks and she jerks towards it, straining, but I don't touch the pack.

I brace my arms on the top of the opening and lean into the shaded cubicle. "You choose to do this now?"

"Not like I'm...doing anything else." She swallows thickly, painfully, but she still laughs.

"You force me to watch. You punish me for the things I said to you earlier in the cave."

"Do you feel punished?"

Yeeshee. "Krakaw. But I will."

"Then don't watch."

"You will deteriorate to ash and bone. Death won't even want you when this is through, when the muuir has worked its way entirely out of your system."

She laughs again, her mouth opening and her teeth gleaming white. I watch sweat bead on her brown cheeks. It's a sweet smell, sweet and sickly. It doesn't smell like her at all, but that doesn't seem to matter to me. I inhale and remember when I…

"Death never wanted me anyway."

Krakaw, he didn't.

"Apply a patch," I say.

She opens one eye and sticks out her tongue. "I'd rather not."

"You'll die allowing the muuir to leave your system all at once."

"Krakaw. I've done it before."

She has? I find it difficult to believe. "You lie."

"Shh," she tells me. "I need to get my beauty sleep."

"You don't need it," I blurt and I'd say that the words came thoughtlessly, but they didn't. It was a thought, it was mine and I wanted her to know it.

She laughs, "I know, I know. What's the point, right? I'm so…disgusting already." A contortion twists her body. Her heels dig into the hard material that makes up the bed. My tail snaps behind me, whipping the air as my mind attempts to solve the predicament before me but there are too many pieces forming puzzles of varying shapes and sizes, and none of their shapes snap together.

"That is not what I meant," I grunt out beneath my breath, but she isn't listening. She's humming to herself now, a tune I don't know. "Take another patch."

"Krakaw. Now eck off, Jerrock."

Jerrock. Not Azza. Not Jer. Jerrock. It feels as if she's using my own name against me, except her tone does not drive me to anger. There is opportunity in what she's said. Because Jerrock does not take orders from his targets. I reach for her pack and rip open the magnetic ties.

She screams. Her whole body trembles with the force of her words as she roars, "Don't ecking touch it! Don't touch it!"

Shock has me lowering the pack to the floor. I attempt to hold her gaze, but she can't. Her chest heaves and her jaw begins to quiver violently, like she's naked on Nobu.

"Don't…ecking touch it. It's…empty, anyway. I took it all." Ah.

Ahh.

This explains her actions much more reasonably than anything else. She has not elected to self-terminate. Krakaw, she is simply an addict who has mismanaged their supply. This explanation should soothe me, but does not. "No muuir left. Only a bottle of ramask I got from some…Rekkaru, and that's almost finished, too." She thunks her bottle to the right of me and I see that it is empty. She is just an addict who has mismanaged her…

A surge of suppressed panic rips free of its cage to tackle me.

I turn on my heels and return to the controls. I clear the search for Eshmiri cloaking shield patterns and immediately target waystations, pleasure planets, and dark worlds like Evernor and Kor — places in the Grey Zone where rules bend and the ones who enforce them are easy to break.

I find a location in the Grey Zone between Quadrants Seven and Eight that suits my purpose, but I hesitate. I have never been to this planet before. I focus on it more acutely and in the murky black yeeyar patterns that appear above me like charred sand, I see that it is an abandoned planet. Like the god of the cosmos simply took a bite out of the side of it, the curve of the planet now makes it look like a waxing moon all the time.

Built into the missing center are landing pads that appear to nearly fall off of the edge of each cliff, reminding me too much of the landing pads of Sky. I shiver. Sky. I have not thought much…

This is not Sky.

I draw up the planet's specifications. It is Q1ZX94 — *Quizzar* is how the pronunciation guide reads, were the planet's marker translated to Meero. Operated by rogue Walrey, it is a planet whose primary function is the trading of illicit substances, namely, muuir.

I reread the line twice over, just to be sure my eyes do not deceive me. What are the odds? It feels suspiciously like the universe or some other guiding force has planned this…yet I know there to be no such thing. There are no gods, but Death comes closest.

I set course for Quizzar and watch the planet draw closer and closer. Closer and closer and yet, we are still far. *We won't make it.*

"If there is muuir in your pack and you neglect to tell me, I will punish you."

"There's no…muuir, Jerrock. If there were, you think I'd willingly do this to myself?"

"You are punishing me for my words."

"I'm not."

"I would advise you to stop."

"Sure thing."

I rise. "I will check your pack to be certain you have missed nothing."

"Jerrock." She grabs my arm when I reach for her pack. Her brown skin looks breakable against the stalyx. Worse than that, though, I can't feel anything of her warmth. There is only a map of datapoints about her vulnerabilities that flutter through my left eye, a catalogue of all the ways I could and should hurt her. I wish I could turn it off.

"Ashmara," I reply.

Her mouth quirks. Her eyes reveal nothing. "Jerrock," she breathes. "What? You don't trust me?"

I hesitate.

"I wouldn't lie to you. To anybody else, yeeshee…but not…to you." Her breathing has become more labored. She struggles as she descends someplace I cannot follow. I cannot protect her there. "I'm not that noble. If I had… muuir…I'd be on muuir."

"Why don't you want me to go into your pack, then?" I ask her, but her reply is cut off by a low moan as she bows around her stomach.

She releases me and covers her mouth with her hand. "I'm going to be…"

I retrieve the absorption cloth from the panel to my left and drag the large white spongey contraption beneath her head. I help her sit up and I hold up her shoulders as she purges. Her bile is instantly absorbed, all but the odor, which lingers on her lips as she falls back into the pod. She is shaking and breathing hard.

"Don't look at me like this," she says.

I hand her water in a small open pouch and a damp towel to press to her forehead and I don't answer her. I merely wait as the cycle begins again.

12
Ashmara

I'm a fan of the underworld. Underworlds, I should say, of any kind. Of all the moons in all the universes, I only like their dark sides. Teeth are like knives. The more jagged the better. And the most beautiful views always have the most dangerous peaks to climb.

But this?

This right here?

This underworld does not spark joy.

Will it end? I don't think it will. Alright, fine. Hand me my muuir pack. Let me bathe in the glory of all my lies. Of course I have more muuir. Hah. Or pagh! That's what the Lemoran Clan Chief Raingar always says. He's such a doof. I wonder how he's doing. He looked mighty fine skewering Tyto on his horns. For such a peaceful brute, seeing him go feral was fun.

Feral feral feral. Sounds like carol, smerol, Harold, Jerrock. Jerrock?

A tight band of pressure tightens further around me. Oh krakaw. Krakaw, krakaw, krakaw…let's stay away from that. Let's dig further through my pack to find my sachet of muuir. I need my satchel. In it, maybe there's a dozen more muuir patches. Who am I kidding? There's at least thirty in there, wrapped up nice and tight for safekeeping. No more powder or leaves or crystals or drops, though. So if I take the patches, I'll have to take a lot, since I'm out of the harder stuff. Who am I kidding? If I take the patches, I'll apply them all. Now. Let's get started. Where is my pack?

I reach for it and feel the band again, getting tight, tight, tighter than a…than a what? I'm an Eshmiri. We're not so intimate. Touchy-feely, sure, but intimate? Krakaw. And the way I'm being held now, I know I've never been held like this.

It isn't nice. It's a prison.

And I'm not a female easily caged.

I struggle.

"That's enough," the voice says.

I struggle some more.

"Calm yourself, Ashmara."

Krakaw. Ashmara isn't calm. Ashmara fights. She schemes. She plots and she plans. She's a ruiner, but a finisher. She's stolen all the stones of the universe just so as not to leave one unturned. And right now, she's going to get her pack, apply a muuir patch or two or ten, and then she's going to depart from this bleak, bleak planet or ship or whatever vessel it is she's in and join the carbon deposits in the nothing that exists between planets and it will be like she never even lived.

Heat presses at my eyes, which are closed. I take a deep, labored breath. I feel a wave rise up in me and I start to thrash more violently now, kicking my legs and moving my arms, thrusting my elbows back into the wall that I've been bound to in an effort to escape it, but I can't. The *thing* holds me fixed. Maybe it's a bed. Maybe I'm in a prison for the criminally insane.

I would laugh at that if I could feel my tongue. I can't be in a prison. I am Ashmara. I don't get caught because the one hunting me always lets me win.

"Ashmara, fighting will get you nowhere."

I've heard that before and they've always been wrong. Fighting always gets you somewhere. Hurt, sure — dead, possibly. But somewhere, yeeshee.

"Ashmara... Ashmara!" The band is cinching me tighter around my stomach and I need to free myself *quick* because if I don't get out of here and soon, I'm going to be sick again.

Stop it! I scream, only I vomit instead. Heat floods my whole body. I roast. A dead animal on a spit. Slice, slice, slice me up. I can't...

...feel...

...I...

I'm not going to make it. I'm going to die in this cell. Yeeshee. I've never had so little fun in my life.

"Ashmara, I have muuir here. It is better to take some and wean off gradually. Quitting altogether, all at once, you could die."

Krakaw.

"Ashmara, I will apply the patch..."

"Krakaw!" I scream. It blasts out of me with what feels like a dying breath, except the breath doesn't actually kill me.

Pity.

"Ashmara, let me do this..."

I start to shiver and shake. Krakaw, I think to myself, and I must somehow be able to convey it because he curses, "You cannot insist on torturing me."

Torturing *him?* I'd have laughed had I the breath.

"Breathe," he says.

Krakaw. I don't think I will.

"Breathe, Rook, breathe!" Someone punches me in the chest. I know who it is, but the bitter child within me refuses to believe that it could be him. That he would ever willingly choose to hurt me like this.

Ha. What do I know? What was I even thinking? That Azza would come back and be able to love me? Like this? I'm such an ecking fool. Disgusting. I spent so long thinking about what it would be like to have him back that I never once thought about the consequences. I thought it'd be like old times. Old times? What are those? Would we play games like kits and there'd be nothing wrong in the Quadrants? But the Quadrants are a mean and hostile place, especially for two orphan hybrids like us.

A wave of nausea rises and passes again and, on its heels, another. It's never-ending.

But…

…eventually…

…it does end.

In a swamp of sweat and vomit, the worst of the rains seem to pass, leaving me like waterlogged soil. Strangely, I feel like I'm being anchored to the ground by the gravitational pull of the largest planet in a thousand suns, and also a hundred times lighter. I'm utterly drained, half dead, near comatose, but still awake enough to feel the brush of something warm against the side of my face.

Still awake enough to hear words spoken in a whisper, "Ashmara?"

"Hm?" I lie limp within the confines of my cage, his bare arms, his bare chest, his muscled legs covered in smooth, yet partially shredded tensile fibers, all coiled around me like a serpent. Maybe, like a Naxem, even. I've heard rumors that a Naxem planet has been spotted by the Gaphalrey telescope in Boshi, the Walrey capital, but those are only rumors and, as far as rumors go, they sound pretty farfetched.

"I have assessed your vitals. You will live."

I try to laugh but the sensation is more of a breathless tightening of my chest as opposed to anything audible. He says this like it's a good thing. Right now, I'm not sure it is.

His cheek again against my cheek…it lingers, comes closer, presses… I can feel his breath… I can feel his smooth skin. His skin. His *real* skin. Against me. The heat in my eyes melts into liquid relief. My head lolls on my neck, utterly boneless.

"I'm proud of you, Ashmara."

I open my mouth to release a sob or a scream or a laugh or a plea, but the energy it takes is too much and guts me.

I either die or I pass out.

But as I do, I change my mind. I no longer hope it's the former, but the latter.

13

Jerrock

Ashmara's body took a beating over the course of the last sixteen solars. That's how long it took for the muuir that has accumulated for rotations in her bloodstream to finally relinquish its hold on her cells and die. It will take another thirty or forty solars for the physical side effects to fade. I was told by the...*proprietors* of this...*establishment* that it would be so. And that she would only be fully free of its grip in the next rotation.

They have seen this many, many times in their caves, usually in clients who become lost in the cliffs of muuir and can't claw their way back out. Most die, the Walrey told me. They were not optimistic about Ashmara's chances and I was prepared to inject a dose of muuir directly into her heart should it threaten to fail, but it didn't. Its tempo rose and fell and exploded and plummeted and skipped and danced until eventually, it slowed to a patter. Like rain on glass on the beaches of Belistar, a small, uninhabited Oosa planet where the rain is never-ending.

I watch her across the small, jagged stone table. Moss clings to the stone walls and ceiling and makes the world smell of dew. The floor however, is dry and warm, surprisingly clean and pleasant. Her scent is not. She reeks of unwashed skin and sand and blood, human and lizard and mine and the other assassin's, but more than anything she smells of muuir. Not even fresh muuir, but muuir in decay. It sits somewhere between rotten fruit and expired corpse left out in the sun. She smells of rot and I...

I smile.

It grips me with fervor. I haven't smiled in so long, I'm not sure it would even be a noticeable expression to anyone else, but I notice. Those muscles are so long out of use that until this moment, I didn't remember I had them. They even hurt a little, which makes my smile wilt and then come again.

Ashmara doesn't see, so concentrated she is on the bowl in front of her. It's Walrey soup, mostly made of honey, which makes it hard for me to understand how they arrive at such a savory flavor. Small chunks of meat and mashed grain and a boiled vegetable I've never heard of before float in the gold. It feels like the first meal I've ever had, the first meal I've tasted. I feel *joy*, a spark of brightness in the dark. The soup is the brightest spot of color in this cave, rivaled only by Ashmara's hair, even unwashed, filthy and so greasy it slicks back away from her face. She doesn't care, doesn't try to improve her appearance. She's just surviving. And I feel...

I don't know how I feel. But I never expected to feel like this. Like I've returned to a place I once knew and think of now with fondness.

"You are a stubborn female." I take a bite of my own soup and chew a foreign vegetable. It has *flavor*. I haven't noticed flavor before, but I do now. It is exceptional.

"Soup tastes like vomit," she mutters down into her bowl.

My smile muscles flex and the sensation feels so impure as to border on scandalous. I do it again, just for the sick satisfaction of it. "You could have taken muuir at any time, but you didn't. Why didn't you?"

She sniffles, wiping her dripping nose on a rag. She's wearing her rags still, even though they are more tattered than the clothing I jettisoned on the ship. The Walrey were happy to have it. They got the better end of the bargain a thousand times over. No amount of soup will make up for the discrepancy, whether it tastes like vomit or not.

"Could you tell them to keep it down?" She flicks her spoon feebly and dismissively at the entrance to the cave. It's wide open. There is a platform there where our ship should be, but isn't. The platform is empty and the buzzing of thousands of Walrey can be heard unobstructed. The view is…spectacular.

Yeeshee. Spectacular.

Words I have never used before rise unbidden in my mind and I feel the urge to use them all liberally, a crazed vocabulary lush. "You'd like me to inform the Walrey who've been kind enough to provide us accommodation, food and muuir that they should avert their flight patterns so as not to pass by our cavern?"

She grumbles into her food, the sound unintelligible to anyone else, but I am a Sky assassin. I have no trouble hearing her.

"You also aren't satisfied with our accommodations, hm? You'd like to be upgraded to a cave without moss?"

"I want a wooden spoon."

"That spoon is wood."

"The color of the sky is dumb."

"Dumb?"

"It's blue."

"Several different shades."

"And the clouds are weird."

"Atmospheric."

"And you can only see one sun. Where's the other suns?"

"I find the only sun in the sky beautiful and the view spectacular. We have the best cave on the planet. Right in the very center. You can see the planet's crust arching above and below us. We are right at the center of the crescent moon, our view bezeled by the planet's edges. Because of that, we can see the atmosphere of the planet and its sky thickly, yet it is a thin atmosphere. That is why I had to inject you with the regulator when we landed, so you could breathe. It's also the reason we can see the darkness of the universe beyond it and just a few stars, even in the solar light. Can you see them, Ashmara?"

She looks me directly in the eyes — actually looks at me — for the first time in solars. Sixteen of them. Perhaps more. Perhaps she hasn't really looked at me in rotations.

Krakaw, that would be an invalid assertion. She has looked at me. On Evernor, she saw straight through my disguise. I was not expecting her to. She failed to see me through my disguise before. Just once. When it mattered.

"Ashmara?" I probe.

She winces without blinking and simultaneously drops her spoon. "Ah. I um…" She reaches for it, but winces in pain this time.

I move my short, sturdy stool around the round table closer to hers and pick up her spoon by the time she's recovered. She does so with a soft moan. I touch her arm, careful to do so only with my biological limb. She's cooler to the touch than she should be.

"Come, Ashmara, let us visit the rain pool."

She rocks back, placing her weight on the rear two legs of the stool. She wobbles and would have toppled over had I not grabbed the short wooden back of the chair and held her in place at this angle. Too high for her to place her feet on the floor, her head lolls back and rests on my arm. She doesn't notice. But I notice. And I feel instantly ashamed for finding enjoyment in the sensation, and then bemused at my shame the moment after. Because the point isn't what I felt, just that I feel. And it all feels so ecking good.

I start to tug her up to stand. She whimpers, "Where are we going?"

"The rain pool."

"Is that like a cleaning tube?"

"Yeeshee," I say, looping her arm over my shoulder. "Except there is real water. I took you once beneath the rain ten solars ago. Do you not remember?"

"Krakaw." She whimpers and moans and sags against me.

Her knees are too shaky to support her frame. I scoop her legs. "You were fully clothed and freezing. The waters were warm — are warm. That is why I haven't risked taking you beneath the rains again. Your fever began shortly after and took several solars to break. You don't feel feverish now, though, just sticky from all the muuir in your sweat."

"Augh...my stomach." She makes pitiful mewling sounds as I hold her close to my body and carry her through a craggy stone archway into the rain pool room. I bring her small stool with me.

"It hurts...feels like I swallowed a thousand angry stinging hroax. I..." She gasps in a way that can only be described as violently as I move our bodies beneath the spray. "Eckingcomets," she says in a rush as water splashes down her face and mine, too. She takes a few more labored, gasping breaths before her pulse calms. I can hear it. Just the one heart. I only have one, too. "It's warm."

"I told you it would be."

She blinks and I can feel her watching me, but when I turn to meet her gaze, she looks away quickly. "Yeeshee. Yeeshee, you did. I can, um, do the rest from here. Thank you."

Thank you. The shock of hearing those words from her is likely the only reason I put her down at all. She cannot stand, so I carefully place her upon her stool. Water rushes over her hair, flattening her curls to her scalp and the sides of her face. They run momentarily brown and grey before the white beneath the filth shines through, pure, if only momentarily. This female lives a hard life. Very little about her could ever be described as pure.

From there, she starts removing her Eshmiri rags. Her hands shake and it's clear her attempt is to be careful with them — is she...even trying to rinse them out?

I make a sound I've never heard myself make before. It is neither elegant nor voluntary and I immediately regret it. The look on her face is scandalous. Her lips are parted and the rains cascade off of them. Her tongue peeks out between her teeth. Her nostrils flare, but her eyes…they first glow white, the light spilling out onto her cheeks, before swirling through with lavender lust and then bottoming out to pink. She's afraid of me.

She looks down, but I take her chin in my stalyx hand and smooth her hair back from her forehead with my biological one. She looks up at me. She has no other choice. And I watch so many emotions flit through her eyes. They are ceaseless. She is weak and unable to control them. It feels wrong watching them like this, exploiting this level of raw vulnerability, but I do not look away. Could not if I tried. I can read everything in her eyes and I know the full depth of feeling she has for me.

She tugs, trying to look down again, but I don't let her retreat. It's cruel, but I've never been anything else. I make her look at me and I force her eyes to confess her love again and again. She is so in love with me. And I wonder…

…I stroke my stalyx fingers down her face, picking up sensory descriptors about her heartrate — too high — and her temperature — too low — and all the ways I'd be able to kill her — too many…

…if she is truly a Drakesh hybrid, and her eyes vacillate between colors like this so madly and lavishly…

…if there is the possibility…

…just the one…

…that I may be her Xive—

I feel a spike to the chest and a punch to the stomach at the same time. My fingers flinch against her skin and my stalyx hand drops down to the front of her garment. I tear a fistful of rags free from the cloth frame they adhere to. She jerks. I tear another. She clutches her chest when her bound breasts come into view. I take hold of the collar of her garment and rip it. In this way, I'm able to pull it off of her entirely.

Her body comes into view. It's thinner than it should be, covered in lean muscle. Her breasts are small and bound against her chest with a single strip of rag, clumsily tied into a knot against her spine. I slice it and she tries to catch it, but her reflexes are shot and she misses. I toss her upper body coverings to the ground where they land with a sodden squish. She watches me with a dumbstruck expression until I drop to one knee at her feet and reach for the ties of her trousers.

"Woah. What-are-you…" She speaks in a stutter, her eyes flaring bright, electric green in panic.

I do not answer, but stand and remove my own trousers. I allow her to look her fill and make no effort to soften my erection. It would take too much focus and I'd rather use my concentration for other things.

There is a complex array of cleaning crystals located behind murky glass panels built into one wall. They aren't necessary, as the rains of this planet are themselves purifying, but are placed there for the comfort of the creatures who want them. I want them.

I specifically want the Oosa cleaning gels and I pull them out of the small cubby glowing blue. The gels glow blue, too. I return with several and crush them in my palm before stepping behind her and adding them to her hair.

Before she can protest, I drag my stalyx fingers gently over her scalp and then back up again. She stiffens, her back unfurling so that she's finally sitting up straight for the first time in solars.

"Uoh—"

And then I go in for the kill. I cup the back of her neck with my biological hand because I can't use it to touch her entirely freely, as I cannot retract my claws, and my stalyx hand cards her hair and runs roughly down her scalp.

"Mhm," she whimpers. It is a heady sound. Even headier? The sensation of her body melting into my touch. She wobbles on the stool as I continue my ministrations, working down from the top of her head to her neck before finally moving to her bare shoulders. Their coloring is…

A growl fills the room and I prepare to fight off the invader, but the realization that that sound was mine follows almost as quickly. I start. I've never made this exact sound before and I wait, wondering how I might make the sound again but arriving at no answers. It sounds not quite like a growl, exactly, but something more like a *purr*.

I firmly smooth the heel of my hand down her back until I reach her hips. I massage the space between them where she has two indents straddling the line of her spine.

"Oh eck…nnhhn…" she gasps.

The purr begins again and this time I can feel it deep, deep within me. More of a vibration than a sound. It startles but does not entirely surprise me. I am… Drakesh, after all. At least, partly.

My hands push lower and I massage the space beneath the top of her pants. She does not protest, so I work my way around her body and when I reach her front, I drop back down into a crouch and begin to work her pants down her hips. Her eyes are squeezed shut and she has an expression on her face that is miraculous and mesmerizing.

"You'll need to lift your hips slightly so I can remove these."

Her eyelids part. Purple and white light spills out. She squeezes them shut again. "Mhm…Azza…"

"Krakaw. Krakaw…" I give my head a slight shake. My wet hair shifts as it streams down my back, almost to my hips. White, just like hers. "I was Azza once, a name that you gave me, but that kit is gone. Let him lie buried."

"Krakaw, don't say that." She spits, "Don't say that!"

"It's true." I touch her face. "Azza died, a kit who would do anything for you. Rotations later, Jerrock was born, a male who will not. I would not watch you kill yourself and now that there is no more muuir in your system, I will not leave you alone to suffer through its absence. Now, stand. Let me remove these."

She rubs the back of her hand over her nose and brushes the water from her eyes. The blue satisfaction in them is marred with grey grief, from the small glimpse I see. But that's alright. She looks beautiful in grey, too.

"Why?"

"To clean you."

"Krakaw. Why…why did Azza have to die?"

This question I cannot answer and any answer I could come up with would not be good enough. So instead I simply drag my red knuckles down her chest, right between her breasts. I wiggle them beneath the weight of her left breast and follow the beat of her heart. "Rook died that solar, too."

She shakes her head vigorously, then more slowly until she finally stops.

I tap her hip twice and she waits a beat more, careful to avert her gaze, before lifting as much as she can. She plops back down as soon as I get her trousers down low enough and I keep her and the stool steady as I peel her pants from her shapely thighs and massage Oosa gel over her skin. Everywhere. I bathe in each of her involuntary whimpers and moans as I caress her legs, from the juncture of her thighs to the tips of her toes.

Sensations spark in my skin, beneath my flesh, across my chest and groin most of all. It is…driving me…

I haul her up against me, bringing our bodies flush. She gasps and says my name as I've told her to say it, only she says it as a prayer this time, rather than a curse. My erection presses into the soft skin of her stomach and I stare down into her eyes, which seem to want to focus on anything but my face when they are open, which they aren't often. She looks enrapt with me and it is an ecking mesmerizing thing to behold, especially when she lets me touch her wherever I want.

I massage my hand down her body, smoothing down from the back of her neck, following the line of her spine until I reach her ribs, at which point I support her weight with my biological arm and bring my stalyx hand down her front. I focus on the way her pulse points change and her breathing quickens and shallows as I discover her body in a wholly new way. I finally venture further south, to the space between her legs covered by soft, dense curls. I part them to find her folds and her forehead falls against my shoulder, banging against it in a way I don't like. She could hurt herself simply trying to be close to me.

"Alright," I say against her forehead. Her eyes are closed and her body is struggling. She's shaking all over again from the exertion and from the next wave of muuir detox aftershocks. I withdraw my hand to safer territory. "Are you ready to return to the bed, Ashmara?"

Her arm tightens around my neck. "It feels wrong, hearing you call me that, like this." I don't fully know what she's referring to, but I still respond to it.

I brush my lips against her temple and say, "It isn't. Azza was a kit who let himself get taken away from you. Jerrock is a cruel assassin who will not. Are you ready, Ashmara? Or would you like to stay under the spray longer?"

Shaking her head slightly, she tries to push herself against me further, as if seeking warmth as we pass beneath the spray, back into the breezy outer room. She will be disappointed. Against my stalyx side, there is little heat.

I scoop her legs when she stumbles and carry her back to the bed. Maneuvering her awkwardly and placing her down on the other stool for a moment, I change the bed coverings, choosing not the softest from the selection but the most absorbent. She sweats profusely in bouts as the muuir continues to clear her system.

Against the pale yellow sheets, her dark skin looks healthier. It's an illusion but it still soothes the ache within me.

"How do you feel, Ashmara?"

She shifts and her eyelids flutter. She flexes her toes and sniffs. "I feel weird. Not right. Like I'm not on muuir." She sniffs again. "Maybe I should take that patch you offered me." Disappointment swamps me until she shakes her head. "Krakaw. I didn't mean that. I just… miss Azza."

"Don't. Azza loved you as only a kit is able. Jerrock has other plans for you." I kneel next to the bed and drag my claw up the outside of her leg. Slowly, I lean in and I press my parted lips to the outside of her hip. I taste her. She tastes of perfection and I revel in how her body reacts. She is attuned to me and when she opens her eyes and looks down her body at my face, her eyes are multicolored. Every color. She is too slow to remember to shut them before I see.

"Will you let me show you, Ashmara?"

She writhes against the bed, body arching in unusual contortions that scream of pain. "I can't. Everything ecking hurts."

"The Oosa soaps will help you and so will this. If you allow me to pleasure you, the endorphin release will help combat the illness."

She balks and reaches up to cover her eyes. "I can't do that."

I pull back.

"Don't…leave."

I touch her again, spreading my hands over her upper thigh and rubbing down her leg and up her waist at the same time. I say nothing, but wait for her to give me the answer I want.

Finally, she tears her hand away from her eyes and they are clear, mostly. It must cost her intense concentration…that she is not capable of at the moment. Because one neon strip of yellow still slips through. Embarrassment. I do not like that.

"I didn't want… I didn't think… You…" Shame flares bright. She closes her eyes. Sweat has already begun to bead along her hairline. "I didn't think you saw me as… a female."

"Is that how it appears to you?" I glance down at the stiff rod of my cock. It is red, a brown swirl of skin wrapping around it all the way up to the tip. The last of the brown on my body that the Sky Architects did not see fit to remove. That, and the small strip at the base of my tail. My cock does not seem to know or care that she is ill, which is a pity as it will see nothing of what it wants while she is like this.

"I thought you saw me as your annoying kin," she tries again.

"We aren't related," I say so quickly I speak over her and trip over my own words. She pauses, as if confused. "It's true."

"How do you know?"

"I pulled your bio strand the first time we touched."

"When you kidnapped me off Evernor?"

I hesitate and then elect not to answer. I will have to tell her one solar, but this is not that solar. "Stop deflecting. Grant me permission. This will help. The Walrey have assured me and I am tired of wasting any more time with them on this planet." The incessant buzzing of the Walrey in the distance only further punctuates my point.

"I… You really would do this?"

"It will be a great sacrifice." I fist my cock and her eyes flare bright, bright purple.

The corner of my mouth twists up.

Her eyes explode in color and I am going to take the fact that I am her Xiveri mate as permission. I lift her left leg at the knee and then part it from the other. I swivel her hips so that she lies at an angle and her left butt cheek hangs off of the cot. Then I slip her knees over my shoulders and lean into her cunt.

I press my nose to her curls. They are so dark and their scent, lavish. I pull her plump lips apart, watching how the claws on my red hand look so threatening against the small, dark brown nub and those flowering lips and the pink at their center.

I am so fixated on her core that I entirely neglect the rest of her body. I glance up at her face, wanting to know if this is alright. The explosion of color in her eyes is enough — would have been, had she not also whispered, "Jerrock."

My back muscles tense, shoulder blades pulling together. I struggle to respond calmly, for I am far from calm. I am *ravenous*. "Lean back. Relax. Close your eyes. Concentrate on the feel of my tongue only."

"Your…tongue?"

"Yeeshee."

"I-I've never done anything like this before."

My stomach dips at her lie, but I don't address this now. "Relax. I will torture you just a little. Just know that unlike any other torture I would inflict, you will survive this."

I angle my chin down and I am still holding her gaze as I press the full flat of my tongue against all of her. All at once.

Ashmara's head tips back. She can't hold my gaze. I do not need her to. I will one solar, but again, this is not that solar. This solar is not about us. This solar is about Ashmara and muuir and their relationship, which is now ending. I could not compete with her other lover. Now, I may stand a fighting chance. And I will fight. Already, she has fought. She thinks it's for me. I know it's not.

Her taste is pure ecstasy and though I have tasted females before, it feels like I have not. It feels so different.

I cannot fully put it into words, but I enjoy her taste. I feel pleasure. It ripples through me, my muscles warming with the exertion I feel after a battle, only this battle has just begun.

I take my tongue to her again, flicking her lips with speed. Her body becomes agitated, so I slow my touch and taste and wait for her to settle, then I flick her harder once again. I drive her up and down in valleys and peaks of pleasure and torture, oscillating between the two, before I allow her first release.

Her legs twitch and spasm beside my ears. I anchor her thighs to my shoulders. "Still," I command. She does not obey. "Still." I smack her outer upper thigh hard enough to grab her attention. "Still."

She settles on a whine and flinches on a whimper. Her chest still rises and falls in great heaves. I smile at her brittlely, in the only way I know how. Her eyes have not stopped radiating light this entire time. I pat her thigh lightly, soothingly, twice in the same place I hit her before. "Good girl." Then I return to my ministrations.

I pull her plump mound into my mouth, sucking forcefully and titillating her lips with my tongue faster and faster and faster. I watch her climb. Watch her body bow and her feet point, reaching for the stars.

She shivers. Tears well in her eyes, which are still multicolored.

I shift my lips up to ravage her small, sensitive pleasure center. Its smooth texture against my ridged tongue makes me feel like I'm a savage being allowed to sample the universe's finest treasure. Not pillage and plunder. Not attack and take. But as the recipient of a gift that was given with grace.

I feel her nearing her edge and I force her to it, inserting my stalyx finger into her dripping center. I command the yeeyar impulses in my body to make that finger vibrate. I know that she likes this. I'd forgotten just how much, because the scream that tears out of her throat astonishes me and makes me laugh.

Laugh.

I laugh against her molten core. I suppose it's a laugh. It's more of a scratchy whimper, but Ashmara still seems to hear it and recognize it for what it is. I thought her multicolored eyes could not be more expressive, but I was wrong.

At that sound, and at the climax of her pleasure, the vibrance of her eyes reflects infinity. The colors are no longer distinct, but blare through her and throw light back at me and then up at the ceiling before she curses, "ECK!" She tries to say more. Something like my name, but the words become muddled and indistinct as she rises and rises and crests and then holds at the peak of her pleasure, with my finger in her tight heat and my tongue inscribing vows over her soft, slick flesh. Vows she'll never read.

And one apology.

Three rotations previous…

14

Jerrock

I have a plan. I always have a plan, but this one is better. I pull up her specifications in my yeeyar sight once more as I stand, hidden in the shadows of Pleasure Alley, watching her as she makes her selection.

Alias: Ashmara the Eshmiri

Species: Unknown

Strengths: None

Skills: None

Weaknesses: Thin skin, bipedal, breathes only oxygenated air, no natural defenses, weak musculature, strong familial ties, addicted to muuir

I focus on the last two attributes longer than necessary. I have attempted to maim and kill the female before, but she has become my first failed assignment. And I have already failed *twice* to kill her. Twice. The first time was shocking enough, but the second time, it became a problem and I am determined to right my course. I have not strayed so far from my training. I cannot have strayed so far from my training… It's just not possible.

I review her specifications again.

Strengths: None

I pull up the specifications on myself drawn up by the Architects and read her strengths next to mine, side by side.

Strengths: partially improved exoskeleton, yeeyar-enhanced musculature, ion iron ionyx'ix-enhanced skeleton, yeeyar-heightened senses, speed, and then the list of my skills begins, becoming so long it eclipses the view in my sight. Items ranging from killing weapons I'm expert with and languages I speak to the more esoteric like proficiency in sexual seduction and indeterminate ability to hold my breath.

Weaknesses: None

I have no weaknesses. Killing her will not be a problem. Failure to do so earlier will be rectified.

Alone as she so rarely is, I watch her hoist her backpack higher on her shoulders. I wish for the suspense to end. It's killing me. Only a short time ago, I stood across from my target, posing as a Voraxian merchant using an Eshmiri cloaking device augmented by the Architects. I did not expect it to work, but she did not notice me, so consumed she was by haggling with me over the price of the muuir I sold her.

I gave it to her cheap, but not cheap enough that it would arouse suspicion. Now, I am merely stalking her through the market, waiting for her to imbibe it. I am surprised an addict like her did not take it immediately.

And then my surprise becomes shock when she turns into one of the pleasure houses. I glance up and note that the sign is scrawled in the Voraxian script — large, blocky symbols that each demark a single syllable but flow to full sentences when strung together. This is the Voraxian and Drakesh pleasure house.

I cross the avenue, crowded with species of all kinds, all of whom have come here to Kor for pleasure or trade, sport or sanctuary. But there will be no sanctuary from me for the Eshmiri reaver entering the pleasure house now. I slip in the crevice separating the lavishly decorated Oroshi house from the more spartan Voraxian one. A side door leading into the Oroshi house hangs open on my right. Green steam wafts from it, and so do squeals of Oroshi delight.

Two doors stud the Voraxian house and are positioned side by side. I slip through the first and find myself in a crowded receiving room filled with Voraxians of varying genders, shades and body types. I receive only a few speculative stares, still outfitted as a black-haired, purple-skinned Voraxian trader, as I move along the outskirts of the room. Werro fiber curtains separate this room from several others. The room I'm in currently appears to be used for costuming. Several Voraxian and Drakesh males admire their reflections while several females exchange tips on which types of garments to wear for their upcoming clients.

I move to the werro curtain, through which I can hear Ashmara's voice. She does not sound like the unintelligent and sarcastic Eshmiri bastard that I have heard speak many times before, mostly over holovids, but twice in person, and I feel...

Correction. I do not feel.

She does not sound like she usually does and I debase myself by lifting the curtain back and using my biological eye to confirm her identification. The female speaking in the strange Ashmara-like brogue is, in fact, Ashmara. I perform a scan of her biology to confirm she wears no appearance-altering device, like I do.

Confirmed, I watch the female speak with a pair of Voraxians, one female, one male. Both wear long Walrey-dyed catacat silks and speak to Ashmara gently, coaxingly.

She shifts her weight between her feet and gives them a short nod. The female waves her fingers in a signal that causes drapes on the other side of the room to open. There, a line of males stands, each wearing differing expressions that range from soft and sweet to rakish and lascivious, each intended to cater to a different recipient's fantasies.

They appear in different shapes and sizes as well, some leaner, some meatier, some tall, some barely taller than Ashmara herself. She is tall for an Eshmiri, but as far as Voraxian or Drakesh females go, she is only average.

She exchanges tokens with the Voraxian male through her yamar box, a relic, but he accepts her tokens gracefully into his life drive and then motions her forward to make her selection.

Her agitation grows and it shows. She keeps touching her hair. I imagine her eyes filled with the brightest yellow — a Voraxian and Drakesh color of embarrassment, or shame — but I cannot see them as her back is to me now.

"I'll go with that guy," she says. Her selection was made with some speed. I have been to pleasure houses before to seek out my targets — it is an easy place to find targets with their guards down — and usually the purchaser is overwhelmed by the possibilities presented by such a selection, but not Ashmara. It would seem that she knew what she wanted when she walked through the door.

A male with red skin and white hair all over is the male for her. His hair falls to his shoulders and is cut to taper around his angular face. He is a mean-looking male but his muscles are for show and his smile is intended to seduce. It clearly has.

He looks like me.

I do not know where the thought comes from, but once it arrives, it is difficult to put down. It is, however, accurate. The Drakesh male with the red skin and the white hair and the mean expression is heavier than I am, bulkier, but only along certain axes. His shoulders are inflated, his outer arm muscles, too, but his abdominals are not as defined as mine are and the muscles in his forearms, thighs, calves and neck are less substantial as well.

He lacks all of my stalyx parts.

I could kill him in an instant and, as he offers her his arm and they make their way up the stairs, I decide that I will.

I exit through the same door I entered and move around to the back. I scale the wall and enter the window to the first empty room I come across. I wait near the door, keeping my ear pressed to it. I hear the male in question ask Ashmara how she's finding Kor, if she's here for business or pleasure. Pleasure, she answers. He grants her a laugh that can only be described as rehearsed. He tells her that she's off to a good start and that he will show her pleasures divine.

"Just pleasure is fine."

The voices are louder and I determine that there is a high probability that they will enter this room. I turn and slip beneath the bed. It is formed like a traditional Voraxian nest, lifted off of the ground and bowled in the center. I lie down and roll beneath its shadow between the supports.

The door opens a moment later and two sets of bipedal feet enter. Four feet plod across the floor, one significantly lighter than the other. "You can store your things in there."

"I'd rather keep them with me."

"Of course." His tone tilts up near the end. I can then hear the subtle sounds of kissing. I prepare to make my move. *It is premature.* Is it?

"But um…" Ashmara starts to cough. "Is there a void room? I'd like to…change."

"There is. Just through there. Take all the time you need. I'll be waiting, heelee."

A door opens and closes. I do not hesitate. I roll out from beneath the nest and I advance on the male standing against the left wall, currently spritzing himself with some sort of scented oil. He never sees me before he dies.

I shift behind him and wrap my stalyx arm around his throat. I crack his neck, delivering him to Death, and I catch the bottle of oil he drops in the next moment. The door to the void room begins to crack. I issue the mental commands necessary to modify the disguise I'm wearing to match that of the male's, currently sinking like a stone in my grip. I allow him to drop to the ground and I quickly roll him beneath the nest into the position I just held.

I turn to face the female just as she exits the void room wearing her backpack and a catacat silk robe that does not at all suit her. The two items clash fiercely, the pack making her look like a rugged thing while the silk robe makes her look so small. I have never seen her small before.

The expression on her face does not help. She looks uncertain. It is…confusing. I have studied every facet of this female, yet it feels like I have not yet come across this particular version of her before. It's destabilizing, leaving me in the dark, as I always seem to be with her. I need to correct it.

"Take it off." The words are mine, but I do not remember intending to voice them.

Ashmara stalls. She looks up at me, her white-eyed mask carefully in place. "What?"

"You heard me." I do not risk turning to face her fully. The cloaking disguise I wear is state of the art, but it is not foolproof. If she looks closely enough, she may able to see imperfections. Fortunately, for me, she can scarcely look at me at all. "I do not repeat myself."

"Are you for real?"

I move to meet her and, with the hand I just used to kill the male whose corpse lies beneath the nest, I rip the silks from her chest. She starts when I grab her backpack and take it away from her and she lunges for it, but I hold it out of reach.

"You have no need of this," I say though I shouldn't. She *does* have need of it. She needs to take the muuir I provided her earlier.

"I do. I want to take a hit before we…"

I simply stare at her. I keep my expression blank and controlled, but inside, a battle wages. I should hand her the pack. I should hand it to her. Why I do not is…

"Okay then. I can um…" She scratches her neck. Her jaw clenches and her feet shuffle back and forth. It's as if she's only just now realized that she's bared to me fully, her body glowing brilliantly in the made-to-feel-natural light. "I guess I can wait."

"On your knees." I toss the pack behind me against the wall beneath the window. When she bends to retrieve it, she will likely see the male underneath the net.

What am I saying? She will die long before she gets the chance.

She stammers, "You said that I'd get to…"

"On your knees."

"I-I paid good tokens for this!" she tries to assert herself. This display is uncharacteristic of what I know of her. She lacks all confidence.

"You said *just* pleasure. And that is what I will give you." I take a step forward and wrap my stalyx hand around her throat. *Squeeze. End it now.* I cup the back of her neck and force her down. She drops to the ground before me with a thunk while my other hand frees the clasp of my pants. It releases, flooding my suit with air and making it possible to peel off easily. She will not see the black of my garment, though. She will see only the brown silk trousers that I want her to see and the red, ridged cock beneath it.

"And that is also what you will give me." I drag my metal finger over her bottom lip, forcing it open.

Her heart beats rapidly and her eyes loom enormously in her face. She looks like she will attempt to say something, but I do not allow for it. I feed the head of my cock into her mouth, watching the red disappear behind her teeth. She cannot see the brown spiral that coils around the shaft, but she can see its ridges, an illusion I create for her. I let them glow violet and she starts, eyes going crossed as she tries to focus on them while simultaneously sucking my cock between her wet, hungry lips.

"Eyes up."

Her nostrils flare. She looks up at me and her eyes flash red and purple. She's angry with me and she enjoys it.

"Suck better."

Her nostrils flare again, but she repositions herself, popping my cock free of her mouth before returning to it with her mouth and both hands. She circles her hands around the base and bobs her head up and down my length. I scarcely feel it. I have been trained well in the art of deflecting pleasure, so that I may never be corrupted by it.

She works efficiently yet clumsily on my cock until I comb my fingers through her hair, reach the back of her neck and yank her off of it. I toss the female onto the nest and crawl on top of her. I grab her ankles and drag them apart, I pull her close…

I should kill her now, simply rip her leg out of its socket…

"Wait!"

Did I voice my intention out loud? I did not, but I still wait, regardless.

I look up and her eyes flash pink and bright yellow and a deep, wanton purple. "Wait. I just…"

I thrust her knees up to her chest and I ignore whatever she was about to say next. Instead, I feel saliva pool in the back of my mouth and make a decision to end this. I drape my body over hers, grab a fistful of her white hair, yank her head back hard enough that she can no longer speak, and then I force my cock into her tight heat.

The pressure is…

I feel my eyelids flutter several times. My mind goes momentarily blank.

Refocus. Center. I think of Pain. I think of his ally, Death. I remember what it felt like to have my cock in the first female I ever rutted, but more acutely, I remember what it felt like to choke her to death. The Architects let me get to know her first. She'd been Drakesh, too. I had not spoken to a female in such close quarters, short of the other assassins I trained against, that I made a mistake. I listened to her. I heard her. Killing her had been…

Necessary. To perfect my craft, it had been necessary and I am a better assassin for it. Killing this female with whom I have no connection at all and who is nothing but an unintelligent pebble in the shoes of greater beings — a nuisance — will take no effort at all.

"…oh eck, ecking eck. Eck…hey, this is…my first time… I like where your head's at, but this hurts like an ecking… I'm on fire down there… Can we stop? You'll still get your payment, but I can't… This was a bad idea…"

I blink many times. Over and over. Her core squeezes around my shaft and the pressure…

I drop my biological hand to her throat and, though I can see my sharpened claws glittering as they press into her dark brown skin, they do not glitter as much as her skin seems to, covered in dew. She is so afraid, but more than fearful, she is ashamed. The yellow in her eyes is not so bright now. Purple flares there, too, but less frequently, blotted out instead by a beige-tan color that I know reflects pain.

I draw my hips back, see the liquid shimmering along my length, see the purple color in my cock's ridges darkening as if the ridges truly were mine and reflective of my current state. I saw my cock in and out of her roughly several more times. She tenses up, scrunches up her face and squeezes her eyes shut until water wets her lashes.

My thoughts hitch and though I attempt to cling to awareness, my mind shorts. This time the moment lasts longer and, when I come to, I no longer have my hand wrapped around her neck. I pull out of her. She releases a pitiful little moan as I do and a single tear drips down her left cheek.

"Whew! Well, that was, um, fun. Thank…" She gasps.

I have my hands beneath her knees and yank. I drag her knees up above my head and I dive into her heat. I offer her the pleasure that the previous male promised and then some, glutting myself on her flavor over and over again. I drive three orgasms out of her and then another two, and then I toss her back onto the nest once she's spent.

I climb back on top of her and toss her onto her stomach. I lie over her, pressing the full length of my body to the full length of hers. We fit…well together. Her ass is round and firm and presses against my hips.

"Lift." I tap her hip twice. She doesn't move, but continues lie against the furs covered in sweat, panting. I slap her hard enough for the sound to reverberate through the room. Her whole body jolts and even though she is exhausted, likely low on muuir and suffering, her eyes beam only purple and white and it is that white that…

Stop. I cannot…

My mind blanks. I am inside of her before I realize that I should withdraw. It is too late. I rut her to the brink of my own orgasm and stop. I do this several times. I am trained not to come, but to fake a climax. To climax is to entertain notions of weakness. It is when I would be most likely defenseless and a target could escape or I could be slaughtered. The latter would be preferrable to the former. I should stop now should I wish to avoid a climax. I should…

The climax happens without my consent. I empty into her body and, though I know that I am sterile, as all assassins are, it still inspires panic. I should not be doing this. I gave her the muuir and that should have ended it. Why did I take her backpack away? Why did I…

"Ow…hey…you're…squeezing me… What are you doing down there? Comets…"

My mind blanks. My arms are coiled around her and so are my legs. Her face is pressed to the furs and my tail is deep in her ass. The tight ring of muscle clenches around my tail and I shiver at the latent shock of pleasure that radiates from it.

"I can't…anymore…" she pants.

I do not like her *can't* and move my stalyx hand around her body to her core. Against her clit, I make my fingers vibrate. My cock is still wedged inside of her and when she climaxes yet again, I come with her a second time.

I rut her all through the lunar. She protests several times. She begs me to continue even more often. She's crying out, whimpering and moaning and repeating the same curses over and over. She lets me do what I want with her and what I want is to sate myself on her flesh and be done with it. But I do not seem to finish. I am not sated.

I only stop when eventually her eyes close and her body gives up. It is a likeness to death, the way she lies, but is so much more peaceful because she lies there smiling. None of my targets have ever lain still with smiles on their faces before.

I stand back from the nest and look down at her. Yeeyar fires through my muscles in small explosions. I am shaking. My hips are bucking in micropulses. My mind does not blank, though I wish for it to now. Instead it moves at the speed of light, drawing up plans and then just as quickly setting them ablaze. I find the recordings my yeeyar sight has taken of the past solar and lunar — ever since I arrived here on Kor — and I erase them. The Architects cannot know…

The last thing I do before I disappear, shaking, through the window, is grab the body beneath the nest so that she will not be incriminated in the male's death and grab the muuir from her pack. I leave with them both.

On my ship, sailing away from that wretched rock, the feeble female lying on the nest amidst the chaos I wreaked over her body, I read her and my own specifications again, side by side. I read them over and over. No longer am I focused on my strengths, but on my weaknesses. Where it says none, I know that is no longer true.

I have one.

But I vow to get rid of her, if it is the last thing I do.

Now...

15

Ashmara

Pulling on my slippers is an odd experience made odder by the male seated across from me pulling on similar slippers. He's smiling. At least it's sort of a smile if I squint and tilt my head just right. I've never been scared of him before. Not in all of his Sky assassin glory. Not even when he held a blaster to my face. But I'm scared of him now. I'm scared of that smile.

I scratch my neck and look away when he meets my gaze with his pretty brown and white and black eye. He's staring. I wiggle my toes in my slippers, the silk feeling like claws sawing into my flesh. It gets worse when I start to tug on the other garments, all silk, new agonies visiting me with every new layer added. I'm so uncomfortable. The effects of a body depleted of muuir is only part of it, and not even the largest part. It's him. He's totally different and it's freaking me out. He seems almost happy and he wears happy like chainmail. I can't cut through it with sarcasm, with a look.

So I don't look at him at all.

There. That's better.

I pull on the rest of my Walrey-gifted clothes, hating all of them. They're light and airy, easy to maneuver in, which I'm grateful for, but they aren't Eshmiri. *I am Eshmiri.* I need to return to my Eshmiri ship where things feel normal. But…will Jerrock come with me now? Now that he's smiling at me? What will that be like? Do I even want him to come?

Yeeshee. No matter what he feels about me, I'll always want him there. Always.

"Here. Allow me."

His hands appear in my vision and my torso jerks upright so fast I get dizzy. The sudden movement causes pain to blitz me in the back of the neck, one concentrated, stultifying dose. I cry out, unable to cage the sound fast enough. Biting my bottom lip, I try to breathe my way through it but I can't do that either, not when a gasp is pulled out of me at the pressure of firm fingers pressing into my nape and massaging me with just the right pressure.

Ecking sinners…

Bless the saints…

It feels so good.

He continues to massage me and I let him, sitting there all slouched on the edge of my cot, my head lolling on my neck like I've got no control over it. I don't have control…he has all the control. He massages me for spans. Solars. Eons. And when he stops, I only come back to myself on his word.

"Better?" he asks me.

"Yeeshee," I whisper.

"Good." He drags the laces across my stupid slipper, cinching them tight. "Are you ready to go?" He pulls the laces of my other shoe tight, too.

"Krakaw." My voice breaks.

He stops moving. Then he touches my face, fingers skimming my cheek before pressing into the indent in the center of my chin. "We cannot linger here. Already, we owe the Walrey for shielding our presence. Two assassins have come within range of their communicators looking for us. They will not stop."

I nod, knowing all this, but that wasn't what I meant. I meant that I want to stay here, with him smiling at me like this. I don't know what will happen once we leave this place, but I'm pretty sure it doesn't involve him being nice. He's never nice. This is nice. Scary, but nice. I'll take the terror of it, so long as it remains just this way.

And I don't want to deal with the fallout after promising myself I wouldn't take the rest of that muuir. I'm off it now, I can't go back. If I take one single hit, it'll all be over. All that work…

I shudder.

"They cannot harm you," he says, and for just a split instant, I have no idea what he's talking about.

I chuckle when I realize he means the assassins. "They most certainly can and will." It's true, but they're still not the ones I'm worried about.

"Krakaw." His voice is harder. More familiar. It… makes me sad. Is the weird, ecked up moment we had together already over? Maybe I should take more muuir again just to get back here. Krakaw. He would *never* forgive me. I can *never* go back. This moment would *never* happen again but now…

He touches my chin.

…there's still a chance.

"No harm will come to you. They would have to pass through me and I will not allow it."

"But there are so many. Like those ecking lizards…"

He makes a sound. I don't dare call it a laugh, but I still react to it. "That is why we will have to infiltrate the Sky planet and tear it down from within."

"Krakaw. Let's not."

"Wasn't that your plan all along?" His hand lands on my knee. There's not enough fabric between us. I feel hot. Burning hot.

"It was an ecking dumb plan." I push his hand off my leg and stand, putting some space between us as I head towards the open mouth of the cave and the rushing winds whistling past it. I need air. More air. All the air. My head is on fire. I feel flushed. My body…sings. "Let's not. Let's head to Kor and hang out with Rhorkanterannu. I heard he bought his female a planet. It's got a beach on it."

"You like the beach?"

"It's not a reaver pit, but it'll do."

"I don't care much for the beach."

"How would you know? Have you ever been to one?" My words come out harsher and meaner than intended. I look up when he doesn't answer. "S-sorry."

I hear his heavy steps and want to move away from him, but there isn't anywhere to go. The wind is blowing hard and there's nowhere to retreat to here, except for the platform I'm guaranteed to fall off and a zillion buzzing Walrey who'd do nothing to break my fall. His hands reach for me. I hold mine to my chest, afraid that if he gets hold of them, he'll pull me open.

And that's just what he does.

He molds his fingers around my wrist and forces them away from my body. He takes both of my palms in both of his and brings them to his lips. He brushes his lips across my knuckles once, twice, before looping my arms around his neck and pulling our stomachs flush. His pale jade robe is parted down the center revealing a sculpted red abdomen and a single red pectoral. His stalyx enhancements cover his left pec and ribs, ending just above his hip bone. He's hard everywhere, as impenetrable as he suggests, making his flimsy little robe look absolutely ridiculous.

So hot. The male is so ecking hot.

Meanwhile, I likely look like a corpse, not that I've had a chance to see myself in any reflective surfaces — thank the stars. And now I look like a corpse ready for burial in this giant yellow sack, so big it could be a body bag if I tucked my feet into it.

He's a feast for the eyes and I know the color in my own eyes is broadcasting embarrassment. I don't want him to see it, but he's made it impossible to look anywhere but at him. He occupies my entire viewpane. There is nothing else.

He lowers his head and speaks directly into my ear. "There are many things I haven't yet sampled." He brushes his cheek against mine. Stalyx against skin. I feel my eyes water. *I abandoned him. I don't deserve this...* "I am eager for you to show me them all."

"You can't possibly want that, Jer."

His nose skims my jaw before lifting slightly up. He brushes his lips against mine. It's so, so quick. So quick. I chase it, leaning onto the balls of my feet silently asking for more, but he denies me with a small, smug smirk. He combs my curls behind my ears and then he…ruffles my hair. My entire throat chokes. He remembers me. He remembers. And my heart breaks all over.

"How are you able to tell me my own desires, *Ash?*" He steps back and goes to the table where he collects a few small items I can't quite identify.

I grab my pack and hoist it high onto my shoulder. "Don't call me Ash."

"Don't call me Jer."

"Fine," I huff, lips trembling. This is…uncharted territory, but I'm… "I'm excited to explore with you, too, Jerrock."

"If we survive the Sky."

"You said we would."

"I said *you* would." He ruffles my hair once more as he passes by me and heads for the platform.

I'm angry now as I shuffle to catch up. I grab his stupid balloon sleeve and tug. "You're not leaving me behind again."

His biological eye blinks. He says nothing, but I'm serious. I won't let him get out of this one. I grip his red wrist and haul him closer — haul myself closer to him, but same difference. "Promise me," I grit.

His head cocks ever so slightly. "You'd believe a promise from an assassin?"

"You're retired."

He does that upper lip snarl again and it makes my own mouth twitch. "Don't worry. I wouldn't believe a vow from a reaver, either. Let's go."

"Uhh, how?" I say, distracted, then shake my head. "You haven't answered the question."

"Our transport is arriving."

I'm just about to press the issue when I make the fatal error of looking up at him as he steps out onto the platform just in time for the wind to pick up and ravage his hair. Eck. His hair. I ecking love his hair. Mine never grows like that. I've tried. I once got my curls to fall all the way down to my shoulders and there, they stopped. They got fuller and fuller and fuller and when I pulled them out long, they stretched halfway down my back, but as curls they just sprang right back up.

It was a dumb thing to be annoyed about, in the grand scheme of things, but as a kit with heightened emotions and nobody around to tell me why I looked the way I did or whether or not I *could* be seen as attractive to anyone in the cosmos — to the Eshmiri I grew up with, I certainly was not — I had been. Now, I'm glad my hair isn't as long as his. It's *his* and only succeeds in making me find him even more magical.

My neck gets hot as I remember the magic he wove over my body. It was unrelenting and ecking brilliant. I want more, but I'll be damned if I ask him for it. I'd rather jump right off the edge of the ecking platform.

Jerrock's been staring off of the platform for the past few moments. He stands so ecking still, it's creepy. No being should be able to stand so still. I wonder if that was part of his training, too. Slowly, I approach. I'm still wobbly-kneed, so I teeter a little bit when a Walrey passes by overhead, buzzing angrily and way too close.

Jerrock still doesn't move, but when I finally arrive beside him, he says, "This place reminds me of Sky."

I'm surprised, though I shouldn't be. There are only two beings alive who have been to the mysterious planet and survived to tell tales of it. And I liberated them both. "What's it like?"

"Like this." He gets his crooked expression and glances at me. His hair whips between us.

I can't ecking help it. I reach out and grab a fistful of his hair and tug it back over his shoulder. I grip it firmly, feeling the thick strands against my palm. They're so big that it takes nearly my whole fist to contain the mass. My hair isn't that thick, but it's twice as soft.

What I'm doing brings our bodies closer together. Too close. He pivots just a little bit, just enough to show his interest, to reveal the expanse of his defined pectorals and abdomen. He's ecking ripped. That stuff never did anything for me before on other males, but it does *everything* to me now, knowing that it's his.

"You know that's not what I meant."

He huffs through his nostrils. They flare. "The Sky planet isn't a planet at all, but a moon. Its orbital pattern spans nineteen different planets, circling one before it's pulled into the orbit of another, then another, then the next. The pattern changes each time. That is why none have been able to locate it. It is an unusual cluster of planets whose magnetic fields, masses and gravitational pulls keep the orbital path of Sky so random.

"The moon itself is small. Its population is made up of the Ren, a relatively unknown species that are all but extinct. Sky was their primary home and few of them have ever made it off of Sky. Niahhorru pirates arrived on the planet eons ago and found it too violent and dangerous. The tribes there were constantly at war. Now, they war only with the Sky. They war over and over, and their numbers are halved every time."

"Why do the Sky even let them live?" This story's hold on me makes it hard to concentrate on my knees, which haven't regained their strength. I wobble towards the edge of the platform when a pack of Walrey — a flock? a swarm? a cluster? — spiral down around our platform, heading to the one just below it. I can't see who's on it from where I stand, but I can hear the loud trills of another Walrey cluster.

Jerrock's hands fit around my arms. He rubs his thumbs firmly across my pitiful little muscles, supporting me as he does. "I don't know. I've never wanted to know. We assassins don't interact with the Ren. They live below. The Sky Architects and assassins occupy the towers," he sighs. "The towers reach so far into the sky that most of the time, I cannot even see the surface. I can only hear the sounds of the Ren as they die."

His talk of genocide and assassins is making me hot, even though it shouldn't. I wonder if he could talk to me like this about muxung dung and I'd find it just as arousing. Probably. He pulls our bodies together and I suck in a hiss through my clenched teeth. His hand smooths down my back, landing on my sacrum before pushing lower over my ass. He palms it firmly, *possessively,* and the motion is terrifying.

It feels like he's revisiting something that already belongs to him.

"Jerrock," I choke. "What are you doing?"

"Touching what's mine."

"That's what I was afraid of."

"You don't want me to touch you?" He lifts an eyebrow and has the audacity to *smile* at me again, like he can read my thoughts and knows already the desperation and depth of my feelings for him. Terror shakes me at the thought. I try to pull back, but he doesn't let me.

"You-you don't even like me. You said as much."

"Did I?"

I fight a little harder now. It's a pitiful effort. Like smoke trying to fight against a violent wind. After a few moments, he releases me and I stumble back, arms windmilling wildly to keep myself upright. I'm breathing hard.

He just stares at me, a look of irritation, maybe, on his face. Irritation, or concern. I wish he had ridges for me to be able to tell…

He did, once. Before I ecked it all up and let him get taken…

"I…"

"I know you are in love with me." His voice crashes through whatever I was about to say next. A cold chill rolls over me along with the next gust of wind, which pushes me closer to him. He turns to face me fully and takes a threatening step in my direction. "I knew you loved me. I've known it my entire existence. As Azza, I knew. I knew even as Jerrock the killer. And now, as just Jerrock, I know still. But when you were on that muuir, I knew you didn't love *you*. I could not fight against that. Jerrock the assassin wouldn't have even stood a chance."

I hear what he doesn't say next, what only his eyes convey. That now, because I'm off muuir, things are different, that everything's changed.

I grimace, thinking of the lies I've told him and of all the muuir still in my pack, just in case I change my mind… "You're-you're giving me too much credit. I ran out…" I lie again. "I'd have taken more if I had some."

"Perhaps, in the beginning, but when we arrived here on Quizzar, I offered you an escape." His yeeyar eye shifts dramatically, cutting up and then down, grey against grey. The silver side of his pate gleams in the bright light. It's so bright, I can barely stand looking at him, but I can't look away. I never want to look away. "You refused."

"I-I didn't go off muuir for *me*," I stammer, doing and saying anything to try to put some distance between us. "I did it for you."

"You may think that, but you would not have given up the substance if you did not want to."

I shake my head fiercely. "I didn't mean for you to see…all that. You didn't have to help me."

"I would not have helped you if I did not want to. Besides, you did the difficult part all by yourself." He cocks his head, brown bio eye narrowing, yeeyar in his other eye forming a frightening-looking pupil. "Our transport is incoming."

I don't turn to look at it. Instead, I shout over the sound of the wind our incoming transport creates. "You have got to stop saving me. I'm too deeply indebted to you. I'll never be able to make it all back up."

He smiles his crooked, jagged smile. "Saving your life is my greatest pleasure. It always has been, even as Jerrock the killer when pleasures did not exist for me. No matter who I become, I can assure you that will remain constant. Come, Ashmara. Step away from the edge."

He holds out his hand. I want to punch it. I want to punch myself. I want to bang both of my fists against his chest until my hand breaks against the stalyx. Instead of moving towards him, I shout, "You have to stop!"

He gives me a funny look.

"After what I did, I don't deserve it."

He lunges forward, grabs my wrist and tugs me against him as he backs away from the edge of the platform until we're standing once again in the open mouth of the cave room. "What do you think you did, Ashmara?"

Heat. Pressure. It all builds behind my eyes. I'm weak, and weak Ashmara struggles with all the feelings she has inside. "You know."

"I assure you I wouldn't be asking if I did."

"I *left* you, Jerrock. I *let* them take you. You suffered for five rotations because of me."

And then his face transforms. The white hairs above his brown eye lift and his lips hang slack. Tension thrums through the thick cords of his neck and ripples down his red chest. The color shimmers against his green robe. Pretty. So much prettiness in such a lethal male. How he ever thought he'd cover it up with a matter displacement shield is beyond me. I'd recognize any version of him.

"Your ship is ready," comes the voice through the two-way translator box the Walrey wears. I move to face the owner of the voice, but Jerrock doesn't let me go. Not right away.

He glances between my two eyes, searching them for something. Eck! I don't know what colors I betray currently. I've always had piss-poor control over my emotions, those colors, but now, off of muuir, in front of Jerrock, it's as bad as it's ever been or will ever be.

He grabs my chin in that way he so often does and I dare only the slightest peek through my left eye. He sees me. He always sees.

He breathes, "Is that truly what you think?"

"Reaver. Assassin. Your ship," the Walrey says even louder.

Jerrock turns to face him and quips, "We're retired."

I snort, unable to help myself, and let him smile his crooked smile at me, then tug me toward the Walrey ship.

"What the eck, Jerrock?" I laugh suddenly. "We're gonna fly out of here in this?"

"We have no other choice. The price of admission for this length of time, and for keeping the assassins circling the planet at bay, was the superior Sky ship. I had to accept whatever ship they had to spare and were willing to give me." He's grimacing, looking ticked the eck off as he stares at the thing.

It's a classic Walrey ship, built for beauty — not for battle. It's beautiful. A brilliant yellow ball with glowing designs carved all over it. They look like vines overlaid against the ball and they glow a darker gold than the sleek surface of the ship beneath it. One section of the circular ship boasts replica Walrey wings, huge and intricately carved so that I can see every vein in the eight oblong wings that spread out behind it, sort of like a gigantic tail.

A blistering laugh leaves my throat. It hurts my chest, which strains with even the slightest inhale, but eck it. "This is ecking amazing. I've always wanted one of these." I feel like a kit all over again, the first time I told Tintin and Gibli I wanted my own ship and they said, *what kind do you want?* And then helped me steal a rickety old oil transport ship off of a fleet of Niahhorru. It'd been rad. That ship had only been the first of many ships I owned. I finally got all the way to a top-of-the-line yeeyar-built Niahhorru ship with a kintarr core.

Had to trade that, though, in order to afford the tools, equipment and time of the specialists I hired to help me free Sky assassins. There were five total that I worked on. Manila was only the first one that lived.

"You…you *like* it?"

"Course. This is a classic Walrey comb, a key part of a hive formation. They only fly these when important shit is happening. We could totally pretend to be Walrey royalty when we approach planets. We definitely won't need to pick up an Eshmiri shield." I laugh again. "No one — and I mean, *no one* — will expect a Sky assassin to fly in this."

"This isn't a Walrey comb. Or any other type of Walrey royal hive pod," Jerrock says behind me.

"I'm confused. Then what is it?"

The portal opens and, since there's no gang plank — why would the Walrey need one when they can fly? — I jump and try to catch hold of the lip. The Walrey laugh at me when I fall and I'm annoyed when I crumple to the ground. I haven't fallen in a climb since I was a kit living with the Lemorans and Jerrock, Azza then.

Thick arms circle my body and I let out a yelp and then a squeal and then a bright laugh when Jerrock doesn't just lift me up into the ship, but *jumps* up onto it with me in his arms. He sets me down on my feet and turns to conclude some kinda transaction with the Walrey. Meanwhile, I stare at what's in front of me. The only thing in front of me. The thing dominating three quarters of the ecking ship.

My jaw hangs open and I don't dare turn around as I hear the portal door close on a gentle melody. The ship rumbles to life. Jerrock's clearly working the controls. Maybe I should help him. I should definitely be anywhere but here, my pack slinking off of one shoulder, standing stock-still and just…ecking…staring.

I clear my throat. "You need any help over there?" He doesn't. "I know the controls." I don't. "Let me just put my pack down and I'll..." I throw my pack into a corner — wait, it's a circular room, there are no corners — against a wall and turn around and take a step and slam straight into a wall.

Jerrock is there, right there against me. My face smashes against his warmth. "It's not a royal ship," he repeats. I know that. Doesn't he know that I know that? I'm not blind! I can see the recessed circular bed in the center of the floor, a gigantic pillow covered in catacat and Walrey-dyed silks and edena hides, likely meant for us, as the Walrey bastards who gave us this pod clearly thought we were Voraxian and lovers.

We're neither.

"It's a pleasure pod, Ashmara."

"Uhh...yeeshee. I see that." And even if I *couldn't* see that, I'd still be able to smell the subtle notes of baranthime and wrexthan — both powerful aphrodisiacs. Eck! I can feel the scents hitting me, stimulating me, making me want to sink into those pillows, throw my arms above my head, and let Jerrock have at me for as long as he likes, to perform shekkur over my body all by himself. "Let me have a look at the controls."

"I have it covered."

"You don't know where we're going."

"Do you?"

"I had a plan — *have* a plan..."

"Wouldn't you rather put the pleasure pod to use?"

My heart trips and stalls. My stomach freefalls down to my waist. My cunt squeezes and my lips flutter, singing soft serenades to Jerrock's dick. And salivating.

The low, low, low endorphins riding my system are nothing against the impact of the memory of him trying to help me. I thought he'd just been trying to help me…

"I thought-thought you just wanted to help me with the-the muuir," I stutter uncontrollably, trying to look anywhere but at his face. Oh ecking stars. Against all the walls are tools of pleasure for every species, every race. Oosa electrodes. Niahhorru nets. Avmar oils. Drakesh breeding belts.

"Hm." That's what he says. That's *all* he says.

"I thought you just thought of me as a sibling. As family. As a Niahhorru pirate views his brother…" I take a step back, careful not to fall into the bed by mistake.

"You said that before. Do you need to hear my answer again?" He tracks me with his beautiful brown bio eye. The yeeyar sees more, though it remains a blotchy blur filling his eye socket. I know it sees more than just my flesh, too, but also how my heart races. "And I cannot speak to Azza's desires, for he was a kit, but I can tell you that Jerrock has found you every bit female in each encounter he's had with you."

Each encounter? I think to myself. I stumble over the pack that I dropped. He merely slides it to the side with his outer foot as he stalks me around the outer edge of the room like a predator stalks its prey — like an assassin stalks its next victim.

"Do you understand now?"

"I-I-I'm not sure."

He closes the distance between us, moving too fast for me to block his approach. I wouldn't have anyways. Because this is everything I fear and everything I want. "We are not related. I do not view you as my kin. I never have. I have always viewed you as a female I want to rut." I stop breathing. He reaches out and presses his finger to the hollow at the base of my throat. "And I cannot seem to resist you when you wear clothes this thin. They make you look like you're vulnerable. I want them off. I want to feel the fire within."

He picks me up and tosses me into the center of the room. I gasp, my belly floating as I fly through the air. I hover at the peak of the arc my body creates before I fall. It seems to last forever. I hit the pillows, sinking into them when I expect to bounce. It doesn't stop my heart from bouncing, though. My pulse, which was already erratic — a side effect of my recent breakup with muuir — can't take it.

He drops the robe from his shoulders, my mouth dries, tongue lolling out, and I know…any plans I had to return to my Eshmiri ship and my Eshmiri ways will have to wait.

16

Jerrock

She is saved by the alarm. My hand is on my belt and my desire to pleasure this female until she's lying in a pool of her own pleasure and cannot remember her own name, let alone the drug-induced spell she was under, is all I can think about. Any pretenses I've ever had, pretending that I am not fully enrapt with this female, are shed. Definitively. Never to rise again. And I...

BLORRRR.

BLORRRR.

BLORRRR...

The blaring is obnoxious and I move to the control panel, extend my wrist towards it and allow the yeeyar in my bones to do its work. Though this is not a yeeyar-made ship, I am able to quickly overtake the controls. This is an inferior ship, however, its function second to its appearance, and though I cannot fully control it, I can read it well enough to sense what is coming towards us...

"Impossible."

"What is it?" she says to me from the bed. Eck. The desire to go to her is strong.

"It's a Sky ship."

"The one you gave up in exchange for this lovely contraption?" I glance at her with my white eyebrow raised. She's sinking into the pillows, feet and hands slipping and sliding in every direction until she's splayed like a star. It's funny and my urge to chuckle outweighs both my lust and my suspicion. I laugh and her muscles give out. She simply lies there, broken, staring up at me with a frustrated, bemused expression. Her eyes shine momentarily every color and my chest, it strains.

A blast rattles the ship, making it feel less like a pleasure station and more like a floating prison.

"Krakaw. And this ship has no defensive systems."

"Give me a hand." Ashmara has crawled to the edge of the bed and clings to the platform for dear life. She looks up at me and there is a moment that passes between us as I take the step needed to reach her, stretch down, and coil my fingers slowly around her forearm. I hoist her up effortlessly and she passes by me wordlessly and heads to the limited control panel, focused. It's for the best. This way, she cannot see my hand, how it flexes as it hangs by my side. My arm feels just as heavy as the knowledge that I have never been asked for help before. Now, she asks me so easily, as if there were only one outcome. As if I'd always help her.

I would and I have.

I step up behind her and struggle to focus on anything other than the heat her body emits. She has her pack between her feet and holds her outdated yamar box in both hand. She jams it into the opening in the control panel I created and sparks fly.

"We're too far from Kor," she mumbles, as if she doesn't notice my presence just behind her.

I fight the urge to palm her throat, wrap my other hand around her hips and yank her against me. "What business do you have with Kor?"

"That's where I'm supposed to meet Tintin."

"You told the reavers that you'd meet them on Evernor."

"It's a diversion we use in case anyone's listening. We say Evernor out loud. We mean Kor." She speaks quickly, flippantly, with trust.

I moan.

She glances back at me and her eyes flare bright purple. I grab her cheeks in one fist and she jolts. "Jerrock," she mumbles, though she really can't speak.

I kiss her lips, which are pressed together from the sides and entirely limp. They're soft and damp, though. The ship shakes again and I close my eyes. "I could do this forever with you."

"K-kiss me?"

"Go into battle with you." I peel my eyes open and though my yeeyar sight never actually stops gathering information, I am able to command it to go dark. It's a strange feeling, being deprived of sight, but it's worth it for my other senses to come alive and bask in the heat of her body, the touch of her skin, the scent of her hair, the sound of her breath.

"And yeeshee," I smirk. "That, too."

The ship rattles. "We might not get that chance. We're not near any Niahhorru or Eshmiri ships… Wait…" She reads the holo projection that displays from the top of her box. It is a visual representation of the star map before us. Two-dimensional, colors all flat. It's a cut above worthless and yet, since I've known her, it's all she's ever used. "Yeeshee!" She whoops loud and long and yanks her yamar box back. "Stay out of sight."

She fires on her communicator and, even though her legs barely seem capable of holding her upright, she still stares into the screen, a confident little thing. Then she says, "Reoran, heelee, I need to cash in that favor." She details our coordinates and explains our current threat. She speaks quickly.

The Oosa response, spoken in flashing lights and squeals, is all that I can see reflected on her face through her flickering holoscreen's privacy shield. But I can tell already that the conversation had between this lowly Eshmiri reaver and the Oosa Dua of the Eighth Quadrant is a pleasant one. Just how pleasant is something I would like detailed more explicitly.

My stomach stirs. I feel thin threads of jealousy tethering me to the ground. I want to cut them and allow the assassin that I am full reign over any and every being she's ever smiled at like that. She laughs at something Reoran has said to her and it is decided.

I wipe my list clean and add names to it, Reoran's just after the three Niahhorru pirates who wanted her for their shekkur and are now stuck on that lizard planet for all their efforts. As she ends the call and I plot their decimation, I note that I feel better. Much better.

"Why are you smiling like that? It's creepy."

"I don't think so."

"How would you know?"

"I know how to moderate my expression to replicate any emotion."

"So what emotion are you going for now?"

"Not creepy. Murderous."

She grins rather than recoils, the little devil that she is. "Who are you thinking about murdering? Because if it's me, then can I have that last shot of muuir first?"

Surprise derails me. "What last shot of muuir?"

"The one in the pocket of your robe. I saw you put it there. The one you bought off the Walrey. The one I wouldn't let you give me."

She'd been in the throes of agony, but she still noticed that. I wonder how, and whether she's upset that I kept it. I reach into my pocket and withdraw the small tan-colored patch trapped between two thin pieces of translucent film. She does not react at the sight of it, as I thought she might, but simply looks from me to it to me again with a small, secretive smirk.

I offer it to her. "You should have it. As a reminder of what you overcame."

She gives it a look, but it is not one of consideration. It's clear as she answers that she's already made up her mind. "Krakaw. You keep it."

I don't ask her why and I don't press the issue. I merely nod and slip the film back into my pocket. I don't know why I keep it. Perhaps, as a reminder of what she overcame. Perhaps, as a reminder of the moment she gave herself back to me. "You are a warrior, Ashmara."

Her eyes dart to the side. She doesn't answer. Instead, she rubs her temple and grabs hold of the nearest wall when the ship is attacked again. "Reoran's patrol should be here soon. Your Sky buddy won't be able to get past them."

"And what payment will Reoran require for such *generosity*?" I step forward, backing Ashmara fully against the wall because I'm irritated with her, yeeshee, but also because this part of the ship is the strongest and backing her against it best ensures that she will survive whatever barrage the Sky ship has planned for us next — and the plans I have for it.

I brace one forearm beside her head. My yeeyar wrist I extend back to the controls. I interrupt the current flight path and take over, pulling the small, useless ship up and left.

"What are you doing?" Ashmara splays both of her arms. She holds onto the wall behind her and grabs my red arm, digging her fingernails into my skin.

"Reoran's fleet will *not* be here soon. We are too far from anywhere for that to be possible and, even if it were, I wouldn't want you to have to pay *extra* for expedited service."

"I don't have to pay Reoran anything for this."

"Then what have you already paid her?"

"Are you... Is that why you want to murder someone? Reoran? She's the nicest Oosa around. Don't murder her."

"Her name is already on my list. Give me one reason why I should remove it."

Ashmara's eyes brighten, turning the most marvelous color. I don't have long to admire that particular shade of bright, iridescent white mixed with fuchsia and taupe. Surprise and confusion. As if she truly does not understand jealousy as a concept — perhaps, having been raised by the Eshmiri, she does not. Or, she does not understand that I might be possessive over her. Hm. I will have to rectify this. Does she not know that she has been mine from the start? Even when I did not know who she was, or who I was, I never let another hold her contract.

"I…" She gasps as the ship lurches in unconventional directions. I do not attempt to lose the Sky ship, but to confuse it as I draw nearer and nearer to it. "You think that I…" She allows her voice to trail off.

I grimace as I maneuver our ship past an incoming barrage of blaster fire, this stuff more powerful than the last. Acidic, it will melt the outer hull of any ship that isn't composed of kintarr or yeeyar, which this piece of frivolous gold most certainly is not.

"I've nev-never been with another being before."

Her blatant lie stalls my anger. I press our faces close together and press our bodies closer than that. I let my full length crush her to the golden wall of this pleasure ship. I rock my hips into her stomach, watch her eyelids flutter. She jerks. She doesn't know what to do with her hands. I love that she is inexperienced and yet, I know better than to believe this lie.

"Never?" I whisper.

"I…"

My moment has arrived. I cannot waste it. The incoming ship is switching blasters — if I had to guess, opting for the short-range high-impact rounds rather than the long-range ones. A hit from a long-range blast may damage the ship, whereas one hit from a high-impact round would tear the ship in two.

I crush my lips to hers, sucking her tongue into my mouth and nipping gently at the tip with my teeth before pulling back. "You'll finish that thought in a moment." I heave my body off of hers, though it takes effort, and move to the door. "Get into the closet and don't come out until I command you to."

She's slow to respond, blinking even more slowly. Finally, she turns to look in the direction I'm pointing and her eyes go huge. "You-you want me to wait in the sex dungeon?"

I grunt. It might be a laugh, but I don't have the time to refine it into anything more gentle. "Yeeshee. Wait for me in the sex dungeon. Prepare yourself for my return."

"Prepare myself..." she says, glancing at the wall of objects for sexual pleasure and the gold cage with cuffs dangling from its ceiling. I wonder if she'll fulfill my fantasy and apply the chains herself or if I'll have to do it for her. The thought makes me salivate and renew my determination to return to her even faster.

I turn away from her as I feel the Sky ship latch. The assassin will attempt to board. Ha. What shall I kill it with? My bare hands? The confidence I feel knowing Ashmara will be here awaiting me on my return is high. Too high? I will not take risks now.

Moving over to the wall of sex objects, I quickly leap and pull the lightning stick from the wall. It's a fully functioning one, too. I've heard the Oosa can sometimes obtain sexual arousal from these. How, considering they debilitate most, I'm not fully certain.

Ashmara stands where I left her, but I gently push her towards the cage and repeat, "Prepare yourself and await my return." I kiss her forehead right before I release her. It was a mistake, because her eyes widen and she simply stands there looking dumbfounded.

"Move, Ashmara," I tell her, but she just repeats, "Prepare myself how? And wait...return?" Ashmara shouts as I move to the door. "Return, Jerrock?"

The Sky ship locks into place, the yeeyar making a familiar crinkling sound as it extends from the Sky ship to cover the doorway of the Walrey pleasure ship. The moment I feel it fully lock, I engage the commands for the golden doors to open. I do not hesitate.

The Sky ship's white interior flashes and I toss the lightning stick into the sliver of space that appears between the golden doors. I fire a blast of my own at the shimmering gold-and-white-striped cylinder. My strike is well placed and so was my throw. The lightning stick explodes over the head of the assassin, showering the creature in sparks.

It rears back, raising a shield above its oblong head. It is almost entirely Avmar, with only a few sections of its long body removed and replaced with stalyx. The shield, I realize, has replaced its front right pincer. The left pincer has also been replaced, this time with twin saws. It recovers quickly and swipes for my stomach. I'm moving forward and one blade connects. It sends additional sparks flying as my stalyx half takes the bulk of the hit. But not all of it.

"Auff," I grunt, the slick, warm heat of my blood spilling over my lower abdomen. Annoying. I can count on one hand the number of times blood has been drawn from my skin by an opponent. And now it's happened to me twice in as many battles.

That does not bother me.

What bothers me is that it's happened twice in front of *her*.

The Avmar and I battle in the short room of the Sky ship. The battle is bloody and gruesome. I am made to bleed three more times. Once on the cheek, once on the upper thigh, once on the outer arm. I am ecking furious as I finally, slowly, agonizingly bring the Avmar down.

It's not a pretty way to die, taking it apart piece by piece as I have. I've finally gotten it slowed down enough to be able to take one of my daggers to the creature's underbelly. The soft section most Avmars have between the folds of their carapaces has been replaced on this Avmar with stalyx, so I have to go through the carapace itself.

I fire six rounds in quick succession and in short range. It is enough to break through. Just as I bury my fist inside of the creature, dagger in hand, I hear a thunk on the floor behind me. I turn, confused and a little unsure given that I saw the holding tanks in the back of the ship were empty. It's just the two of us, the Avmar and me, and now the assassin is dead. I should be alone.

The Avmar drops beneath me in a puddle of its own innards. I pick my dagger up and toss the handle, catch the blade. I prepare to release my weapon into the chest of whoever dares to intervene here and now when I see *Ashmara,* of all the universe's rebels, lurch ungainly into the ship.

She's holding a weapon at shoulder height and, seeing me, flings it at me as hard as she can. Her aim is perfect and I'm too focused on how weak she looks in the knees, yet how conversely determined her expression is, to defend properly against it. I lift my forearm to block the incoming object, but the rubbery texture bends around my arm, grazing my cheek before bouncing off of it. I catch the thing and turn the object towards the light.

"Interesting choice."

"I thought so." Her gaze is lost in the carnage of the room.

I grimace. "It isn't pretty."

"I've seen worse."

"Have you?"

"Krakaw."

I smirk and gesture towards her with the enormous green Oroshi dildo in my hand. "You don't have to watch."

"Watch what?"

"I'll jettison the corpse." I move to the control panel and insert my wrist into the hifelai, letting the yeeyar connect and take over. I hope that she listens and does what I tell her, though I don't count on it. "Go back to the other ship. There is another Sky vessel incoming," I lie. There are two.

"Are you bleeding?" Her eyes round. "Is that blood?"

"Go back to the other ship and get in the cage. Lock it."

She comes towards me instead, slipping twice on the Avmar's innards. I lunge forward and catch her elbow before she can fall in it completely. It isn't toxic, per se, but it isn't good to linger in its fumes or get its innards on your skin. My skin, fine, but not hers. "It cut you? Isn't their venom toxic?"

"Not fully and, even if it were, not to me."

Her fingers trail over my chest. It is distracting. "Are you sure?"

"I'm sure." Her concern. It is...

"Why?"

"The Architects modified the venomous assassins so that their venom becomes instantly lethal. They infuse all assassins' blood with the antidote. We are immune to our own venom and the Architects, for all their hubris, never expected us to attack one another. If you manage to liberate any more assassins before I manage to kill their creators, I suppose they will need to modify their approach."

"Krakaw."

I give her a look.

"*We.* No more I or you. Just we." Her voice trembles. She's angry with me.

I feel a smile on my lips, though inside my chest hurts. She must know. "You must know." She has to know. "You have to know…"

The look on her face tells me that she has not even considered it.

"Ashmara," I breathe. I brush the backs of my bloody fingers across the plump curve of her cheek. Her color is still weak. "You must know that a trip to Sky is a one-way journey, one that I plan to make alone."

A thousand emotions pass over her face and ripple across the fabric of her gaze. I imagine that I can feel it and that it is soft to the touch. She opens her mouth and starts a hundred sentences, shuts it, then starts a hundred more.

I grip the back of her neck and prepare to pull her into a kiss, but she resists my hold. I don't force her.

The ship lurches. I take a step so as not to lose my balance. She wavers in my arms. "Eck you, Jerrock," she spits before ripping out of my grip, her soft curls slipping through my fingers. She turns her back on me and goes to the other ship. Why does seeing her follow through on my command feel like this?

I touch the wound on my stomach which, by comparison, doesn't sting at all.

I go to the command panel and track the movement of the other ships, trying to focus. Now, there is a third ship to add to the mix. This one has a hold of our two ships and is towing us. It is moving slowly. The Sky ships are closing in. I wonder what the Oosa ship that drags us is doing…until I suddenly grin.

A fleet of Oosa ships suddenly blasts past us. There must be a hundred of them. There can be no less than that, I'm sure. They immediately descend on the incoming Sky ships in a flurry of blaster fire. I watch the scene unfold. Watch the battle take place. The Sky ships fight together, as I knew they would, and they make a good stand, clearing the battlefield of at least ten Oosa fighters before finally being obliterated. Fractured yeeyar flings into the nothingness of space like the tentacles of an enormous hevarr taking its last breath.

The ships explode apart and soon, the ship markers disappear from the hifelai. Gone. But no great sacrifice is made for free. I want to know the cost. And then I see where we are headed and my anger flares brighter as our conjoined ships begin to dock.

I turn to track Ashmara down — I want to be near her when we disembark — but she's standing right there. I almost run her over in my haste to make sure she's alright. She stabs me in the stomach with a blunt instrument. "Ow," I say, simply for the purpose of eliciting a reaction from her. It works. She frowns.

I'm waiting for her to say what it is she's going to say, so I don't look down to see what she's doing with my wound. I have some idea when I feel heat followed by a soothing balm. "So you've decided to let me live after all?"

She doesn't speak. I can feel our momentum slow. "We're nearing a port."

Silence.

"Have we reached Uoustar?"

Silence. But she cannot keep her eyes clear. They flash pink and red and black, even. She's not just angry with me, then. She's livid. And afraid. *And possibly even afraid for me.*

"How did you gain permission to dock at Uoustar?" I demand.

Silence.

"It is a planet on which no non-Oosa are allowed."

Silence.

"It is a great honor to be invited. I have heard of only two other beings ever to gain entry. The second Rakukanna of the Voraxian Federation, first of such a title, was a known mistress to the Oosa Dua of the time. Her arrangement with the Raku, then, was not a Xiveri match, but purely political."

She snorts and lifts the healing wand from my stomach to my outer arm. She still won't meet my gaze even though her eyes betray everything.

"The second was a Sky assassin." That gives her pause. "He managed to make it to the surface and execute his target before he was detained. He managed to escape captivity then, too. Now their policy, I believe, is to execute assassins on sight."

"They won't execute you."

"Why?" My gaze narrows. "Because what you offered Reoran is of so great a value she'd lift not one Oosa policy but two just for you?"

Her eyes flash with color. Fire and flame. She's livid. Incensed. Infuriated. "She's a friend. An ecking friend, Jerrock."

Friend. I truly do not even understand the concept.

Her brow relaxes. She eases back onto her heels. "You don't know about friends." Shame. It surfaces in her gaze like an enemy I want to vanquish. I want to address it, but first, I say slowly, "Friends. They are like your Eshmiri hoard. Those you associate with…"

"Associate with?" She scoffs and pivots one shoulder away from me. "Krakaw. Tintin and Gibli are my family. My fathers. They pulled me off of that ship after I waited there for who knows how many solars for you to come back. They fed me, made sure I had clothes. Held me when I was sick or scared or cold." Heat blasts through me and the chill that follows is the only reason I am able to overcome it. "*Friends* are like Reoran. Like Rhorkanterannu and Herannathon, like their mates, Deena and Nalia now, too…"

"And what am I to you?"

"I don't know." She shoves the healing wand against my chest. "Friends don't go on suicide missions without each other. Friends don't lie to each other. Friends don't hurt each other's friends, either. Reoran owes me a favor because, in one of my raids, I rescued two Oosa. That's it. That's all. End of story. After we leave this place, you and I can go our separate ways. I'll go hang out with my *friends* and you can go try to take on the entire Sky planet alone and get yourself killed in the process." She shoves the spear end of the healing wand into my gut, right where the wound once was. It smarts, but I don't allow myself to react to it. Pain is inconsequential. Pain is nothing.

Then why do her words hurt so much?

The ship emits a thunderous sound as it finally reaches land. It shudders before it settles and then the gold Walrey ship is pried loudly and forcefully off of the open doorway to the Sky ship we stand on now. I could keep the doors closed with the yeeyar connection I have to the ship, but I allow them to part. I don't know why I let her walk away from me.

Standing in the doorway, she slings her pack up onto her shoulder and says, "Good luck finding the Sky planet without your key or any friends to help you find one."

"I don't need friends to get a key. I just need to kill a Sky assassin."

"Krakaw, you need to *not* kill a Sky assassin and simultaneously harvest the key from their body while making sure you don't die in the process. Trust me, I should know. I've liberated three Sky keys from the bodies they belong to and guess what, Jerrock?"

"What?" I ask, though I don't need to hear the answer. I have a plan. I will find an assassin, retrieve their key and kill them. No matter how long it takes. And, given how rapidly we are being attacked by them, I know that it will not take very long.

"Every time I ever retrieved a key, I wasn't alone. I had friends there to help me. But good luck. I'm sure you'll be fine on your own. Just don't expect to see me around. I know how it feels now and I get why you didn't want to have anything to do with me. It's too hard to watch your *friends* kill themselves, no matter how quickly or slowly."

The gold shell of the ship is pried free of the Sky ship. I am about to shut the doors, locking her in here with me to finish this conversation, but I hesitate. What would I say? And in that hesitation, she jumps down into a brightly lit world without me.

17
Ashmara

Reoran is the first being I see when I jump off of the ship, leaving Jerrock behind. Her guards attempt to block her way forward, trying to protect her from me, as they should, but she shoves her big blue body past them. It collides with mine and I give her a hug, letting her pull me into her warmth in a hug unlike any other. I'm halfway lodged in her body when I hear a stir and open my eyes and see the Oosa freaking the eck out at the sight of Jerrock in the doorway.

A blast fires at his head that he just narrowly manages to avoid before I throw both arms in the air and shout, "Hey, hey! He's with me!" I repeat the words in the high Oosa trills and let my eyes flash with very specific emotions for good measure. It's the hardest language I've ever tried to learn and I'm still not sure my attempts at translation really work. Half the time, I can't control my emotions well enough to fabricate the colors that appear in my eyes, but I still try.

"He's with me," I repeat to Reoran directly.

She hesitates, peeling her jelly body off of mine. Completely spherical, she lights up from within as she trills. In Oosa, she asks me if I'm in trouble and when I tell her that I'm not, she has the audacity to squeal, "Is this *him*?"

I grimace, hoping to the high heavens that Jerrock never bothered to learn the Oosa language. I smile at Reoran grimly and give her a single sharp nod. She squeals even louder and rolls past me, nearly knocking me over before she reaches the edge of the Sky ship. Her spherical form distends, molding to the lip of the entryway before pulling the rest of her weight onto it. Jerrock has angled himself away from her, looking very much like he'd like to retaliate. The guards are going absolutely berserk, flooding past me like thunderous blue river water as they chase after their leader.

I start to laugh — or would have had my gaze not lifted at that exact moment to Reoran and Jerrock inside the starch-white ship, two contrasting and beautiful colors. Red and blue. Fire and water. The water encompasses the fire and completely douses the flame. Because love will always do that. I just wonder…can Jerrock ever be anything other than hate?

I watch the two of them interact until I'm sure Reoran is safe before moving through the crowd, searching, searching for the one I'm most excited to see. I don't see her immediately and I would — she stands out from the Oosa, an otherwise homogenous species. But I know she's here. She's never too far from Reoran.

For now, I take a breath.

Maybe, my first breath that I can remember. Without the muuir in my system, everything feels…

Duller.

I huff and ruffle my hair. It's hard not to want to dig into my pack and retrieve the muuir I told Jerrock wasn't there. Especially now that I know his plans for us. For me. For leaving…

I inhale and try that whole breathing thing again. I move to the edge of the landing dock. It's a natural platform, the kind you might land on when you get to Lemora, only there aren't any pad pads here to lead you off of the low plateau. Also, this plateau isn't brown rock or green moss or grass, but pink.

Pink and blue swirl together in the packed earth beneath my feet. I stare down at it, watching it roll into a brighter orange before melting away into green and blue and purple once more. It's beautiful here. So incredibly beautiful.

My breath catches when I reach the edge of the plateau and lean my elbows against the natural pink wooden barrier. The sun is a bright yellow bulb in the blue sky. The sky is lighter than the Oosa blue and totally cloudless. It makes it almost unbearable to look out at the world of Uoustar, the most beautiful planet in all the Quadrants. Because without the clouds, there is no shadow to hide the loveliness. It just is, with nothing to get in its way.

The world of Uoustar is composed almost entirely of pools with an endless maze of pathways in between. Each pool is a varying shimmering shade of pink, purple, blue, or green. Pools stack on top of other pools, shelves made of rock holding pools at different levels, water spilling from one into the next, creating mosaics of swirling color.

Oosa themselves fill many of the pools, splashing and laughing and coupling in the water. Each color, I've been told, has a different effect on the swimmer. I've never been in the pools myself — I always thought that muuir would make a bad bedfellow to any other natural toxin, but now…

Now I'm not sure.

Eck it. Maybe I should couple with an Oosa in one of the pools.

My name is called from the right and I turn to see a smaller Oosa rolling towards me. She's surrounded by twice as many guards as Reoran and is just as excited to see me as I am her. I run towards her. She rolls towards me. We collide in a pile of liquid limbs and shaky humanity.

I don't feel so great. That stupid soup was the last thing I ate. But I could stand forever to hug her like this.

"I missed you, heelee."

She replies with something similar, calling me *brachard,* an Oosa word meaning something like 'loved one.' It's what Oosa call their family. No one else. And I'm touched, just as I always am.

I give her a soft pat and she envelopes my hand in her Oosa flesh. She asks me how I've been and I tell her I found the one I've been looking for and he got me off of muuir. Her excitement agitates the guards at her back. They are trained to repress their base urges, so as not to be distracted, but at the sound of her excitement, two of them begin coupling in plain sight.

Reoran returns to us then and collides with the Oosa in front of me, Dloroora. Dloroora is Reoran's kit and is widely considered top contender to replace Reoran when the Oosa hold their next election in seven rotations. The Oosa live so long, seven rotations might be the term of three Rakus of Voraxia.

Dloroora tells her mother of my *accomplishments*, she calls them. I laugh at the word. If only they knew the rest of the story. It's hardly one that makes me look good.

Reoran responds with equal parts excitement and glee — the Oosa are always gleeful. Or horny. Or murdery. They're good beings. She tells her fully grown kit that she's met the male in question and guides her away. Jerrock is trying to get to me through a throng of Oosa bodies eager to touch and couple with him. I laugh, even though I don't mean to — I'm still mad at him. I think I knew this was his intent all along, but hearing him say that he's planning on going without me — out loud — hurt more than it should have.

Jerrock replies in trills and whirrs that surprise me as he carefully disentangles his limbs from outstretched Oosa parts. It's clear he's learned *some* of the Oosa tongue, though he can't communicate in it as well as I can since his ridges have been removed and he doesn't shine with color. *And it's my fault.*

He comes towards me, but I don't really need to see him now, so when Reoran and Dloroora invite us to join them for a meal and offer us a place to rest or relax for however long we want, I accept.

Jerrock stares at me over the tops of Oosa bodies — some nearly as high as he is, but most rising to my chest height — and offers me no expression. No indication of whether or not this is something he wants to do. But I don't really care if he stays. I don't want him to expect a goodbye from me. If he wants to leave me behind, it should be now.

As we're led away from the ship, I'm funneled close to him by the guards flanking us. I tell him, "You should leave now. Just take the ship and go. They won't stop you."

"Which ship?" Reoran asks me as she leads the group down the path towards an enormous tiered castle set on the hillside. The castle is Oosa blue and shaped with huge round parapets and balustrades and ovoid structures that soar into the sky. It looks like a doll's castle from far away, but as we roll closer, it looms huge and gobbles us up.

The inside is opulent, as is the Oosa way, and our meal takes place inside a great blue hall, seated at a low orange table. We're served all the Oosa delicacies and then some and by the time I'm finished eating, I'm completely stuffed. Reoran's team has to literally roll me away from the table when the solar is done.

I'm deposited in a blue bedroom, alone, and left with the promise that I'll join Reoran and Dloroora in the heefeegee pool the coming solar. I agree, even though I have no idea what that is, and I sleep. I sleep a sleep that makes all other sleep jealous. I don't dream and if I dream then I dream only of lovely things, like pink pools sitting against a yellow and blue horizon.

I don't dream of Jerrock.

18

Jerrock

I watch how easily she converses with the Oosa all through dinner, or whatever meal this is on this planet with a sun that only sets for moments in shades of lavender. It's as if she's one of them. How seamlessly she adapts. She speaks Oosa better than I do, using the colors in her eyes to replicate their colorful trills. I've never seen a Voraxian or Drakesh do that.

I am not allowed to sit beside her at the table, but as far from her as the table's length will allow. It annoys me. The Oosa near me are mostly comprised of Reoran's guards, leaving Reoran and her progeny, Dloroora, to surround and occupy my female at the other end of the table, regaling her with tall tales of pleasures received across the vibrant cosmos. Reoran even says something about her disappointment at her representatives having lost the bid for the human hybrid that is the current miriga of Lemora's Clan Raingar.

Ashmara replies in equally expressive gestures, telling tales of her own. When the dinner is finished and Ashmara has lost her ability to converse as eloquently as she was able to earlier, given that exhaustion and wine likely leaves her emotions more raw and their colors less stable, the dinner guests depart or couple in alcoves against the walls. I am last to leave the table. When I do, I leave surrounded by Reoran's private guard, who lead me to a sleeping chamber. I wait a breath for them to depart the outside halls and immediately leave it and go to Ashmara's room, fully intent on concluding our earlier conversation.

My rage towards Reoran was misplaced and I want to confront Ashmara about it. Why she lied about her relationship with the royal Oosa family. I want to know why she drank Oosa wine tonight and let them carry her out of the room, happy and so well sated she did not seem to care for her own safety. Granted, she had to know I was there and would let nothing happen to her, but she also didn't seem to care either way.

I didn't like that.

She didn't look for me as she was wheeled from the room in a floating pool of Oosa bodies. Reoran seemed to know that something had *happened* between us, as she put it. She didn't ask what, just told me to fix it and that, until I did, I'd be in a far wing of the castle, away from Ashmara.

Clever. Because I scoured the castle only to realize that she'd put me in the room next door to that of my female.

The doors in this wing of the castle are all locked, but I have no trouble letting myself into her room. She's set up no precautions. Not even a simple barrier. She simply lies there in her bed, nestled into lavish blankets filled with a gel-like substance that the Oosa seem to prefer. They wrap around her and cover her and she looks so content lying among them, a small smile I've never seen her wear before strung between her cheeks.

I know her smiles. I know *all* of her smiles.

I know the smile that's mine.

I know the smile she wears for others.

I know her tired smile, her brave smile, her concealing smile, her nervous smile, her arrogant smile, her tough smile, her bitter smile, too.

But this smile? This smile right here? It makes me ravenously vengeful, and gloriously content. She looks so at peace, I'm almost happy to let her lie like this without interrupting her.

Because this smile is all hers. I cannot take that away from her. So even though I am only *almost* happy, I let her sleep.

I take a seat beside her in the bed, careful not to wake her — *unable* to wake her given the strange, thick and fleshy texture of the bed. And I watch her. And as I watch her, I strategize about what I will tell her when she wakes. And when that grows dull, I try to imagine what it is she dreams about that gives her such an expression.

Me, I decide. She's dreaming of Jerrock.

19

Ashmara

Whatever the Oosa put in the ecking water is…well, I know what it is and right now, I find it marvelous.

I let out a huge sigh, mouth open, chest full of breath. I exhale. I exhale and exhale and exhale. I inhale and stretch my arms and exhale again and let the tingles run through me. On the next inhale, I have no choice but to settle on my back and extend my hand down my body. Between my thighs, there is a restlessness I've felt before, many times, but I've only gotten to act on a handful of them.

I'm never alone, always in rooms and cabins and pods full of Eshmiri — and that's only when I'm not stuck in some holding cell somewhere. My latest venture into detention was in a Sky holding cell and it wasn't exactly pleasant. Jerrock put me there. My body still aches with the memory of being pinned to the wall he chained me against, but I don't think about that now. I don't think about the way Jerrock the assassin looked at me, *hating* me yet unable to transform his hurting touch into a killing one.

I think about the way Jerrock the free looked at me when he offered — I swallow hard — what he offered.

He offered me something so selfless, it seemed, I was so embarrassed. He didn't have to do that, such an obscene and salacious act. His tongue… I'll never forget it.

I slip my hand under the fine fabric of the Walrey garments I'm still wearing and touch my lower belly. It tingles wildly beneath my fingertips. The sensation is nothing like muuir. I still feel entirely like myself. I can still think entirely clearly. I can still remember his words, each and every one, even though I was hurting so badly in the moment.

Relax. I will torture you just a little. Just know that unlike any other torture I would inflict, you will survive this.

That's what he promised, but I'm not sure I did.

I conjure a new image now and picture him looming above me here in this Oosa bed, all smiling and sweet. He'd ask me if I want more pleasure… *"Yeeshee,"* I breathe.

I wiggle my fingers beneath the curls that cover my sex and touch my soft skin and laugh just a little. Krakaw. Jerrock would never ask me so nicely like that. He's rough with me. It scares me just as much as it arouses me and makes me absolutely terrified to know what he'd be like if we were actually *together* like that. My memory unintentionally jumps to that *other* solar, but I shove it away. Not before sweat breaks out on my forehead as I remember losing my virginity to a male at that pleasure house, though.

I thought the male I chose from the selection looked kind and gentle and that he'd go easy on me, but he'd been rough, bordering on cruel in a way that, now, makes me think of Jerrock…and makes me sick to my stomach knowing it wasn't him. It feels like, by seeking out that other male, I gave up on Jerrock. In that moment, I guess I had. I'd lost all hope of finding and rescuing him.

Now that I have Jerrock back, my biggest fear is him finding out that I was with another male. This Jerrock that I've awoken seems possessive and territorial. I don't think he'd like it if he knew another male had pleasured me. He might not forgive me for it.

I might be mad at him now, but I don't want him mad at *me*. I don't want him to know. I wish I could just purge that memory from my mind but right now, I can't seem to repress it. It burns, wanting to exist, wanting its recognition for what it was — a lunar I'll never be able to truly forget. I draw on it as frustration makes it impossible to achieve my climax, so I just give in. I revisit that pleasure house and the male who took me in that nest, only this time, I replace his red Drakesh face with one that's half covered in stalyx.

"Yeeshee, Jerrock..." My fingers rub more roughly, but I keep tripping over the memories, unable to keep up the illusion that it was Jerrock in that pleasure room with me, and then being horrified of him discovering what I'm thinking about.

I'm also not that *skilled* at anything related to sex, even when it comes to pleasuring myself. I can count the number of times I've had the chance to do this on one hand, and the amount of times I've succeeded is even less. Frustration bubbles in a different way and my expression twists. The good vibrations rippling through me are rising and racing to nowhere and it's here, at nowhere, that they plateau and drift.

"Ugh." Tension leaves my body. Frustration kills my mood.

I sigh up at the ceiling, which shimmers blue. There are no windows in the walls, but the walls themselves are translucent and I can see that the solar light is bright, whatever time it is. It's probably time for me to get up. The longer I'm here, the greater the risk to Reoran, and I don't need to put her or her kin or the other Oosa here in harm's way.

Rhorkanterannu, on the other hand? I don't mind one bit.

I pull my hand out of my silk trousers at the same time that harsh words rip like a whip through the air. "Continue."

I freeze, my mind running into rubbery Oosa walls and bouncing back. "Krakaw," I gasp, blinking up at the ceiling, terrified to look around and face the horror of my ecking reality. Embarrassment doesn't know the female I've become. This is ecking humiliating.

"I was not asking. Take it off."

My mind shutters. *That's what the male in the pleasure house said to me.* I shake my head. "What the eck are you doing here, Jerrock?" I'm proud of how hard my voice sounds as I prop myself up on my elbows. I jump. Holy ecking moons. He's right ecking next to me! If he reached for me and if I reached for him, our fingers would touch. Two arms' lengths separate us on this big, weird ecking Oosa bed. And he's just watching me. His legs are stretched out in front of him, his green trousers looking dull in the strange blue light.

Not his eye though.

His brown bio eye is full of fire. His jaw is hard and clenched. The white of his hair drapes over his shoulder in tangles, down the red side of his chest. His muscles ripple as my stare drops down, down, down to the massive bulge on the front of his pants. My mouth salivates. I think of the male I'd rutted in the pleasure house, wishing it was Jerrock's cock I'd had a chance to taste.

"Take it off."

"Jerrock!" I blurt, even louder this time, memory making my gut clench. "Stop."

His head tilts slightly. He looks ecking pissed. "On your knees."

I blink many, many times, and then I blink again. I don't like this coincidence. I don't like it at all. "I'm not ecking around, Jer. Get the eck out of my room. I don't want to see you right now."

"On your knees."

I'm scared now. Really scared. I jerk back, narrowly avoiding being grabbed. I jerk my wrist back just in time and Jerrock grabs only blanket with his stalyx fingertips. "You came to this planet for pleasure, did you not? *Just* pleasure." He licks his lips. The cords of his neck muscles thicken in pulses. I start to ease off of the bed as he rolls onto his knees and starts to shift towards me, looking every bit a predator. For the first time in all the rotations he's been chasing me, I feel like prey.

"That is what I will give you," he whispers as he crawls towards me, "and that is what you will give me."

"Krakaw." My face flames with heat. Mortification and shame and rage hit me briefly before I'm overcome with an even greater urge — to flee. The coincidence… it…it can't be…

"Yeeshee," he says to me.

I fall off of the low bed onto the floor, landing hard on my wrists. Jerrock has no sympathy. He continues to stalk towards me, looking like a male possessed.

I survey the room, trying to find a weapon to defend myself with. My pack lies close by. It's always close by. I lunge for it, but Jerrock beats me to it and snatches it off of the ground. He tosses it onto the mattress behind him so that I'm separated from it by the immovable wall that he is.

"Eyes up," he says while angry tears bubble in mine.

"You ecking lying bastard." I choke. I'm so humiliated. It can't be. It *can't* be.

Jerrock pauses in his advance. "I'm many things, a bastard is one of them, a liar is not. You're the only one who's lied between the two of us, when you told me you'd never been had before. Why did you lie to me, Ashmara?"

I have to get out of here. I need air. I need a weapon. I need to stab him. Yeeshee. Stabbing him will make me feel better. But first, I need to know for sure... "Was it you, or some other Sky assassin?"

Rage makes his shoulders arch back. His bottom jaw flexes and so does his biological fist as he says, "You really think I'd have allowed another assassin to rut you like that?"

Oh eck. It really was him. The male I remember, that I wished was Jerrock, actually was. My chest burns as the clarity washes over me. I'm...I'm...I'm angry and bitter and elated and scared but most of all I'm just overwhelmed.

In a flurry of movement, arms and legs all working at once, I slip and slide and scrabble over the floor. I lunge for the door and slam it shut behind me just as I hear Jerrock slam into the wall. Eck!

"What the eck, Jerrock?" I shout over my shoulder. "I'm not an animal! Don't chase me!" I race down the halls, which are decorated with Oosa divans and plush seats — absolutely nothing I could use to maim the brute with.

I make it down the hall and into the next when Jerrock slams into my back. I scream as my feet leave the ground and the front of my body collides with a rubbery blue wall, his back like stone as it traps me there. I'm trapped! My breathing is hard and my adrenaline is high but my brittle, broken limbs spasm in a last-ditch effort to save myself. I use all of my force to push against the wall, gaining just a little extra space, before I let the tension in my body go all together.

The push and release gives Jerrock momentary pause because despite everything, he won't hurt me and I can count on that. When his arms reach out to stop me from shattering against the wall, the cage I'm in opens just a little. I drop to the ground, out of his grip, and throw myself away from him. I lunge towards the staircase, falling down most of them. There are many Oosa in the grand entryway and they don't pay attention to me until I collide with them, bouncing between their bodies.

"Jerrock is being a bastard!" I shout when I spy Dloroora in the doorway, light from outside cascading through her translucent flesh. She's a darker blue than the other Oosa, bordering on charcoal. The assassins that held her managed to inject some yeeyar into her flesh, but not enough to take over her body by the time the reavers and I broke her out of the ship. Now, she doesn't light up quite as brightly as the other Oosa, but that doesn't matter. It really ecking doesn't. She's just as spectacular as any of them, never more than when she answers, "Should we kill him?"

I hear the sound of his boots hitting the ground as he jumps down the stairs, clearing the entire grand staircase in one go, and I release a scream and a laugh and a cry and a shout all in a single, garbled word, "Krakawstopdon't!"

Because I'd never want to hurt him. No matter what. Not even if he wounds me and carves the soul off of my bones.

I sprint out into the light, sliding to a stop on my left foot. I feel fire slide down my entire side as I remember being shot there during our last altercation. He didn't shoot me, though, another assassin did and Jerrock retaliated against him. *He didn't even know me then, but he still fought for me.* I close my eyes, feeling pressure behind my sternum build and build. I need to find somewhere safe to run before I explode, but there is nowhere safe here. There are only open fields and pink and purple pools where Oosa bathe and couple freely among them.

I don't have the time to decide what to do or where to go. I head right, racing down a well-trodden — or rolled — path. I take the first offshoot, and then the next and then the next, losing myself in a maze of Oosa pools. Down at the bottom of a hill, the Oosa bathers become fewer. Pools at the top levels of the plateau stacks are well-occupied, but down here, where water ripples and cascades in glittering rainbow waterfalls, I'm almost alone. Almost, except for the male hunting me.

I head for the first of the colorful falls, intending to hide behind it. I know it won't work forever and see a stone near the edge of the pool. I reach for it, stumbling as a sudden dizziness makes me wobble, but I get lucky and my fingers close around it despite my struggle.

I grab it at the same time I feel a presence draw near. He came out of nowhere and now he's so close that I can smell him even stronger than the minerals radiating from the falls or the pools above and below them or the rocks surrounding the pools. His presence is stronger than the smell and the pull of the sun. Standing, I'm prepared to turn and smash his stupid silver head in with my purple and green shimmering stone, but before I can take so much as a breath, I'm grabbed from behind by impossibly strong arms.

The red and the stalyx overlap around my waist as I'm hauled up against his chest. "Give it all you've got little fighter," he whispers into my ear, "because when you're finished, it's my turn."

I grunt as I throw my full weight forward, trying to untangle my limbs from his. Trying to untangle my soul from his soul. It's no ecking use. He outweighs and outmaneuvers me a hundred times over and right now he's got himself pressed against me everywhere it counts. His other hand grabs my wrist, twisting it back until I cry out in pain and drop my rock.

His lips linger against the side of my face. "You think you had any right to give yourself to another male?"

He wrenches my arm behind my back, straining the shoulder socket and hauling me against him even tighter, keeping that arm pinned. His now free hand slides across my collar bones to my neck and when he squeezes it too hard, I remember everything I've been trying to repress from that solar in acute clarity and in an entirely different way.

"I can't believe you did that… You *tricked* me into rutting you…and you…you were mean…"

"And *you* were mine. Always mine. From your very first breath." His voice is hard and violent as it cleaves cleanly through my words. "You deserved punishment for trying to give another being even the smallest piece of you. I simply corrected you."

I shake my head, twisting my neck as much as he'll let me, which isn't very much at all, so that I can speak against the silver side of his face. "You are an ecking asshole."

"I remember how yours felt." His tail curls around my left ankle, so I lift the opposite foot and bring it down on his instep. At the same time, I use my arm pinned between us to scrape the skin of his lower abdomen, reaching for his dick. But I don't think either of those things affect him as much as when I try to headbutt him. I slam my temple towards his stalyx cheek, but before I make contact, he wrenches away from me, releasing me. I'd think it was a defensive maneuver if I didn't know that my attempt would have hurt me a lot more than him. He'll always protect me, won't he?

I burst forward towards the pool, though I don't know what for. It's not like a little water will stop him as I dive beneath the curtain of the waterfall. The water. The damn Oosa water…it has a tingling effect as it splashes over me. It's also cool — a contrast to how warm it is inside the small, dazzling pink and yellow cave. I turn to face him and watch the water cascade over his hair, wetting it to his skin as the falls part around him like a curtain.

He stalks towards me and…and I don't back away. I don't want to back away. I want to run towards him, but only if he'll let me keep him forever. His gaze skids down my body, taking in my skin until I'm raw and exposed, and something flashes in his expression. His lips part. He comes within arm's reach of me and lifts his fingers towards my chin, but withholds his touch.

"I'm sorry," he says, voice no less rough. It almost makes the words sound strange, off, wrong. They are wrong. *He's* wrong. He's wrong about so many things.

I can't ecking stand it. I don't know what emotions I'm flashing now. Maybe all of them. *Maybe* all *of them.* Because there's nothing of me left. My chest heaves and I step into his grip and grab his thick neck with both of my hands that no longer tremble because of the muuir, but because of how overwhelmed he's made me.

"I should kill you," I scream through clenched teeth.

His expression shutters as he says, "Yeeshee, you have every right."

"You rutted me…you rutted me when I thought you were someone else." I squeeze tighter. It's having no effect except for helping me exhaust myself.

He says nothing.

"And the way you treated me. It ecking terrified me. I thought you were going to kill me."

"I *was* trying to kill you…"

I shake my head. "I wouldn't have been scared if I'd known it was you." I lick my lips and warily confess, "I *wanted* it to be you." I use both hands on his throat to wrench him down to me. I kiss him hard, biting even harder, until I taste blood on his tongue. He lets me.

I score my nails down both sides of his chest, hearing how they screech against stalyx, but also feeling how his biological skin burns beneath the nails of my other hand. They're dull and don't really hurt him, but I wish they would. He deserves punishment, too.

"All this time..." I say as he matches my feral kiss with one of his own, one even more violent. I barely have the time to come up for breath, but speak in moans whispered between his lips. "You let me think..."

He lunges at me, pressing me against the warm cavern wall, his arms caging me in. He brackets my face with his forearms and shoves his knee between my legs, keeping them apart. A sinewy limb that scares me at first wraps around my other ankle. Using his knee and his tail, he pulls my legs apart.

"What? What did I let you think?"

My breath hitches with my next words. I stutter, struggling to get anything out past my fear, my concern, my terror, my love, my need. "You let me think that I made a mistake."

"Mistake?" His lips pause against the side of my neck where they'd been biting and suckling the sensitive skin behind my ear. "What mistake?"

I drop my hands from his shoulders, sliding my palms over his chest before circling them around his back, wanting to touch him everywhere, trace his every scar, feel the place where his stalyx and biological skin come together, explore his every seam. "That I gave another male what I wanted to give to you." He tenses beneath my touch. I don't let that deter me from this small, singular truth. "I had plenty of chances to bed other males, but I wanted the first to be you. I went to the pleasure house when I lost hope of ever finding..."

Everything is in motion. I'd thought I had a fighting chance against Jerrock all these past rotations that we'd been locked in our deadly battle. Now I know the truth. Just like when we were kids, he's been letting me win this whole time.

He's never moved with such controlled speed or strength as he does now. One moment, my back is against warm rock, damp clothing plastered to my skin, the next I'm lying on the floor of the cave, my clothes lost somewhere in the wind. Oh krakaw, there they are…

He bundles them up beneath my head. His pants must be with them, too, because I don't see them anywhere. All I see is his erection, long and red, roped with brown skin. It's ridged and thick, the head bloated around a small glistening slit. Beads of milky white cum streak down his shaft. My mouth quirks suddenly at the realization that sweeps me.

"I should have known."

"Known?"

"I should have known the male in that pleasure house wasn't who he claimed to be. His seed was white like yours. Voraxians have blue seed, don't they?"

He freezes and narrows his eyes as he kneels between my parted thighs. He sits up on his haunches and lets his gaze track down my body, absorbing every detail gluttonously. I don't care what he thinks — or rather, I'm not afraid of what he thinks of me. Because I've never known confidence, not really, but I meet it here in one single moment as I take in the look on his face as he watches me.

Hungrily.

"Are you suggesting that I made a mistake?"

I reach for him, but he shoves my hand away, so I touch the center of my chest. He watches the strokes of my fingertips so avidly that I test him by sweeping my touch back and forth between my breasts. His head swivels from side to side as he tracks the motion. I rub my left areola and silently scream victory when his tail whips into focus and coils around his cock. As he starts to jack himself off with his tail, I no longer feel so confident. My throat is completely dry and I know I've started to sweat again. I've never seen anything so erotic and I'm grateful for the cool spray of the nearby waterfall on my skin.

"Krakaw," I whisper, because his gaze and his touch will accept no other answer.

"I didn't think so. I don't make mistakes."

"I make enough for the both of us."

"Make as many as you like. I'll fix them all."

His back bows, chin tilting up. His nostrils flare and his hands scoop my knees deftly, even with his eyes closed. He lifts my legs up high and spreads them wide. My tailbone no longer touches the ground. His tail tightens around his cock what looks like painfully and I lick my lips inadvertently when more of his seed spurts out.

Oh stars. Oh comets.

Ecking yeeshee.

Ecking krakaw.

A sudden fit of terror cracks me over the head like the rock I'd aimed for Jerrock's skull, this time making a connection. He uses his tail to guide his shaft towards my center. I'm hot. I'm hot and I'm afraid. The mushroom head of his erection is painted half red, half brown, the colors clashing and not at all melting together. Everything's going to change. If not for him, then for me, and he won't even be watching me as he turns my entire universe inside out.

"Wait," I gasp, breathless as I speak. His tail unfurls. He presses just the tip of his cock into me. "Wait!" I shout, the word echoing loudly off of the walls of the cave. I'm having trouble breathing. I think I might burst into tears, but I'm not sure why, not sure why I'm stalling. What am I waiting for? *To not feel afraid. To not feel like I'm the only one falling...*

"Jerrock, wait! Wait, Jerrock, please wait..." He didn't the last time. When he was *him*, I begged him to wait, wanting to back out of the moment. After the fact, I was glad I didn't, but this time I want things to be different.

"Jerrock."

His eyes peel open. His nostrils flare again. His eyes look a little bit crazed and there is the starkest and sharpest tension threading every muscle in his chest, neck, arms, thighs, face and fingertips. "Yeeshee?" he grinds out, the word so rough as to hardly be intelligible. His teeth saw back and forth. He bares them at me like an animal. If I wait too long to do this — to fix his mistake — he's going to take me like one. It'll feel wonderful, I know — I know, I've felt it before — but it won't be us.

It won't be us.

It takes enormous strength and effort, more than I have, to prop myself up on one elbow. The position is awkward, my ass hanging a few inches above the hard stone ground. He looks furious, lethal, really as he watches me, his one eyebrow drawn towards his stalyx forehead. He watches my other arm as I free it from beneath me, balancing my entire weight on just one elbow now as I stretch forward, towards him.

His gaze is distracted by my chest. He glances at my breasts and a low growl slices out of him and makes me flinch. I touch his low belly. He tenses and his tail slaps around my wrist, prying my hand away from his skin. He wants full control. He wants to take and to dominate, but I'm not my normal self. I'm someone else without muuir as my backbone. I'm me.

"Ashmara, lie still…"

"Krakaw." I shake my head. "I-I'm sure you've done this before with other females." He flinches and I don't need to know more. The sinking in my stomach is quickly shoved aside. I don't need it here. "I know you've been trained by the Sky on how to pleasure females. I know because I've been…experienced…I've experienced it. I liked it. I liked it a lot, I really did, but I…" I'm shaking. I try again for his stomach, meeting resistance from his tail and fighting it. "I'd like to try."

"Ashmara…" he growls, low and deep. His hands slide from my knees to my ankles. He yanks them forward and I slide over the smooth stone, dropping onto my back once again. He leans forward to cover me, bracing one arm by my face and sliding his other hand beneath my hips, popping them up.

"I'm not a toy, Jerrock." I grab the outside of his arm and squeeze it as hard as I can. "And I want to be… *present* for this. I know I can't be if you're everywhere. I can't focus. I'm overwhelmed."

"You'll be…present…later," he huffs, sounding like he's going to erupt. Sounding like he's bordering on pain. "This first time, I will lead…"

"I know you could bring us both to pleasure in a heartbeat, but let me fumble my way through it for the first time, *please*. The second time, you can do whatever you want to me."

His eye flashes. The tension in his neck is taut as a cord. His gaze bores down into me and he looks furious all over. "Why?"

"I want to go slow."

"Krakaw. I *can't*. Now that I'm free to do whatever I like, I've never wanted to do anything more. I want to *devour* you. My restraint is…" He shakes his head roughly, white hair spraying over my chest. "I can't wait for your fumbling." He pushes against my mound, which is slick and hot and swollen so badly it hurts. His cock jerks against my clit and we both hiss.

"Jerrock."

He meets my gaze and I watch fire and fury cloud his expression. He's going to thrust into me — I can feel it — and I'm going to love every instant of it. It'll be a hard rut, a fast one, a claiming one, one that's brutal and all his.

But I want this rut to be mine, a claiming in the way that comes most naturally to me.

My hand, clutching the outside of his arm as if it was driftwood and I was lost at sea, moves to the stalyx side of his face. I rub my thumb beneath his eye, watch the yeeyar shift, and take a deep breath. I focus on his face with every ragged piece of me. "Okay, take me."

An expression flits across his face as he stares between my eyes, but it's gone too quickly to catch and, in the next moment, Jerrock's length is pushing into me and I'm moaning wildly, but…I'm also being lifted.

My head kicks, jerking back momentarily before I manage to regain control of it as he pendulums our bodies back, lifting me into a seated position on top of him, one in which I'm impaled on his hot, hard length. It fills me up so greedily and hungrily, I can barely breathe — and then I stop breathing altogether when he keeps going, keeps rotating us back until he's lying flat on the smooth cave floor, staring up at me.

He places his hands on my hips and squeezes them hard enough to leave bruises. I cry out as his erection fully impales me and I sink into the pleasure of this new, wonderful, beautiful angle. I see stars and hallucinate the ends of their explosive lifetimes before coming to.

"Ashmara." His voice drives me back to the present and I look down at him to see his face and his pained expression. He's baring his teeth at me like a beast locked in a cage and says, "You better ecking move."

I sit up higher on his cock before letting my full weight slam back down. The ripples of pleasure that radiate throughout my body compound exponentially when his head kicks back into the stone. I repeat the movement, Jerrock's hands on my hips squeezing but not guiding as I jerk my body up and down and up and down.

It doesn't take long for me to start panting and for my knees start to hurt, so I slide my feet underneath me and push up into a squat. The position makes me feel incredibly unsexy until Jerrock's eye flares open and his hand slashes out and touches my clit. It *vibrutes* and I crack apart on a scream that sounds like I'm being murdered.

Coming back to this reality is, in some ways, more difficult than a muuir come-down but is also so much better. I'm sated and heavy, but electric and alive. I realize I'm completely slumped over his chest, my sweaty forehead pressed to his collar bone.

"Ashmara." His voice cracks and I have to use both hands to press my torso off of his.

His face is…unrecognizable. It's completely pained, his yeeyar eye entirely blown black, while his other eye looks purely panicked. He looks *stressed*.

"Ashmara, *please*, let me take over. You're too ecking slow."

"I can...let me..." I say, bouncing as his hips buck up and his length slips so easily in and out of me. "Let me rut you." That wasn't what I meant to say at all, but I go with it. "Tell me what you need."

"I...need..." His hand flexes as it reaches towards my face. His lips stutter. He doesn't seem to know what to say. "It hurts."

"Where?"

"Here." He touches the center of his chest, right where his silver and red halves meet.

My heart. Oh, my weak, human heart.

I nod, knowing exactly what he means. "Muuir was the only thing I could find to make it better...until I found you."

He moans even though I've stopped moving, writhing like he's being tortured. I lean down and lick the space he just pointed to, then taste my way up his chest. The stalyx has no flavor at all, but his red skin tastes like salt and spice, a rainstorm, a vicious thunder. I chase that taste up to his neck and bite it before working my way over his jaw and finally to his lips. I kiss him, not hard, but so, so softly.

His mouth parts on an exhale and he moans like the beast that he is. It echoes against the cave wall and his hips jerk up simultaneously. He slaps the ground with one hand before slapping my ass. "Hey!" I squeal, a laugh rising up and out of me as he suddenly stiffens, then empties into me in a fit of anguish.

He empties and empties and empties, body shuddering, chest convulsing like he's a robot that's short-circuited before finally finding peace. I can read it in the lines of his face, and knowing that I was the one to put that expression there is a high that I know I could never have achieved on muuir.

Never.

I ride the wave of his chest as he takes deep, painful breaths that eventually calm but never settle completely. He opens his eye and grunts, "Stop smiling."

"I'm not," I lie.

He snorts or laughs or whatever that sound is that he sometimes makes for me, but the laughter fades and so does the peace until violence is all that remains. "Alright, you've had your fun. It's my turn."

He tackles me into the waterfall, tossing us into the pool beyond it and, in tingling Oosa waters, we wash our pain away until only one thing remains.

And I'm too chicken shit to put a name to it.

20

Jerrock

The feel of her sloppy cunt squeezing my cock in its vise is too much and never enough. I've rutted her in six different pools, nine different times, and now we lie together in a bed in the castle, limbs tangled together, staring into each other's eyes.

Well, she stares into my one bio eye. I stare into her soul. Her eyes are bright with every color of the universe. It makes me want to sheathe myself inside of her once more but...and I'm nearly embarrassed to admit this, I'm fully drained. She's depleted my sac and, though my hips twitch, wanting inside of her body, my softening cock needs a break. I've rutted more in a single lunar before, but never like this.

Truly, never like this.

Never with her fumbling lips and hands and goofy ecking laugh chasing me down paths I can't claw my way back from. I'm lost in her oblivion and I'd like to remain here, lost.

I touch her temple. Her eyelids droop. The solar has set and the only light that remains in this room is that of the moon. It beams through the translucent ceiling, turning her white hair to a light blue.

I whisper in the lunar's cool embrace, "Why did you not tell me that the female you rescued from the Sky was Reoran's kitling?"

She yawns contentedly and smiles softly as she settles into the mattress. I pull the blanket up over her shoulder. Is she warm enough? I pull her closer and taste her lips once more. They're swollen and likely bruised. I don't ecking care. I should, but they feel too good and I'm a selfish male.

"I don't know," she answers groggily.

I am annoyed by her response. I comb her hair behind her ear. Her curls are getting longer. They fall nearly to her chin. I tug on one curl just for the simple satisfaction of watching it spring back again. "She had already been experimented on when you arrived aboard the ship?"

She nods.

"You see, that doesn't make sense."

"Hm?"

"The Sky don't experiment on one target among many, and they wouldn't do it on board a regular ship."

"That's nice."

I huff, enjoying her soft expressions. She's such a soft female. I love that her reputation among the Quadrants is something other, something wild and raucous and reckless. No one knows this soft female here. Even if I currently do want to strangle her, again. I suppose she has that effect on many beings. But from now on, only I get to do that.

"It isn't *nice*. It means that you are lying to me again. Either you attacked a Sky vessel with experimentation facilities, much like the one I attempted to quarantine you on with the other two hybrid females—"

"Only Manila is a hybrid. Nalia is full human," she interrupts.

Surprise stalls my accusation. "The female with the spots is entirely human?"

"Yeeshee. Pretty cool the humans can all look so different, huh?"

Cool. Huh. Such a mild descriptor for something wholly marvelous. Very few species boast such diversity. That alone should be celebrated. "You are evading the question," I mutter with a shake of the head. How easily she distracts me. I hang on every word she says.

Her arms windmill as she fights free of the blankets and tries to squeeze herself even closer to me. There is nowhere for her to go, not unless I unzip the seams of my soul and pull her inside. It won't work. I've tried.

Instead, I pull her as close to me as possible, tucking her head beneath my chin and inhaling the scent of minerals on her skin. Free of muuir. Mmmmhh. I inhale deeper. "So which was it? You took on an experimentation facility, or these are two separate…"

"I went back for her."

I still. My hands, which had been rubbing soft circles between her bare shoulders, still. "You did what?"

"The Sky ship," she yawns, "they'd already separated Dloroora from the others and taken her someplace else. Luzu, Retro, Uuni, Gibli, Hunhun and I went after her while Tintin stayed behind and made sure the Oosa found us okay. We got her out."

"You fought another assassin?"

"Krakaw. We just stunned him with that device we used on you. It didn't work so well back then, but we've perfected it since."

Fury fills my chest. Pride, too. I jerk the blanket up to her neck, wanting to smother her with it. Instead, I shape it around her to form a cocoon. "Do you have no instincts for self-preservation?"

She just sighs, "I didn't go for Dloroora because I wanted to get something from Reoran. I did it because it was the right thing to do. It was what I wish someone would have done for you."

She flings her words out into the room like they're meaningless. Like they aren't ripping me to shreds. I've faced no opponent, no weapon before like this. "You're a fool."

"Mhmm."

"You're so ecking fragile, Ashmara," I say, though I nearly call her Rook. "I fear with your stupidity," *her selflessness*, "that I won't be able to protect you."

She sighs again, so sleepy, so content, so unaware that my heart has taken a leap and threatens to pulverize its way out of my chest. "That's the great thing about these big, ecked up cosmos, Jerrock. You don't have to do anything alone. And I've got friends." She laughs lightly in her sleep.

I huff, "I'm chaining you to me. You won't leave my sight. Not again."

"Not until you leave me to go for the Sky all by yourself." She starts to push away from me, both palms against my chest. I don't let her go, but I do let her rotate so that her back and ass are pressed against my chest and hips. The motion causes my cock to stir. Maybe, I should...

Krakaw. Shh...

I press my nose to the back of her head, breathing in the scent of her hair. She smells ecking incredible no longer on muuir, just her. "You'll get into trouble if I leave you alone, won't you?"

"Hm?"

"Perhaps your recklessness has given me cause to reconsider."

She smiles. I can't see her face, but I can feel it all throughout my body. "You mean it? You'll stay with me?"

Nothing will tear us apart. I will find another way to save her. I know it's the wrong thing to do — that my plan is the only way to ensure her safety — but maybe, just maybe, we can find another way together. "Yeeshee."

"Someone told me once never to believe an assassin," she says.

I chuckle. "I'm retired, remember?"

She huffs a laugh and I tense, worried that she will press the issue further, but she doesn't. Instead, she nestles further against my body. It is a clever move because it makes the thought of leaving her truly inconceivable. My mind shorts at the prospect.

"Relax. I can't sleep when you're tense like this." She squeezes my hand between her breasts. My stalyx hand. She doesn't care that it isn't real.

"Does it bother you, the way I look?" I look at my stalyx arm gleaming in the moonlight and feel... something towards it.

"Krakaw," she sighs. "Krakaw. Sometimes I just miss..." Her breathing softens, shallowing out as sleep comes for her. But I want her here, with me. As I promised, nothing will separate us. I want to exist wherever she does, even in sleep.

I goad her, prodding her in her stomach. Her muscles are soft now. Earlier, I loved tasting their edges. "My human flesh? The same color as yours." I trace a path over her shoulder now before bringing the blanket back up to her neck, back over us both.

"Krakaw," she says, shrugging the blanket off again. "I miss…your ridges. You could always control them better than I could, but sometimes you'd let your colors slip."

"Hmm." A rumble slips through my teeth. It is deep and comes from the chest. *I'm purring for her again.* I feel…

Too much. I feel far, far too much for her to attempt to ascribe something as meaningless as a word to such depth.

Instead, I hug her to me tight, holding her, squeezing her to the point of pain. She grunts, but lets me do what I want with her. She's mine and voices no complaints. I kiss the back of her neck. "I see your colors. I love seeing your colors. Love provoking them. Love seeing them shine like a beacon for your Xiveri mate."

Ashmara jerks in my arms and when she looks over her shoulder at me, her gaze is bright and shimmering. She must see her colors beaming in the dark because she shuts her eyelids over them, white lashes fluttering. The last color I saw from her was her yellow embarrassment.

I shush her. "You have nothing to be embarrassed about."

"My…my…you…"

She sniffles and buries her face in the pillows beneath us, but I use greater force to pry her arms away from her face and force her to look at me. Propping myself up on one elbow, I loom over her and chuckle through my nose. I kiss her forehead, then take her hand and place her palm on my cheek. I guide her fingers over my yeeyar and stalyx face where my ridges used to be.

"Don't worry. My ridges would be shining just as brightly for you, if I still had them."

She gasps so dramatically, I can't help but laugh outright. She flinches from it, or perhaps from my words, and stutters, "Are…you…saying…"

"Was there ever any doubt in your mind?" She's sniffling and looking all soft again, prying my soul open and having her way with whatever she finds, whatever is left. "I am a creation of the science of the Architects of Sky. Only something greater than science could have stayed my hand time and time again. I should have killed you. But no Xiveri can kill their other half…"

I have barely finished speaking before she bursts into tears.

I begin to laugh full and from the belly then as I fall back onto the blankets and coddle her to my chest. I crush her there, where I plan to keep her forever. As long as forever allows. As long as I can stave off Death. But I will not think of him now.

Now, I will think of laughter.

I laugh into her hair, and kiss every place I like. "Whoever would have thought Ashmara the Eshmiri, the feared and the fearless would ever succumb to her emotions like this?"

"Why…can't I make you…succumb to yours?" She huffs.

I stare down into her multicolored eyes and feel…just feel. I shake my head softly. "Ashmara, you already have and you still do. Each and every solar I feel limitlessly for you."

21
Ashmara

I finish hugging Reoran and Dloroora goodbye and join Jerrock on the Sky ship. Jerrock was sure the Oosa would steal it and sell it or strip it for parts, but I just laughed and told him, that isn't how friendship works. That isn't how love works. They wouldn't take from us just because they can. And besides, they want the sex ship more, anyway. The Sky ship is colorless and ugly and made for containment and killing. What use would a race of colorful, free-loving and only occasionally violent beings have for it?

Our Sky ship takes off and aims for the stars, coordinates set for Kor. Jerrock stands beside me and we watch the hifelai star map illuminate different constellations, asteroids, comets, and the other celestial bodies that make up the Quadrants and the Grey Zones in between them. Jerrock points certain bodies out to me, offering tid bits and facts about the planets I've never been to before.

"And what did you think of Uoustar?" I ask him as we finally pass out of Quadrant Eight, and out of the safety of Oosa territory. That's as far as friendship will take us, at least for now.

He steps behind me and wraps his arms around my body. I let my pack slide off of my shoulder and hit the floor beside our feet so that he can hold me more tightly. "It was…memorable."

"Memorable." I laugh. "That's the best you can do?"

He laughs his funny Jerrock laugh, too. "What did you think of it?"

"Fun. I had fun. Did you?" I turn around and circle his neck with my arms. I smile up into his face and am only half teasing when I ask, "Actually, do you even know what fun is?"

His grin doesn't falter, though something in my chest clenches at his slight pause.

I continue, "Amusement? Pleasure? All the good stuff?"

His grin morphs into something else. Something deadly, only because it's so sincere. It makes my colors glow and that's even before he has the ecking audacity to look at me gently and speak even more gently than that. "The only fun I've ever had is you."

I shove him off of me and quickly wipe my eyes. I *refuse* to cry. I take my pack to the edge of the room and pretend to reorganize it for a third time. "You're a jerk."

He laughs in that gruff way he has, then comes and squats down before me. "Why? Because I don't feel the need to lie to you? Unlike you and your incessant lies to me?"

"I'm not a liar," I lie as I paw past the muuir shoved way into the bottom of my pack. I know he's still got one strip in his pocket. I saw him put it in there this morning. I don't know where he hid it while we were in the pools, must have been somewhere in my room, but what concerns me more is why he's kept it.

"Liar," he sneers.

I grin at him and shoot him another wink. He asks me what the gesture means and I shrug, then hand him my yamar box and say, "It's a human thing."

"Hm. I suppose I have some studying to do. Someone once told me that there is a human manual containing a guide that will help me learn how to woo my human mate." He grins at me.

I shoot him an acerbic look. "I have it on good authority that the being who told you that is a fool."

He nods, considering, and tosses the yamar box up and down lightly in his fist. "True. But even a fool can be correct on occasion."

"You're insufferable."

"And yet, you love me all the same."

I open my mouth, but falter at the sound of that word coming out of his mouth. It sounds so...so *scandalous...*

It sounds so ecking good...

...that I can't speak, so I just continue smiling at him while he continues smiling at me, and we're just smiling at each other when the hifelai starts to bleep.

Jerrock's expression transforms so suddenly, I don't even have a chance to say goodbye to the Jerrock that existed in the rains of Quizzar and the waterfalls of Uoustar, the one that was so happy. Jerrock the killer returns just as swiftly, his aura of danger sweeping over him like a cloak as he stands and moves rapidly to the controls.

"They keep finding us," he hisses and my soul sinks. I thought we'd have more time than this, but I guess the universe has other plans for us.

The idea of feeling guilty crosses my mind, but I shy away from it. The truth is that I don't feel guilty even though a better female than me probably would. Mostly, I'm surprised that he trusts me even though I've lied to him and keep lying to him. He hasn't asked me why or how the Sky keep finding us so quickly and it doesn't seem like he's even thought to ask me. Not even once. Huh.

I watch him take over the navigation from the autopilot and power on the blaster systems. "How many are there?" I ask him.

The fact that he doesn't let any emotion play on his face tells me everything I need to know about his answer. "More than there have been."

Ah. So, this is the end. "They were waiting for us on the edge of the Grey Zone, weren't they?"

"It would appear so." The ship lurches. He's going to try to outmaneuver them. I wouldn't dare doubt his abilities, but I also know not to doubt the other assassins' abilities. And there are a lot more of them.

And I've seen this coming.

I've been waiting, actually.

"Well, it's about time," I huff, bumping his shoulder with mine. I offer him a grin, one that's different than the last grin I wore and makes me feel like my old self. The one who existed before I freed Jerrock and liberated myself from muuir. *I freed us both, didn't I? But only because he saved me first.*

His bio eye rounds. The muscles in his cheek tick. He's smiling, but it's not a pretty sight. He looks *stressed*. "Don't be worried, Jer," I offer with a glib little chuckle. I don't like seeing him stressed, so I try to lighten the mood. "It's gonna be alright."

His hands drop from the controls. His shoulders angle to face me. He makes for an intimidating sight, but I knew that already. I've always been a little bit afraid of him. But I'm more afraid of how much and how deep my love for him is. It's a well with no bottom, from which all the universe's wonders can be drawn at will.

I draw on it now and brace myself, trying to stand tall and firm against his wrath.

"Don't be mad. You knew…"

"What. Did. You. Do?" He punctuates each word with a grunt and shoves his nose down to mine. The kind, doting, yielding male I knew is gone. He presses forward, leaving me no choice but to retreat.

I stagger a step backwards and he keeps coming towards me. "Jer…"

"Do not call me that."

The ship's alarm sounds. I wonder what it means. "How much time do we have?"

"Until what?"

"Until they board, or blow us out of the sky?"

"Ha." The sound isn't a laugh at all. I stumble back and back some more until I hit the wall, my head clunking dully off of it. My feet trip over my pack. Ah. My trusty, trusty pack. "You think they want to blow us out of the sky?"

I don't. I know what they want. "Krakaw."

His wide, stressed eye narrows to a slit. The black part in the very center of the brown is barely a pinprick. "You know what they want, don't you?"

"You told me, remember?"

A little surprise flickers across his expression before it goes grim. "On board the ship, when I took you from Evernor. I told you then," he whispers, as if trying to remember himself.

"You were trying to scare me."

"I was trying to warn you," he hisses.

"Whatever." I shrug, feigning nonchalance. Does he hear my heart, the way it's pounding? I hope not.

"What are you hiding?"

"Nothing."

"Why aren't you afraid?"

"What have I got to be afraid of?"

"Everything. What they have in store for us."

Us. Funny. There is no us. There was only this lovely, lovely intermission. "Sure."

"What did you do, Ashmara?"

I hear the sound of a gravity wand wrenching our ship off of its path. Several gravity wands would be necessary to pull a ship this powerful out of its flight path, but I don't doubt that's exactly what they have.

"Was it your intent to kill me all along?" He presses his hand to my neck, but not with any sort of intention.

"Kill you?" I pull his hand away from my skin and step over my pack, sliding along the wall towards the holding cells. I haven't forgotten how well they double as escape pods. There are two. Just our luck. "What makes you think I want to kill you?"

"Because they will board this ship and I will fight every last one of them to ensure that you live."

"How many are there, Jer?" His expression tightens. Wow. There must be even more than I thought. I smirk, "How many?"

"You haven't changed at all."

I grin. "You've changed a lot."

The alarm blares louder and Jerrock stands up and moves away from me. The look on his face is one of pure disgust, touched with just a hint of desperation. "Don't get in my way." He starts for the weapons panel. Good. That's where I want him. Right where I want him.

This ship is smaller than the other Sky ships we've been on, which is also good. That'll keep this simple. Ha. What am I talking about? It was never going to be simple, but it was always going to be easy, so long as I let myself love and be loved.

I move to stand in front of him and lean against the wall with my bare arms crossed. I'm wearing a garment the Oosa gave me after Jerrock all but shredded the Walrey silks I'd been wearing. It's a full-body suit — blue, of course — made out of a rubbery synthetic fabric. It cinches at the waist and has no sleeves, a high collar with a small V, and the pants go all the way to my ankles. Jerrock is wearing something almost exactly identical, only his is more blue-green than blue-purple.

He pulls a weapons belt out from the storage container. It fits him snugly as he slides it on. He begins holstering weapons onto it, blasters of varying sizes and knives, many knives, a lightning stick. It's cute. I snort.

"You'll stay near the holding pods and you'll take one if things appear to be going in the assassins' favor," he says.

I snort again. He gives me a glare. I can feel something happening above us. "They're here, aren't they? Using gravity boots? Are they going to saw their way in or try to override your yeeyar controls?"

"They can't override the controls of an assassin while he's living. Not from outside of the ship, anyway."

Because they need the hifelai's override code. I smile, knowing this already. "Ah. So, they're coming in the hard way, then?"

He doesn't answer. "Get near the pods. Better yet, get in one." He stands to his full height and comes and grabs me by the arm. "Be ready."

I look at the two clear tubes tucked into a small room — you can barely call it a room, either. It's more like a little recessed alcove. They shimmer with white light. I examine the one on the left, deciding that that's the one I'll use. "How do you open the door?" I nod at it.

Jerrock's ear cocks up. I imagine he's hearing something I can't. Then comes the thud. They must be on the roof. I hear the sound of drilling and know that whichever assassin it is will be inside soon. We have maybe instants to spare. Heartbeats.

A grinding sound echoes dully around us as Jerrock grabs my arm and tosses me towards the holding pods. He goes to the one on the right and slides his finger across it in a specific Sky symbol, like a star with seven points and three dots below, two above. I memorize it, along with everything else about him, all the things I never want to forget. He turns to me as the translucent door whooshes open and he cocks his head towards it.

"In."

I sigh as the sound of the drill echoes louder and louder. "Have I told you how handsome you are?"

"Now's not the time." He hesitates, looking strangely shy, even with an arsenal of weapons strapped to his belt. "Later."

I laugh. I laugh a laugh that's so full of laughter it makes Jerrock's murderous impulse flare and become momentarily docile. I use the moment to my advantage and advance on him. I smooth my palms over his chest and scrape my nails over his neck in a way that I know he likes.

He shivers. "Ashmara…"

I lean into him and he reacts ravenously. He molds his hands around my back and yanks me into his chest. I tug on his hair hard enough to pull a gasp out of him. He kisses me hard. I kiss him back harder. Both of us kiss like it's our intention to bruise. I want to savor this moment forever, but the sound of the drill is getting louder and I know what I have to do.

I lower my hand down his chest, scraping along red skin, instead of silver. I follow the seam that brings the two colors together all the way down to his abdomen, to his belly button. He clenches his abs as I circle it through the blue Oosa fabric.

"Ashmara…" He breathes, "Wait for me in the holding pod. We will finish this after I kill all sixteen of them."

Sixteen. I would whistle if my lips weren't already occupied. It's not an insignificant number. And assassins, no less. But as it stands, I'd rather do this.

I slip my hand under the curtain of his hair and cup the back of his neck. I pull him down even further, pulling him close as my other hand finds the flap in his jumpsuit and slides between the folds, searching…

"Ashmara, stop distracting me."

I laugh against his lips. "I like distracting you."

"Get in the pod now, please."

"Please." I smile. "I've never heard you say that before…"

"You have."

"Not like this…" I lick his upper lip and my hand shifts subtly from the center flap of his jumpsuit to the left pocket. He doesn't react as I find the small, crinkly little slip, lighter and thinner than a piece of true paper. But no one uses paper anymore.

"You'll never hear it again."

"I'll never forget it." I kiss him deeply, refusing to let him reply. I kiss him with every piece of me, hoping to communicate the depth of my adoration through this last, final touch alone. I pull back and don't try to curb whatever my eyes are doing, as if I ever could. I let the rainbow of emotion that I feel for him spring forward, that brilliant glow.

I wait for him to focus on it, to smile ever so slightly at the shimmer of my eyes, to relax…and then I knee him in the groin as hard as I can.

He buckles, but only somewhat. I think it's the surprise that gets him the most. He hisses through his teeth and I'm quick as I snatch the lightning stick from his belt and stab him in the stomach. His weight slips into his heels — he doesn't lose his balance, but it's enough.

It's enough.

I shove his shoulders back and kick him in the upper thigh. He looks shocked and takes an active step back — I knew I could never really beat him in a fight. But I count on him letting me win, because he lets me win every time. He steps back, right into the pod, and the moment his weight registers on the scale, the door zips shut.

He shakes his head and licks his lips and looks at me — looks at me — and it's the cutest ecking thing, because he looks just a little lost. He lifts his fists and they thump uselessly on the inside of the pod. He thumps them against the pane a little harder. I panic and know that I need to release him immediately, but first…

I run to my pack against the wall and hoist it up onto my back after I retrieve two things from inside of it. The first is the Sky key I've been carrying with me all along.

"You ecking…" Jerrock starts as he watches me withdraw it. "You've had it with you this whole time?" His voice is muted and warbly through the pane, but I can still hear his fury well enough.

"Of course." I take the glowing Sky key into my hand and toss it up and down, admiring its weight for a moment. It's shaped like a small, angry star, spikes jutting out of a sphere at awkward and uneven angles. Each key has a different shape. I've seen three so far and this one appears the most pained. It looks like it hurt to create. It looks like it hurt to endure and to bear, and now all that pain will be erased. All of it.

"Why did you keep it with you, you fool? Why not leave it on your ship with Gibli and Tintin and the other reavers?"

I laugh, "Have you not been listening, Jer-bear? They're my *family*. And that's not how love works. I'd never have let them keep it. Even when they tried to fight me for it, I stole it back."

I mimic the pattern he made across the surface of the pod to his left, then I toss the key inside. Meanwhile, behind me the sound of the grinding becomes deafening. I know if I were to look over my shoulder, I'd see whatever weapon they're using peek through. I feel the pressure inside the cabin increase and quickly pull on an oxygen mask from the compartment near the sleeping bay.

At the same time, I hear the thrashing of Jerrock's fists on the inside of his pod. He's going to break through, there's no doubt in my mind. I've got to act *now*. I've got instants. Heartbeats. I go and stand before him and press my palm to the outside of the cage I've enclosed him in.

He stops fighting for just an instant, long enough to ask, "Why not get rid of it? Toss it into space?"

"You were so determined to leave, to go for the Architects, I needed to make sure I had a way to hunt you down if you ever did. Besides, you think you were the only one with plans to take down the Sky?" I shake my head. "You didn't have to live with the regret of letting them take you the first time. I was always going to kill them. All of them. For what they did to you and for what they did to me, too. Granted, I had hoped to be a *little* more prepared when they came for me, but hey. Gotta work with the tools I'm given."

I shrug and chuckle a little. Oh yeeshee, I'm going to die. I wanted to fight the Sky, but I'm not sure I ever really thought I'd win. I just wanted to free Jerrock. I only ever really wanted him to live and I've got to make sure they see him die to do it.

"You could have given it to the Oosa. The Sky would hesitate before crossing them."

"That's not how love works."

He scoffs, exasperated, "You can't possibly love all the universe's creatures."

"Why not?"

He seethes, struggling past his rage, past such foreign concepts. "You could have given it to me to carry. They would have never suspected it had been removed…"

I laugh a wet, sloppy laugh and look into the cage I've trapped him in. "That's not how love works, Jerrock, and in case it wasn't clear, I may love all the universe's forgotten kitlings, but I'm ecking *in love* with you…"

"Ashmara, you ecking rat," he seethes, filling up the entire frame of the pod, looking every bit like a caged demon. "You had the audacity to be furious with me for suggesting I leave you behind when you intended to leave me all along."

I grin at him. Then shoot him a wink. "Pretty shitty, huh?"

"When I get out of here, I'm going to wring your skinny little neck."

I smile and step back out of the small alcove. At the same time, I hear something thunk down behind me. Even without the sound, I know the assassin has breached the ship. I know it by the look on Jerrock's face. The panic. The pain.

"You're going to have a long life, Jer. Don't waste it looking for me. You won't be able to find me without a key."

"Ashmara, you fool. You think I'll stop looking for you?"

"You won't be able to find me. You don't have a key and you don't have any friends with keys, remember?" I laugh gleefully and glance over my shoulder at the only one I care about. "And this is a one-way trip, don't forget. Don't bother looking, because if you ever find me — which I doubt you will — I'll already be long gone."

I hold up my hand, show him the muuir I stole from his pocket now trapped between my fingers. I hoist my pack higher up on my shoulders, planning to take Jerrock's muuir along with all the rest of the muuir I'm still holding. Because eck it, right? When I go out, I'm going out in style.

"Ashmara, what is this?" he roars. "Some sick punishment for what I did all those rotations ago?"

"Punishment? Are you crazy, Jerrock? This isn't your punishment, this is my redemption."

I turn my back on him just as the second assassin drops down into the ship. Then the third, then the fourth. They're all shapes and sizes. I don't care what they look like, though. I stretch my hand out towards the hifelai. I had Manila teach me the patterns, the shapes. I can fly one of these fairly well now, not as well as Jerrock, but well enough for this.

"Bye, my Xiveri," I tell him.

The crack of his fist on the pane lets me know that my time with him is up. I swipe my hand over the hifelai and touch the pattern across the yeeyar. It doesn't react to me, not right away, but I enter the override code as I feel Jerrock trying to exert his force through his own yeeyar, even from there.

Thud, thud, thud, thud. Assassins fall through the hole in the ceiling, which is reinforced with an Eshmiri shield that prevents the vacuum of space from sucking us all out. Against the artificial gravity of the ship, the assassins' feet all sound so loud as they storm forward and close in, trying to stop me. I can't let them.

I slam down on the controls and both holding pods release. Jerrock's goes first. The second holds the Sky key. This one I've set to detonate and it does in five, four, three…

The explosion rocks the ship, blowing a hole through some part of it. I curse as I start to slip towards it, the oxygen tank flying off of my face and the pull of space constricting my throat and pulling the air right out of my lungs. I can't breathe at all when the first assassin reaches me and grabs me by the waist. He tosses me over his shoulder and together, the assassins move in a solid unit, so synchronized it's almost creepy. They carry me up through the hole they created and into a ship where I'm deposited in a holding pod much like the one I just jettisoned Jerrock out of.

I hope they don't call my bluff, these assassins. I hope they don't realize that the Sky key was removed from his skin and assume that, when the Sky key exploded and deactivated, it was inside of him. I hope they leave the one intact holding pod floating in outer space. I hope they forget all about him, just like I hope he forgets about me eventually, because he's always been right. This is a one-way trip, a story with only one ending.

The assassins turn away from me and begin conversing with one another. They say very few words. Only a couple. Mothership, sky, breed and horlax.

I hold up the little strip of muuir between my fingers and focus on it, rather than the sight of the brutally shaped assassins on the other side of the murky pane. I hesitate, then I reconsider. I turn their words over in my mind. I don't need to take it yet. I'll wait to meet the monster that everyone fears first. Until then, I'll relax, close my eyes and do what I do best. I'll dream of Jerrock.

22

Jerrock

The explosion of the other pod fully engulfs mine. I cannot deny her genius. Or her stupidity.

She truly thinks the Sky do not know that I'm still alive? A joke.

She truly thinks I won't come for her? Ha. Ahaha. Ha. Haha. Ha.

And yet…

She still got me here.

I watch the Sky ships converge, forming a safety arc around the central ship carrying Ashmara. Now that they have the most wanted female in the cosmos, they will not risk losing her. Not like I risked losing her.

I would decommission myself, were I not the only thing separating Ashmara from finally meeting Death. *She is already dead. I'm kidding myself.* I underestimated her and let her trick me. She *pushed* me and that small action that I *allowed* to happen killed her.

If it were only that simple.

They don't just want to kill her. If they wanted to turn her into an assassin, that would be something I could work with. Just to kill her, against their true, nefarious desires, would also be a gift. They want her for the horlax. The Architects have been trying to find a female capable of being bred by that monstrosity. It was an Egama giant once, but it's since been spliced with so many different species, its origins are entirely unidentifiable. What they created is a revolting, violent and utterly soulless thing.

I slam my forehead against the pane, if only to attempt to shake the image of *it* climbing on top of her from my mind. It doesn't work. It doesn't help. I watch and wait, wondering if any of the Sky ships will bother attempting to blow me from space and end my torment here and now.

But they don't. Instead, they just…leave. I can scarcely believe it. Did Ashmara's stupid plan work? It wouldn't be the first time a plan this stupid worked against an assassin. All of her stupid plans worked against me. Yet, they don't come for me. Whatever the reason. Perhaps, they hesitate to entrap me because to do so, they would need to pull me aboard the ship — too great a risk, given my reputation. Or perhaps it's as simple as this: leaving me here, knowing what Ashmara is about to endure, is a far greater punishment than Death.

Besides, I will meet him regardless.

On the edge of the Grey Zone, there are no trading routes, no travelers. I have no beacon of any kind to signal for aid. Even if I had one, no one would stop for me. No one would pick up a Sky assassin, let alone a failed one. I have no friends.

I watch the Sky fleet leave with the only thing in all the cosmos that is precious to me and I plot murder. I plot murders. I enact them over and over again in my mind. I picture the mercenary who threw her over his shoulder — a Tevalope hybrid with Niahhorru arms — and imagine digging my blade in between the sinewy muscle of his lower arms, cutting them off and beating him to death with them.

Then I picture strangling her... Yeeshee. Strangling her while I rut her into submission. *Yeeshee...*

My breath grows erratic and I calm it by closing my eyes and inhaling and exhaling shallowly. I have limited oxygen supply — eight solars before I run out. Eight solars to come up with a plan that puts me in the vicinity of another planet.

I open my eyes and use my yeeyar sight to scan my surroundings. The Sky ship is unusable, even if I could return to it. The hull has been blown apart. The only other useful object in range is... My hand drops down to the lower pocket of my pants and I grip the bulging material.

I still have Ashmara's yamar box. Her outdated yamar box.

I withdraw it from my pocket and stare at it for a heartbeat. Black, it can function as a communication device, but it only responds to her signature. My pulse picks up. *Hope.* I crush it. There is no hope, but there is something.

There is something.

I puzzle my way around the box, searching for ways I might unlock the device without breaking it. It takes little effort. It only takes blood. I slit my own wrist to allow yeeyar to escape in its purest form and I use it to crawl into the device and unlock it from within. I fire on the communicator and say Gibli's name.

The answer is immediate. "Ashmara? You are not Ashmara." His face tilts to the left.

"Gibli." I calm my voice, but it doesn't help. I am rage, contained only by this ecking pod Ashmara put me in. "Come get me."

"Latching onto your coordinates," he tells me. "Be there shortly!" He waves and grins and disappears, leaving me in stunned silence. He...he's coming to help me.

I oscillate between shock that he's agreed to come for me and fury at how long it's taking him to arrive. But I don't panic. Krakaw, I do not. An assassin does not panic.

But I'm not an assassin anymore, am I? I'm an obsessed ecking lunatic.

I slap my palm flat against the pane. It's been a solar. The oxygen in my pod is getting thin. I have to do something. But what? I need to...

Wait.

What is that?

My yeeyar sight focuses far beyond the range of my biological eye. My *human* eye. I see stars, infinite constellations of them, but coming closer I start to see something I half don't expect... Past the debris littering this small section of space, I see...I see...something moving.

It's a ship. I know that it's a ship. And I know exactly which ship it is, but I struggle to believe it. My heart pounds. They've come. For me, Ashmara's reavers have come. No one but Ashmara has ever done that for me before. Why would they come? They should have forsaken me. They love Ashmara, they are not my friends, they should...

That's not how love works.

The words roll over in my mind, and then they roll over again and again as the Eshmiri reaver ship pulls into place directly above me. A portal in the bottom of the ship cranks open, the sound echoing as I'm swallowed up inside of the large black hole and into their loading bay.

Thunk. The sound of my pod clanking down on the floor below. I do not wait, but fight my way out of it, bloodying my knuckles in the process, scratching the eck out of the back of my stalyx palm. I feel bloated with rage again as I step out of the fractured shards of the Sky holding pod and into the loading bay of the decrepit Eshmiri ship.

My hand shakes around the yamar box, the beacon that saved me. The beacon that will save her because I'm coming for her. *I'm coming for you, Ashmara, just hold on…* But what time does she have? *Very little.* The air in their ship is dense and damp, the scent of rust and metal and oil permeating everything and yet, there is one scent that is distinctly absent from such a constellation of odors, a scent as familiar to me as the sickly-sweet stench of yeeyar being injected directly into the vein.

Her.

Ashmara's scent was once sweet like muuir but in the past solars, I've come to realize how fragrant it really is. A deep, bone-tingling aroma. Something that smells like a planet I've never been to before. That's distinctly her.

I miss it.

A chaos of stomping feet sounds all around me, first behind and above me, then directly above me, then slightly further away before they grow louder again. A horde of Eshmiri I know by name but not by face appear before me. I always thought they all looked the same, never thinking to distinguish any of them. I've never had an Eshmiri as a contract. Few want to kill Eshmiri. They rarely cause a ruckus, preferring to stick to their lawless planets in the outer corridors of the cosmos. All except for these fools, only they are missing their matriarch, and the biggest fool among them.

I watch their faces, their expressions, how they change. It guts me, slicing me open from neck to navel. I didn't expect this reaction, but the disappointment I feel grows momentarily larger than the rage. I have let them down. I let down her fathers, the males who took care of her when I couldn't, the males who continue to take care of her when I have failed.

One of two I do recognize steps forward in front of the rest. He holds a blaster across his chest, but he doesn't point it at me like the others do. I find myself fixated on this. Why doesn't he attack me? What does he see in me now? A friend? I cannot imagine that.

"Ashmara?" he says, his gaze pinned to her yamar box. It takes me until that moment to realize that I still have it locked in my grip.

My fingers spasm, the stalyx unsure of itself in ways it's never been. "She…"

"You left her?" one of the others says, his expression delightfully murderous as he swivels his weapon my way.

"I *failed* her," I tell him, wishing for a fleeting moment that he was an Architect and could cause me immeasurable pain.

Collectively, their shoulders sag, and for a moment, we all simply stand there. No one says anything.

Time seems to take a moment to compose itself before resuming and when it does, it's the smallest of the

Eshmiri who swaggers his way forward. He still has his blaster pointed to me as he speaks, though his gaze swivels among his comrades. I know his threat to me is only halfhearted and that fact further guts me.

"We go get her back," he says. "She would do the same for any of us."

The Eshmiri closest to me releases what sounds like a laugh, though the undercurrent of murder makes it sound too eerie for that. "Yeeshee, she would, but we have insufficient weapons. We spent the last of our tokens to free *him*."

My entrails soak the ground around my feet as the wound keeps reopening, though it never closed completely. My jaw smacks shut and I bare my teeth at the reavers as they all attempt to speak at once. They shout and argue about plans, about weapons caches they could raid, about trading vessels they might successfully overtake, about attempting to rob the Niahhorru of their Sky key, about attempting to rob the Lemorans of theirs, but somehow, in this moment where focus is paramount, all I can think about is what Ashmara said.

About love. *That's not how love works.*

About friends. *You don't have to do anything alone. And I've got friends.*

I think about these things over and over until I realize that I have decided on our path forward before I find the words necessary to voice it. When I do, I gather my strength, all of my courage, and I speak over the horde of Eshmiri reavers who are not just friends to Ashmara, but family who love her. She was right when she said that that's not how love works and I think I've only just now begun to understand. Whys don't matter, nor do reasons. In fact, pointing to reasons would be entirely pointless because that's *not* how love works. And that's not how my love *for her* works. Reasons are not what's stayed my hand time and time again. And reasons are not what convinced me to go back for her. But I will.

And I will need help to do it.

"We will not rob or steal from anyone to retrieve Ashmara."

They go silent, then two in the back giggle wildly at my suggestion before they all join in.

Nerves I am unaccustomed to feeling bite at me. I take a step forward. Eight blasters swivel in my direction, held up by five sets of arms. Gibli still hasn't pointed his own weapon at me, a fact that does not go unnoticed.

"We will not steal or rob. We will *appeal* to Ashmara's *friends,*" I say, trying out the word, though it doesn't even sound like I'm speaking Eshmiri anymore. It just sounds *wrong*. "Which of Ashmara's friends currently holds a Sky key?"

"Nalia," Tintin says slowly.

"She is mated to Herannathon of the Niahhorru," another reaver adds.

This is good. "Any others?"

"A Lemoran Clan Chief holds another."

This surprises me. "Which one?"

"Raingar."

This is bad. Very bad. I grimace, but am undeterred. "We will need firepower, even with a key in our possession. The Niahhorru will not offer theirs freely and the Lemorans do not engage in warfare for any reason. They are only known to defend their keeps. We will need the Voraxians to ally themselves to our cause. Is there any reason to suspect they might? Does Ashmara call any among them friends?"

"Krisxox!" one of them shouts. The others laugh uproariously. "They are best of friends." The Eshmiri shriek with delight.

I feel that I am being laughed at, but I don't have time to question it. "The Lemorans may lend their support if they known the Voraxians are involved. They have been known to cooperate in the past. The Niahhorru will be a larger problem, though perhaps, since they aided in the rescue of Clan Chief Raingar's miriga, they might…"

Gibli cuts me off. "We are reavers. Reavers don't ask for help because it won't be offered," he shrugs.

"Unless it's to rob. The Niahhorru like to help us rob."

"They might be the only ones to help us, but reavers and pirates can't take on the Sky alone. You can't count on *friends*. Reavers work alone."

They're all talking again, voices rising in volume. I shout over them. "Friends," I say, "may not be a concept assassins or pirates or reavers know well, but I know a race that values this concept highly."

The reavers all glance between each other, giggling slightly in confusion.

"Humans."

The collective *oooohhhh* the reavers issue is so coordinated it nearly makes me chuckle myself. Would, if I could, but every spare moment I have is spent on hallucinating the horrors being inflicted on my…

"The Clan Chief Raingar's miriga is a human hybrid and so is the Rakukanna of Voraxia. If the Hu'Raku of Voraxia is also a human it could be that we can appeal to a race that does believe in *friends*. And despite what Ashmara may say aloud, she is not just Eshmiri. She's a human, too, somewhere beneath her reaver skin. Let us try not the way of the reavers, this time, but the way of the humans."

Silence.

Tintin is the one to break it. He laughs and offers me a shrug. "Where do we start?"

I grin at him, my chest inflated with the most damning and daring of emotions. *Hope.* "We start with the Niahhorru."

23

Jerrock

"Interesting." The four-armed leader of the Niahhorru stares into the holoscreen while the reaver ship charts its course towards Voraxia. "I did not think I would ever have the pleasure of speaking with a Sky assassin on such…amicable terms."

I grip the back of the command chair as I attempt to control my vitriolic expression. I doubt that it works and when I *accidentally* rip the seat free of the metal bolting it down, I know it hasn't. I continue regardless. "That is exactly why I have contacted you now. In the hopes that your…amicable nature may extend itself to our current predicament."

"Let's meet him, if for no other reason than to rip him apart," comes a voice not visible in the viewpane, but that I easily identify. It is Deena's voice, known mate to Niahhorru pirate lord Rhorkanterannu. Her pitch is high compared to that of the Niahhorru as she speaks in slightly accented Meero. *"This is the dick that kidnapped Nalia, isn't it?"*

Rhorkanterannu grins with one edge of his mouth. His skein is dropped into place, shielding his eyes. He is ready for battle and we are not even in the same room. In the same Quadrant. "It is," he says to her, rubbing his chin.

"I don't even know why you answered the request to speak to him."

"Curiosity," he replies, his attention sliding somewhere I cannot see. "Interest. It would not be the first time."

Silence, then. I wonder what he means, finding his phrasing curious, but I do not dare ask him about it. Right now *everything* is on the line. Everything.

"So, you want my Sky key," he says. "And you say Ashmara has been taken by assassins."

"Correct. Ontte."

"He probably killed her and is trying to get to us."

Rhorkanterannu grins a little more broadly. "It would be a foolish strategy to use Ashmara to try to get to anybody. She has more enemies than friends…"

"But *you* are friends."

"We…" Rhorkanterannu considers, but it's the voice in the background that says, *"Why are you hesitating? Of course we are. Ashmara may be a bitch, but she's our bitch."*

I growl at the insult, yeeshee, but even more at the claim. "She's *mine*."

Rhorkanterannu's eyes flash, his skein fluttering. He tilts his head at an almost imperceptible angle and his lips press together more firmly, then curl. All of these are things I doubt another would register and none of these are reactions I would miss. I am trained in this. But in this instance, I understand nothing.

"Very interesting," he says.

"What is of interest to you, pirate king, is irrelevant." The insult whips out of my mouth before I can censor it.

Everyone knows that the leader of the pirates looks down on kings. To insult him now is…

"Fool," he calls me, but he surprises me then in a way I do not anticipate. He laughs. "To mate a human makes us all foolish. It is a folly I can well understand."

I grit my teeth and attempt to wait with patience. The Eshmiri crowded behind me are decidedly impatient and are talking openly now of attacking Kor, the Niahhorru base, for the simple pleasure of it now that Rhorkanterannu has made them wait.

Rhorkanterannu's gaze pans over the Eshmiri surrounding me, all talking loudly in their high-pitched brogue. He seems to be making calculations. Niahhorru always are. Finally, he exhales sharply, "I cannot help you."

"You can, you choose to deny your aid."

"The nerve of that guy, hey?"

I snarl even louder and Rhorkanterannu sits further forward on his chair. He doesn't like my irritation with his female and I hate that it is suddenly a sensation that I can understand — even empathize with. "You acknowledge that Ashmara is a friend, yet you deny her when she calls."

"We aren't denying her, we're denying *you*." The face of a human female appears in the holoscreen, looming larger than her male's. She looks absolutely furious to see me.

"It is one and the same."

The lower two of Rhorkanterannu's arms reel the female away from the screen. He pulls her back against his chest and breathes against the side of her neck in one long inhale. His skein flutters on the exhale and my envy that he has his mate close, to hold, to touch, to keep safe makes my toes curl in my battered Eshmiri boots. I want to kill the both of them, and yet I must sit here and debase myself to ascertain the whereabouts of the only one I care for in this entire universe.

"You abandon her to her fate, either way."

The human female's eyes focus on me even as she clutches her mate's lower hands around her stomach as if using them to anchor her, like gravity. "Are they going to turn her into one of you?"

"There is no *you*. I was freed. What they have in store for her is far worse…"

"What are they…"

"Deena, centare," Rhorkanterannu interrupts before returning his attention to me. "We cannot offer you aid. We have too little firepower and it is too great a risk."

Fury eats at me, and I agree with the Eshmiri around me, silently vowing to join their quests for revenge. "Then provide me only with the Sky key."

"That will cost you."

I hesitate, wondering what I have to offer. I come up with nothing. Then, I wonder how someone who has *friends* might play this game, what she might offer. Maybe, she wouldn't have had to offer anything because she would have already allied several Niahhorru pirates to her cause. She would have made more friends, even back on that lump of a planet filled with lizards…

Of course.

"I know where three pirates abducted by the Sky are currently."

A pause. "Where?"

I do not require a vow to give me the key in exchange for their location. I don't, because Ashmara wouldn't. She is a foolish female. She wouldn't care. She simply would tell him. So I do. I tell Rhorkanterannu and Deena about the planet, how to find it, and its inhabitants. As I finish, the Eshmiri alert me to the fact that we have begun to near Quadrant Four.

"Why did you abandon them there?" Rhorkanterannu asks.

"I wanted to. Ashmara didn't. We left them because I did not allow her to make another choice." Another truth, one that could hurt me, but she is owed that much. "Even now, I am glad we left them there. They wanted her for their shekkur."

Rhorkanterannu grunts out a laugh that Deena echoes. "I'm not so sure that I blame you," he says, before pulling Deena's long hair off of her neck and resting his chin on her shoulder. "What do you think, little pirate? Should we help him?"

Deena pretends to consider, but only long enough to kiss her mate on the cheek. "I suppose he can have our key. It's technically Gibli's, anyway."

"Don't tell him that." He smiles, then grows a little more somber as he returns his attention to the holoscreen in front of him. "The Sky key is yours, however, I cannot offer you fighters. I have too much to protect. Leaving Kor now is difficult…"

"Not for me, it isn't." A new voice chimes in and I see the door to whatever room Rhorkanterannu and his female are talking to me from open.

The human female with the flame-colored hair comes closer to the holoscreen. She's wearing impressive battle armor, but that isn't what startles me. Her eyes blaze black, brilliantly. She steps up next to Rhorkanterannu, a second Niahhorru pirate at her back that I know to be her mate. Herannathon.

He glares as he sees me, all four of his hands clenching into fists.

"My mate doesn't have any interest in doing anything to you but killing you, but I'd like to help." She crosses her arms over her chest and I notice some unusual-looking weapons at her belt. They look like mok biz batons, but have varying tips, some serrated, some electric, some blasters, all of them deadly. "Manila and Ashmara are my friends and, after having heard Manila's story, I don't blame you for what you did. Ashmara is the most shroving psychotic female these Quadrants have ever seen, but we'd miss her if she'd never crossed our paths.

"So, we're in." She slaps her male on the shoulder and he grunts out an angry, noncommittal reply. "Herannathon will gather a team. You tell me where you'll be and I'll bring the Sky key to you myself." Her eyes cloud black and I wonder what sort of transformation this is. Ashmara seemed to think she is pure human, but this is something different.

In either case, I offer her a nod in gratitude. An unusual sensation for me, I do not know that I have ever felt it before.

"Then that settles it. It looks like the Niahhorru are on your side after all, assassin. Herannathon and Nalia will bring you reinforcements. We will coordinate with Gibli on our rendezvous destination. He has access to our private channel. Deena and I will support you from here but assassin, let me tell you, if you think you will align the Lemorans to your cause, you may just take the title of most psychotic creature in the cosmos from the female you intend to rescue."

I do not reply, but offer him another nod while Gibli turns from me and begins to plot a course to our rendezvous point — where we'll meet *after* we get the Voraxians and Lemorans on board. "I will see you shortly Nalia, Herannathon."

Just before the line of communication closes, I hear the female called Deena offer a shrill rebuttal to her mate, "If Nalia's going, then so am I. She shouldn't get to have all the fun without me."

24

Jerrock

Spans later, I have negotiated my way onto the small planet of Heimo and have been granted an audience with the human Hu'Raku of the planet. Her mate, Krisxox, sits on her right and on the holoscreen occupying the entirety of the small, stately foyer of this relatively small home are the Raku and Rakukanna of Voraxia and their small kitling, a hybrid with purple skin. She is older than the other two hybrids who sit before me, each one bouncing on one of Krisxox's knees.

Though I attempt to be direct and clear, the kits continue to distract me. With swirling brown and red skin, the two little kits look just like me. Like I did, once. It is like looking into a strange mirror, seeing what my life could have been had I had two *parents*, had I been loved.

And I would trade none of it, because in this reality, Ashmara and I might never have shared the same breath.

I have made my demands, voiced my requests, made my appeal. Now, I sit and wait. The Hu'Raku is first to speak. She stands quickly, garnering the attention of both kitlings, who look up to her with fascination and awe.

One has white, frizzy hair, the other's is brown and straight to her shoulders.

"Of course we'll assist Ashmara. She has done more than assist us. And the Sky planet…while I don't generally approve of warfare, it seems to me that the Sky Architects are servants of pain and that their creations are not willingly made and should thus be liberated. The Architects themselves should be placed on trial…"

"There is no cage capable of holding them," says her mate. "If we go for them, we go to eradicate."

His female grimaces. She nods once. "Tri-God forgive me, I can think of no other option."

The Raku, the Rakukanna, and even her mate starts at this. "If Sv-the Hu'Raku is willing to enter the humans into battle to save one of our own, then it must be a battle worth fighting." She nods and looks to her mate. On his word everything hangs, and yet, it is a moot point. Because his Rakukanna has already decided for him.

He nods, a small smile playing on his lips. "You said *friends*. It's a concept we had not heard of before encountering these humans. But Ashmara is one of these…*friends*. You are not, but that does not seem to matter. My Rakukanna and the Hu'Raku of our people have already spoken. You have our allegiance. Who else have you allied to your cause?"

I take this moment to patch in Rhorkanterannu. Krisxox groans at the sight of the male that appears in the holoscreen to his left. "You," he hisses.

"*King* Krisxox," Rhorkanterannu replies.

But before either of them can begin what would surely be a battle of tongues, I light the other holoscreens, revealing the faces of all five Lemoran Clan

Chiefs, the Oosa Dua Reoran, a cluster of Oroshi Gibli contacted, a pack of Tevalope that owe Tintin a favor, and the hybrid Hypha female Manila. "And this does not include the countless bands of Eshmiri who have jumped at the opportunity to help us, too. By Tintin's latest count, we are two hundred and sixty ships bearing upwards of a thousand warriors, excluding Voraxia's reinforcements."

"You agreed to assist the Sky assassin, Raingar?" Raku says, speaking to the Clan Chief of Lemora directly.

The male sulks while his miriga beams beside him, shining like a star. "Of course we did. We love Ashmara." Love. That word again. The humans use it so freely, carelessly even, yet they always seem to mean it when they do.

"The Clan Chiefs of Lemora abhor Sky practices. We have lost many valuable members of our community to them," says Clan Chief Reyna. "It is time to put aside our differences and put a stop to them."

"And to put our past lives behind us," the miriga of Clan Raingar says. I wonder if she can ever truly understand how much her words resonate with me. "We need to work together in this."

Her mate simply emits a soft grunt, "Pagh."

The Hu'Raku and Rakukanna of Voraxia grin. It is the Rakukanna who says, "I suppose you should up your ship count to two hundred and sixty-two."

As I give her an inquisitive glance, the Hu'Raku says, "The Xhea and Okkari of Nobu will not want to miss out on a good battle, and I'm sure they'll have warriors interested in joining, too."

"These numbers are strong. More than I could have asked for — than *we* could have hoped for," I say, gesturing to Gibli and Tintin at my side, who are busy on their yamar boxes, coordinating with our other *friends* as to how to proceed, trying to enlist others to our cause, too.

"We have found the Sky planet using the key the Eshmiri sold to us," Clan Chief Bebette says, though she's interrupted.

"Sold to *me. I* paid for it…" Raingar grumbles, settling only when his miriga places her hand on top of his arm. She looks impossibly small next to him, yet she stands tall and as she smiles at him it is clear that this female, too, has a male who would bend gravitational fields for her.

"We also have coordinates for the planet. We will broadcast them now," Herannathon says.

"There is only one problem." My attention returns to the Raku of Voraxia. He leans forward in his seat, making the simple piece of werro wood appear like a throne. "With an army of this size, the Sky will see us coming from Quadrants away."

Rhorkanterannu in his holoscreen grins, stands, and brushes off the forearms of his lower arms using his upper hands. "Leave that to me."

25
Ashmara

Solars of pure darkness pass. The tube stuck into my arm keeps me fed. I don't have to urinate or defecate, which should scare the eck out of me, but nothing is more terrifying than the darkness. Time ceases to exist in its embrace.

So many times I reach for the muuir patch in my pocket, the one that Jerrock held. So many more times, I reach for the muuir in my pack. I even take the patches out and, using touch alone, I count them. There are thirty-four. But I don't take any. I tell myself that it's because muuir sucks in the dark — it's a solar light substance, meant to be enjoyed beneath a sun, or at least the harsh glare of an Eshmiri torch — but I'm not even sure that's the real reason I keep the peels on the patches in place.

I drift in and out of sleep. I drift in and out of desperation. I drift in and out of dreams but after enough time passes, I pull myself away from all of those containing Jerrock. I don't want him here, back with the Sky. I can't bring him with me. I drift in and out until, finally, I'm released.

I scream as the tube retracts violently from my body. I fall. The bottom of the holding cell drops out and I go with it. I land painfully on my left leg. Ecking comets. Doesn't feel good. Doesn't feel good at all. I reach for it and find the ground beneath me. It isn't rough and textured but hard and smooth. It's not cold, though it might as well be. Everything about it is unforgiving, why shouldn't it be cold, too?

I open my eyes. The room I'm in is white and looks just like most of the Sky ships I've had the pleasure of seeing the insides of. "A real beauty, this one," I offer on a cough. "Though the decor could use some sprucing up." My words come out in a grimace as I shove my hands beneath my chest and prop myself up.

The room is a sphere, very much larger than a ship. There is nothing in it except for me and no sign of an exit. White lights shine from the tops of the walls, radiating from the surfaces themselves, giving them an ethereal, almost pretty glow before dimming into solid walls. When I clear my throat, black splotches of yeeyar move through them at lightning intervals. It's creepy, but only because it's accompanied by the sensation of being watched. *Especially* because.

I wonder when the Architects will show their ugly faces. Since Jerrock refused to talk about them, I don't have any clue what they'll look like. What to expect. I *expect* to see more assassins, but I don't see those, either. Just yeeyar running through the walls and occasionally the floor and the ceiling.

I'm not left to wait too long, just long enough to get fully acquainted with my new holding cell, which, the longer I stare at it, has begun to remind me less of a cell and more of an *arena*.

Buuuut I won't think about that now, especially not with my hand twitching for the muuir in my pack as a random unmarked section of wall suddenly fills with black.

Like ink, the black congeals, amassing itself in one concentrated area before spilling *inward*. It moves as if a strong hand is dragging it out of water, a bucket of oil being dragged out of a well. Sinewy like a muscle and smooth like skin, it ripples out of the wall like living ink. I don't love it. I don't love it at all. And I like it even less when the…the thing *talks* to me.

"Prepare yourself to breed the horlax," it says, speaking in stilted Eshmiri but with an accent I've never heard. The accent is so distracting, I almost miss the meaning behind its words.

"Wait. You — you thing without a face — want me to *breed* with an ink blot?" I laugh with force, clutching my stomach and doubling over just for the theatre of it. Sir Ink — or maybe it's a Madame Ink? — doesn't answer except to shift and shimmer in the air. More black streaks through the walls, looking like liquid. The lights of the room brighten then dim before a prickling awareness causes the hairs on the back of my neck to stand on end.

I turn in time to see the walls of the room closing back together, closing *it* in. Against the white and occasionally black room, the sight of the colorful creature is jarring.

It has a huge yellow head, no lips, so as to better show off a mouth full of jagged and serrated shards of bright white teeth. A black tongue lolls out between them and hangs about four feet long. It whips at the air as if sensing through it, and slowly, it draws forward along whatever scent path pulls it. It has no ears and half of its bald pate is covered in the same reinforced stalyx Jerrock is. Its eye has been removed and replaced with a yeeyar shield that covers its entire forehead. Its nose is a pair of serpentine slits that remind me way too much of my lizard friends — so much so that I shudder. Its neck is as thick as my waist. It towers over me by two full body lengths and is nothing but a straight shot of muscle.

The creature's muscles look so heavy they seem to weigh it down, though I wonder if it even matters when so much of it is covered in stalyx. Most of that stalyx is covered in spikes and most of those spikes are barbed.

"Holy suns..." Sheer astonishment blitzes me and I just stand there agape for way too many moments, because I have none to spare. Meanwhile, Sir Ink has clearly done his duty. Now, the ink blot disappears back into the wall. I chase after it. "Yeeshee! I'd love to eck an ink blot! That sounds ecking fantastic! Wait!"

I slam into the wall so hard my wrists buckle. I bounce off of the hard surface and struggle to keep my footing while keeping weight off of my left ankle. It hurts. Who gives an eck if it hurts? I curse myself. I've got a bigger opponent to worry about.

I turn back around to face off against the creature of nightmares. "You must be uhh...Sir Horlax — can I call you Sir?" Sir didn't work so well with the ink blot, though, maybe I need to try something else. "Lord? How about Lord?"

It releases a bellowing roar that makes my whole body jump. The sound is horrifically loud, shatteringly so. It scrambles my thoughts and I stumble even though nothing has moved. Or has it? I'm not sure where I am. From what Jerrock described, I must be in one of the Sky towers high above stolen lands.

"Alright, not Lord then. How about Sire? King? King Horlax?" The thing tracks me with its giant yeeyar eye. I didn't realize how much I relied on Jerrock's bio eye to give me clues as to what he was thinking until now, because the yeeyar betrays nothing. I wonder what the horlax sees in my eyes now? Fear? I doubt that. I know I should, but I don't really feel afraid of it.

I knew when I shoved Jerrock into that pod that whatever end I'd meet would be a brutal one. I really don't want to breed this thing and I have no intention of bringing any kits into this universe, let alone a horlax prince. My hand strays to my pack. I reach inside and almost feel relief.

Finally.

It's been too long, the muuir answers me, like an old friend. *But muuir never really was a friend, was it?*

I grab the pouch of muuir and unfurl it, never letting the horlax out of my gaze. Not that I can see anything else. He covers half the distance of the room in just a few strides, using both of his meaty arms and strangely short legs to walk. In him I can identify not one species, though I know he must have been someone, once. I feel bad for him. I wonder, if you liberated him, would there be any memories in there at all from any other life?

He roars again and the screech tears me apart. My mind flickers black and I almost drop my muuir. Not the muuir! I scramble and grab it and hold it close to my chest. I start to peel the adhesive film off of the active sides of each of the patches and get ready to apply them. All at once.

Comets, muuir, how I've missed you. The little strips smile up at me against my palm and they don't have to say it, I know they've missed me, too. *But that's not love. It's really not.*

The horlax's tongue lashes out, extending another three feet and smacking the air in front of my outstretched hands. "Woah there, buy a female a horn of hibi first," I shout, cantering back.

The tongue lashes again and I see that it has tiny, bright green pustules covering most of it. Kind of like the ones he has covering his cock.

He's naked, his spiked metal and occasionally biological abdomen leading down to narrow hips that boast a cock so thin and long, I didn't understand what I was looking at, at first. Shaped like a pyramid, the thing has a freakishly narrow tip. Thoughts fleetingly cross my mind — how far up it would go, if it would hurt, what would rip — before I back away from it. Because I know I'm not going to make it far enough to find out. I won't allow that. *But I don't have to give in, do I? I could fight.*

The preposterous thought crosses my mind at the same time that I finally get the thirty-fourth piece of film free. Now, I have all of the strips staring beautifully up at me from my palm. I have to do it this way, because if I applied them one at a time, there's no way I'd be sober or coherent enough to apply the rest after a certain point and just a few won't kill me, or even knock me out enough to avoid feeling what the horlax has in store for me. But thirty-four? Yeeshee, thirty-four is plenty enough to kill me. Actually…I reach for my pocket…it's thirty-five…

Krakaw, that belongs to Jerrock.

Jerrock. My hand twitches. The thing lets out one more roar. A final surging thought surfaces within me and it carries images of his face, of the metal-made monster, of the brown-skinned hybrid he was before, of me and him, and of him letting me win time and time again, and of the few times he didn't let me win but took me for everything I had, and then plundered in search of more.

There's sweat on my skin and I look up in time to see the horlax charging for me, all teeth and metal and claws. Thoughts of Jerrock fall by the wayside and I release a grin.

I was right from the beginning, no need to be sidetracked.

Because there's never been a better time for one last muuir trip.

26

Jerrock

The pirates' machine is breathtaking. I have never seen such an achievement and I plan, first thing I do once I have Ashmara back in my arms, to steal it.

"Engines off. Too many signals will create interference with the mothership. Any yeeyar keys outside of the Niahhorru mothership must be turned off," Tebvarannos, a member of Rhorkanterannu's crew, relays orders through our speaker, as well as the speakers aboard every other ship in this armada. We are five hundred and eighty-nine ships strong, each ship a different shape and size than the one beside it. "This is too many, Nikkowerranorru. We've never run the machine with this many before," he says, though it's clear he's not speaking to the rest of us.

A muted reply. "Eh. If some of them get scrambled, who cares. Let's get on with it."

I would voice an argument if the Niahhorru hadn't cleverly turned all incoming broadcasts off. Now, all I can hear is their lead engineer, a male called Gerannu, attempting to placate Deena and fire on the device, which he does in…

"Five," says a human's voice, the one called Nalia, "four…three… The Sky have recalled many of their assassins. We'll be meeting two hundred and forty-nine assassins in open airspace surrounding Sky. There are sixty-three more concentrated on the planet itself… Two… Everyone ready? Good. One."

And suddenly my body is no longer a part of myself. I'm not flying, I'm not moving at all, I just am not where I was a moment previous.

Nausea stirs in my gut, but it passes quickly, even more quickly thanks to the immediate blaster fire this hunk of a ship takes. "Uuzu, Retro, the shields!" I shout, but they are already there.

The Eshmiri work as a single machine, racing around their decrepit one, firing on canons and blasters, activating shields and pulses. I man the controls and my flying is impeccable, controlled, targeted. The Eshmiri, on the other hand? They fire at will.

Niahhorru, Oosa and Oroshi ships flank me as I make my way through thick purple clouds and into the atmosphere of the planet. The blue-green world shimmers far below, its elegant curve decimated by the black stalagmite towers that mar its horizon. I head for the tallest one, the one most heavily guarded.

The battle that takes place across the sky is pure carnage. An Eshmiri ship beside ours falls, as does an Oosa. Our ship is not going to survive the battle, but that's alright, it doesn't need to. It just needs to get us to that…final…platform.

Boom.

An explosion shakes the wing of the ship. I grab the controls and force us up, just a little farther before the engine gives. We crash through the Sky docking platform and into the tower, the entire ship's weight causing the tower to sway. Reinforced yeeyar does not break or burn, but absorbs the chaos that hits it. The seat I'm in breaks free of its perch and I lurch out of it just before it slams through a hole in the side of the hull and explodes out into empty space.

I turn towards the back of the ship, currently engulfed in flame, and I charge right at it. I release a series of coordinated blasts, slice through the side of the ship and plunge into the tower.

We've crashed into a training room, where assassin creations are sent to compete against one another. You are only elevated to the status of an assassin after surviving the training. If you are deemed defective, the defective part is replaced. If you are deemed redundant, then you're decommissioned, your body incinerated.

Memories slam into me like knives causing me to stumble over the pristine white floor. I fling up a mental command and the yeeyar in my system reacts, doing what I tell it to do. It opens a door at the far end of the training room, one I leave open in case one of the Eshmiri manages to make it off of the ship and…and what? It would be a greater risk to the Eshmiri to leave it open than to simply close…

Whoosh. A blade slings past my face as I move into the corridor. I duck, narrowly avoiding it impaling me in the biological cheek. A whooping sound fills the hall and I look up and see three assassins barreling down the hallway towards me, one of them creating the sound with their mouth.

Tension threads my body as pain lances me through the ears, the sensation like needles. I grimace and fight against it, moving forward to meet the first assassin. Our blades clash, our stalyx body parts, too. I flag when the creature behind it begins its sickening whoop all over again, my mind becoming hazy. I take a blade to the thigh. It's hard to stand. Krakaw...krakaw, this can't be it. I've made it this far and the horlax...

A weapon slams into the face of the whooping creature, a long, sleek baton. An animated grunt sounds off behind me followed by a guttural cry, "Jerrock, get down!"

I fall, obeying the order though I do not know why. A lower position will put me at a disadvantage relative to the assassin I'm fighting, yet...I fight with *friends* this time... I fall regardless.

I hit the ground and, above my head, watch sprays of blaster fire hit the chests of the assassins, over and over and over again, accompanied by an ear-piercing screech, "Take that, you dead-eyed, shrov-for-brains assassins! Hahahahaha!" The wail is filled with delight and followed by another female's deep chuckle. "Deena, stun the assassins. We're meant to *stun* them."

"Oh shrov." A lull in the blaster fire causes one of the less injured assassins to stand and slink its way forward on Oosa legs and a Voraxian tail. It whips its tail at the assailant over my head, but I launch my stalyx arm up, grab the tail and sever it with my Voraxian sword. A model from Nobu, it has a curved and serrated edge. It cuts beautifully. I've never used a weapon to rival it. Simple, yet clean, cold and deadly.

"There we go." A blast sounds and I duck again, a burning sensation grazing the outside of my Drakesh arm as sparks shower over me.

The assassins in the hall roar in pain and in defeat. I imagine all three would have decommissioned themselves in that moment at such a failure, were they capable of movement. I kick up onto my feet, taking in the sight of the three assassins glued to the floor and walls by a sticky, glowing web made of a material I've never seen before.

I turn and see two human females, so small compared to the assassins they fight against, standing in the hall smiling at me. One carries what looks like a mok biz baton, the other a blaster almost as large as she is. It's this one who waves at me. "Jerrock, right? Nice to meet you, I guess. Now, can we get this show on the road before my mate catches up to me? He never lets me use the big blasters."

I can't decide if this female is insane or simply daft and decide that I don't care, so long as she doesn't point her blaster at me. The other female, however, watches me with greater suspicion and I know why. I've done her a great wrong.

"Thank you for coming," I say, though I can't believe the words are my own. I've never *thanked* anyone for anything before. *I didn't even thank Ashmara for freeing my mind. I will though. I will. Stars, please ensure I get the chance.*

"I owe Ashmara a thanks, so I don't need one from you now," says Nalia.

Deena nods. "I may not like it, but I'm here for her, too, because I owe her a couple."

I nod my understanding, because I also know that love doesn't work that way. Even if she owed them nothing, I don't doubt these humans would sacrifice all for her. "We must continue." I turn from them, starting down the hall, but Nalia calls me back.

"There's a better way. One guarded by only two assassins, not eight."

Shock renders me speechless, but I still trust the female enough to follow her when she backtracks down the hallway and takes the next. She follows a path I would have never thought to take, but that leads us nonetheless down routes that are entirely free of assassins.

"What is this?" I ask her and though the question is not well formed, she still understands what I mean.

"When you took me onto that Sky ship, your buddies inserted yeeyar into my system. Apparently it didn't take. Now, I can track Sky keys. They read in my sight as clearly as coordinates. That's how I know there are eleven Sky keys active on this floor. Eight behind us, but closing in. One just at the end of that hall."

I tense, distracted from her fascinating biology by the fact that this means... "You cannot sense another presence?"

"Centare," she says, hesitating. "But there *is* an active Sky key in that room and it looks...odd." She looks worried. Her concern plays out on her face in a way that makes me lose control.

Krakaw. Krakaw, krakaw, krakaw. She cannot have been given to the horlax already, she cannot have. The Architects would have kept her to run tests, to ensure that she would be capable of bearing the kit of that abomination... And yet as I fly down the hall, the scent of sweet, sweet muuir in the air gets thicker. It's a scent I know well and that I know belongs to her.

Krakaw. She hid muuir from me. She had more with her. The ecking...*reaver.* If she took too much muuir to escape the horlax, I will never forgive her. Not for finding a way out, but for giving up on me. She did not think I would come for her. She did not think I would be able to.

I throw open the door to the training arena at the end of the hall and burst through the opening my yeeyar creates. A body lies slumped over in the center of the room, a massive thing covered only in metal and rage. It's six times my size, larger than any Egama has ever been, but that does not stop me from charging straight at it, because I don't see Ashmara. If it lies on top of her, it will have killed her, even if it had been told not to, and I don't see her in the room.

Where is she? Did the Architects take her? Has she already been successfully bred? It doesn't matter if she has, I will free her from them and from that, too. I will not let her body be used as a vessel of malice. Her life is her own and if she chooses to hate me forever for my failings to protect her, then I will liberate her from me, too.

Even if it kills me.

I leap into the air and prepare to slam my blade down through the back of the horlax's neck when all of a sudden a weapon flies through the air towards the red skin over my beating heart. It's a knife. A radium knife. The one that I used to kill lizards on that alien planet only solars ago. It feels like forever. And only one being in the cosmos could have such a blade on them now.

She lives.

Her aim is true and firm and fierce, but I am so shocked by the realization that she might just be alive that I don't react quickly enough to stop it from grazing me. "Jerrock!" she shouts and the voice is her own, unaffected by pain or even by muuir.

I feel the brush of metal against my chest, piercing my skin so gently…before the blade is knocked off of its path by a mok biz baton. My feet hit the ground, the baton hits the ground, the blade hits the ground, Ashmara stands up.

Hidden behind the huge horlax, Ashmara had been invisible from where I stood. But now, looking up at her from where I crouch, I rake my gaze over every inch of her, finding not a scratch.

"Wh-wh-what?" I stutter. Have I ever stuttered before in my life? "You're alive."

"Of course I'm alive," she says with a wild, wide grin, which she casts towards the females who have entered the room behind me. I watch them congregate around their *friend*, wrap her up in their arms, tell her kind things I wish I could also tell her about how they are glad that she's safe and well and unharmed.

Her gaze continues to stray to me. She takes a step towards me and stumbles. The small act makes my heart want to rip out of my chest. I rush forward and catch her. She laughs as she gives me her weight and lets me pull her fully against my body. I want our clothes off. I want to feel her shape.

"So, did you miss me?" she says, trying to be glib. I don't answer. Cannot. "Jerrock? Are you shaking?"

I crush her lips with mine, kissing her for everything she's worth. Krakaw, for everything I am worth. I pull back only when I feel her struggle to catch her breath. I clutch her face in my hands and I make her a vow, "I would have followed you even to meet Death. And I will punish you for this."

She simply smiles, reaches up and pokes my nose with the tip of her finger. "As far as I'm concerned, this just makes us even." She raises up onto her tiptoes and breathes against my neck. "But I'll take my punishment any way you'd like to give it."

I bark out a laugh that causes Deena to cry out, "Shrov! Did he just laugh? Creepy…"

I ignore her and ask Ashmara, "How did you kill the horlax?"

"Oh, he's not dead," she says, giving his nearest limb a light kick. "He's just on a wild, wild ride. Having the time of his life, I'm sure. He'll wake up eventually. That much muuir won't kill him. I was just hoping by the time it wore off, we'd be best buddies. While he's high out of his mind, I've been telling him jokes. So far, I think he thinks they're pretty funny. My backup plan was just to cut his dick off. Would be kinda hard to breed me then."

My disbelief wars with my pride. "You are a foolish reaver."

"And you're a pretty lousy assassin." She grins. "I didn't think assassins knew how to make friends and here it looks like you've brought them all."

I smile down at her and softly touch her cheek. "And then some."

Deena's voice cuts in. "Uhh…guys?"

"Deena, get back!" Nalia screams.

I turn in time to see an Architect lunge from the wall directly at Deena. I throw myself in its path and it collides with my stalyx chest, scraping against it deeply enough to leave scars, even in metal. I roar and roll onto my back and then onto my feet. I duel the Architect, drawing it away from the females, using every ounce of concentration I have not to be impaled by each yeeyar splinter it throws at me.

"What is it!" Deena shouts.

"An Architect," I reply between heaving breaths. The Architect has drawn blood four times and has yet to reveal itself.

"What the fuck? It's not solid!" Nalia shouts. "How do you kill it?"

"It was once…a biological thing." I duck and dive, cut and dodge. "It still…has a heart. Pierce it."

"Females," Ashmara says, "don't let that ugly ecking Architect touch him. He's *mine*."

Time passes. The battle continues. The four of us are flagging, though the Architect is not. We have succeeded in making three attempts on the heart, which has revealed itself four times, but none of our blasts, stabs or spears have stuck.

"It's too well guarded," Ashmara huffs at my side, weaseling herself there every time I attempt to place her at my back. Deena's ammo must be running low. Two of Nalia's batons have been obliterated.

"We should fall back, find the others," Deena pants.

"Oh shrov…don't look now, but I think that ugly thing has brought a friend." I turn and see Nalia's assessment rings correct. A section of the wall becomes black before a yeeyar form appears…and then comes a third. "Eck, Jerrock…how many of these things are there?"

"Six."

"Six?" The panic in Ashmara's voice doesn't make me feel good. Because I feel it, too. I've felt it since we saw the first one.

No one has ever gone up against an Architect and lived.

The Architects begin to move in sync with one another, surrounding us, pressing us closer and closer together until all four of us stand with our backs nearly flush. We are outflanked and outgunned. We need…

The first of the Architects lunges. This is it. My final moment. I leap to throw myself in front of Nalia, but just as I get one foot off of the ground, the wall to my left explodes.

The Architect redirects, lunging through the smoke. I hear a curse uttered in Meero, followed closely by, "Deena, there you shroving are. Don't you ever…Shrov! Nikko, get that shroving…"

"Stab it in the heart!" Deena screams.

Nalia shrieks, her baton flying as another Architect attempts to close in on us from the right. Ashmara shoves her out of the path of the Architect just in time to avoid its strike. I charge the Architect, resuming my dance in this deadly battle, Ashmara moving to my right. I find that we move in sync and together, we manage to divide the Architect's attention.

"Ashmara, centare!" Nalia cries.

Ashmara pitches forward, attacked from behind. I turn and the Architect I had not seen punches me with the full force of its yeeyar and I take flight. I slam into the opposite wall and collide with the floor. From there, I look up helplessly as two Architects close in on my female… I roar out my rage just as another hole in the wall appears. There stands a female I recognize, Manila, her arm outstretched, her command over the yeeyar in this place the same as mine — unwavering. She has two Eshmiri at her side, Gibli and Tintin, along with a dozen Eshmiri I don't recognize.

They burst into the room with…with *darts* in their mouths and begin firing them around at every dark entity they come across while, in their midst, Manila begins blowing on a *whistle.* I grin and nearly laugh, despite the pain rolling through me and the panic affecting my pulse, because I know the Architects do not expect this. They would not have seen this coming in a thousand eons. Such a crude tool wielded by such a wily bunch and the effect…the effect is nothing short of mesmerizing.

The Architects hit with darts begin to *disintegrate* around the area of the dart, the mesh of yeeyar holding them together unraveling and exposing their hearts.

A blast fires through one, the weapon belonging to one of Rhorkanterannu's pirates, perhaps the *king* himself. I lunge for Ashmara, wrapping her up in my arms as I spin her away from an Architect and it falls, looking to grab hold of anything in its last fit of desperation. I pull the radium knife from Ashmara's back pocket and stab at the heart box held aloft by a few black strings only. The heart is a strange shape, like a lumpy star.

That is a Voraxian heart, or a Drakesh one. And as the yeeyar collapses in a puddle of spilled ink around a defunct Sky key and a biological heart with a protective shell encasing it, I think it feels, in many ways, like I'm killing myself. Not all of me. Just a part. I watch the organ, slick with copper blood, take its final beat. This Architect was not born this way. It was made.

This could have been me…

A hand finds mine in the dark and pulls me back and I look into two eyes beaming with light and love sitting in a dark brown face spattered with blood and I smile.

Krakaw, it could not.

27

Jerrock

It takes the better part of a solar to eradicate the remaining Sky Architects and another two solars to capture the surviving assassins. Even without the Architects to guide them, they do not lay their arms down. We fight through the lunar, we fight through the solar until it is done.

And then all of a sudden, it is done.

The Voraxians busy themselves attempting to make contact and make peace with the creatures of this planet, and provide them aid, where needed. The reavers are busy providing the antidote to one assassin at a time, liberating them until the ionine runs out, which the Lemorans are happy to replenish. The Oosa have gone back to Quadrant Eight, taking the Oroshi with them. The pirates are busy scavenging the towers for technology and hoarding it away.

I snort at the sight of Nikkowerranorru attempting to drag out an entire Sky weapons kit, four times his own size. "Get away from that before you blow us all to the sky!" Gerannu shouts after him.

I stand on the edge of the platform looking out at half spears of broken towers wrapped up in orange winds. A cloudy purple breeze blows by. All I hear is chaos. All I feel…

A small hand slides into mine but there's something between us, separating her skin from mine. "This belongs to you."

I look down and see a slip of muuir against my palm, the one I carried. I toss it into the wind, then grab her around the waist and quickly pull her in front of me against the edge of the platform. If I let go of her, she'd fall to Death's embrace. But she doesn't seem frightened of him. Perhaps, I shouldn't be either.

Because more interesting than death is love, is life.

"Neither of us needs it anymore," I tell her, pulling her closer still. I want to feel as much of her against as much of me as decency will allow. I want to feel her on my bio side, against the warmth of my skin.

"That's definitely true. After seeing how bad the horlax looked on muuir, it makes me wonder how I could have ever taken the stuff willingly. He looked wrecked." She chuckles and slides her arms around my neck and we just stand there and hold one another while the yeeyar twitches beneath our feet.

I grimace, thinking of how monstrous the acts against the creature were. "He is at peace now."

"I hope so."

We stand for some time more, thinking of everything, nothing. Exhaustion and adrenaline war for my attention, but they both lose, as they will lose every time. Because she has all of it and then some.

"I can't believe everybody came and fought the Sky for me," she says, sounding so genuinely surprised I have to take a moment to pull back and examine her face. She does not seem to understand her magnetism.

It's a facet of her character that's both lovely and fascinating. She stands out like a sore thumb wherever she goes, yet in all settings is so natural at the same time.

She is a wild thing.

She is a soft thing.

She is twelve ounces of perfection in a ten-ounce cup.

And no matter where she goes, one thing I'm finding clear above all else — she is loved. She is so immeasurably loved.

"They are your friends. Of course they came for you."

"Friends? I've tried to kill at least half these creatures before. Just talk to Krisxox. He'll tell you how friendly we are."

I chuckle, having heard the story from Hunhun and Uuni before. "You should be more surprised that they rallied behind *me* to come for you, when I am the most hated male in the cosmos."

Ashmara smiles up at me, her grin as bright white as her eyes until they shine all the colors, all at once, all for me. The canvas of the sky has nothing on such majesty. "The most hated male, Jerrock?" She clicks her tongue against the back of her teeth. "Krakaw, you are the most loved."

With that simple declaration, she places my hand on her chest over her heart and I am taken to new places, to new worlds, to new galaxies.

Suddenly, she laughs and I can tell that it is directed at me this time. "Is that a little tear there in your eye, Jerrock the assassin?" She tries to rub her finger beneath my bio eye, but I beat her to it and snatch up her fingertips. I kiss every one.

"Of course not."

She just squeezes me tighter around the waist as the next harsh breeze rolls through. She wavers on her right leg given that her left one is injured. I will fix it, though. I will fix everything for her for eternity. For forever. And occasionally, I'll let her fix me, too.

"Krakaw? Not a tear? Then maybe a little color. Just a spot of blue?" she teases.

I don't care what color she pretends she sees. For her, I am all of the colors under the stars and within them. For her, I am weightless. Because for me, she is everything.

"Perhaps, but only a little, then."

She squints and cocks her head to the side while behind her, I can see her Eshmiri arguing with a cluster of pirates over which Sky ship they get to strip, because despite the current state of their hunk of junk, the Eshmiri want to fix it. They don't want a new ship.

They say it's family, too.

"I guess I'll have to try harder to elicit a reaction out of you, then." Her eyes flash purple.

My shaft, swollen already after the heat of such a battle, begins to thicken, stiffen and yearn for her. "What did you have in mind?"

Her left eyebrow lifts and she bites her lower lip in a way that makes me instantly, fully erect. Then she has the gall to lean forward on the balls of her feet and excitedly say, "Gibli says there's a big kintarr deal going down between the Lemorans and the Walrey over that disgusting honey you served me once. We could go steal some of it. Or Deena and Nalia are planning a huge mok bir tournament on Kor. It's supposed to be even bigger than the one on Evernor." Her eyebrows waggle, all hints of suggestiveness gone. I laugh. "What? The stakes are high. Half the known Quadrants have made bets on who will win. Nalia's entering. My tokens are on her, always."

"I wouldn't bet against her." I comb Ashmara's blood-soaked curls behind her ear, grateful that so much of the blood doesn't belong to her, but to creatures who can't hurt her anymore. Too far gone, the horlax…was decommissioned.

"Manila also told me about a new planet. Small and far away, it's supposed to have some killer parties — if you survive the giant snakes, that is." I am about to ask a question about this mysterious place, but excitedly, she continues, "Or we could check out Deena's beach planet. Heqama? Hebama? I can't remember what she named it, only that there are humans living there now. But not too many. There's still uninhabited parts of it. Wild places we could explore together.

"We could join the pirates on their next raid, too. They said they're harvesting some kind of substance — supposed to be even more rare than kintarr and just as powerful. Planet's small and rugged. It doesn't have access to any of the other Quadrants, but apparently some of the beings that live on it can breathe fire. Could be cool to see, krakaw?"

"It would indeed." I rub my thumb across her forehead and across the smooth skin of her chest. I feel her heartbeat, just the one — thump, thump, thump — even and anchoring.

She perks up, eyes alight with mischief in shades of silver and green. "Or we could try to find Earth, the planet the humans came from, and see what's left of it. Or we could…"

"Yeeshee," I tell her.

"Yeeshee what? Which one do you want to do? We have a lot of time to make up for," she says, giving my body a tight, tight squeeze.

I smile, because she is right and also because she is wrong. She is my Xiveri mate. There is nothing but time for us. Eternities of it, in every life born to us in these Quadrants and beyond. I lean down and brush my lips over hers and against them I whisper, "All of it, my little fighter. I'll do all of it with you."

And that's a wrap! The full length novels in the Xiveri Mates saga are complete with Ashmara and Jerrock's story. Enjoyed it? Leave your review Amazon.

Sign up to my mailing list to find out what projects are next in store for me, including details on the exclusive Xiveri Mates collector's and NSFW editions coming out soon: www.booksbyelizabet.com/contact

Haven't had enough Xiveri Mates? Visit Revatu for a Xiveri Mates quickie. Keep reading for a preview or for ideas on what to read next!

Then, complete your collection by adding Exiled from Nobu, Jaxal and Lisbel's story and the shortest novella, to your shelves.

I'll see you again, my friend,

Elizabeth

Taken to Revatu

Xiveri Mates Book 10, a Novella (Latanya and Grizz)

Crash-landed on an alien planet where everything seems to want to kill her, nothing is worse than the male she crash-landed with. She'd rather jump right off of the edge of this cliff than give into his demands, even if jumping means landing in the arms of a huge, tusked green beast who says she's his.

Available on Amazon in ebook or in print anywhere paperback books are sold

1

Grcyxz

I watch the space junk arc across Revatu's perfect green sky in great balls of blue fire. Beautiful. I set down the chrxzyt nut I've been separating from its fleshy outer shell and look across the small orchard at Bebetu and Orick. Orick's upper lip curls back even further, revealing the tips of his tusks. He slings his shearing blade over his shoulder. I stake mine into the ground — a challenge. I don't need a blade to best him and take whatever this haul of space junk brings in.

Bebetu sneers, her tusks jutting from her lower jaw to press into her upper lip — a miniature version of my own tusks, which are among the thickest and sharpest in our pride. The large flaps of her ears twitch in irritation, or perhaps anticipation.

I take off at a run, make it to the edge of Revatu before they do, and then jump off of the edge of the island.

2

Latanya

Rax! Rax, rax, rax. "Rax!" I shout the word out loud that's been repeating in my mind on an endless loop.

He's got me cornered. Rock and a hard place take on a new definition. Rocks aren't my problem.

Negunn is my problem.

The cliff behind me is my problem.

The frothing pink water below it is my problem.

And my biggest problem? This brown, gelatinous, raxing magma goo that's creeping slowly across the forest floor — somehow not disturbing the trees or the bushes at all, but meanwhile incinerating the remains of the wrecked pod I had to bash my way out of. The tracking device built into the hull that I had hoped to use is gone. I don't even know if my parents crashed onto this planet or another one, or if they made it anywhere at all.

Maybe, they're still lost in space.

What if they die there? What if I never find them? My heart seems to pound against all my organs at once, everything squeezing tight in terror as I look across the shrinking space between Negunn and me, hating him beyond any hatred I've ever felt toward him before.

And I've always hated him.

But right now, for all I know, the only beings on this planet might be me and Negunn and, even if we were literally the last two souls left on this planet, I'd still prefer the magma. I glance at it just as the last of the kintarr exterior of my pod's hull crackles spectacularly in a show of color and light, and then dies.

Alright, perhaps I prefer the fall.

I glance over my shoulder. There's only about a dozen steps between me and the cliff's edge. I glance at the trees towering above me, some leaning out over the steep, death-defying drop as if in defiance of gravity, completely unconcerned for the frothing pink waters below. Some of the branches and the thick vines hanging from them look close enough to touch... If I were to jump out over the water, I might be able to reach the one...

But I won't.

"Come on, Latanya. You know you never had a choice in this."

Maybe, I'll have to fight.

"That's not true." I ball my hands into fists and Negunn glances down at them.

He laughs. "We can do this the easy way or the hard way."

"What's the easy way? Because with you things have been hard our whole lives." I slam my fist down onto my thigh, which trembles in the aftermath of the crash. Maybe, the shock. Maybe I'm injured. I wouldn't know. My adrenaline is thrashing wildly through my body, making me hot, making me want him to attack. "I don't understand you! You're a Quadrant One prince. The females all think you're attractive. You're from one of the wealthiest lines in the Quadrant. You could have any female you want!"

His eyes narrow when I say that and his smile slips into something more menacing. A frown. "Not any female."

"You want me because I don't want you?"

"Why don't you want me?" He gestures to his chest, which is bare because it always is. He knows how he looks. He is the prodigal son of Quadrant One, every prince's perfect archetype. Gold skin that shimmers in the light, rainbow-colored hair that falls in perfect waves to his earlobes and never looks mussed no matter how many times he runs his fingers through it. Striated eyes that are turquoise and gold and pink. I've seen him naked before at the royal bath houses and he's got a gigantic cock and is perfectly fit. Muscular thighs. Manicured feet. He's rich. He's intelligent. On paper, there's no reason not to want him.

Except, I'd rather take the magma. Or jump for the trees.

"You're a creep!" The magma is casting heat. Fifty feet away and closing in from the left, it isn't moving fast, but if it gets within a stone's throw, I won't have any choice but to follow the path to the right — the one Negunn is blocking.

"You're just an adopted hybrid oud," he sneers the insult. It's a universal insult for hybrid bastards, the lowest of the low. It stings when he says it, even though he's said it before. My mom told me that words only have power if you let them, but I'm not sure that's true.

"Your mother is hideous and your father was outcast from the royal family for mating her. Their union is frowned upon by the universe. Even though he is your mother's Xiveri mate and her horns flake white for him, they couldn't reproduce. That's the only reason you're on Quadrant One at all. Because no one else in the entire galaxy wanted you besides two freaks that couldn't produce a kit of their own."

I grit my teeth, bored of this. Insults against my parents are insults I've heard before and I don't care for them. They used to bother me when I was younger, but my spine was tempered and steeled by the love of my parents — the two greatest beings in this universe, of that I'm sure — and I have no time for this. There's raxing magma coming!

I cock my head and wipe my hands off on my shift — the threadbare tunic all that's left after I shed my heavy golden outer dress. "And you ask why I don't want to be with you…"

"Come with me, consent to marry me, and I'll step off the path and make sure you get out of here and stay safe against whatever beasts inhabit this planet." He gestures to the magma with a flick of his elegant hands.

"I'd rather jump."

"Then do it! Because I'm not raxing moving unless it's with your consent and your hand." He licks his lips and brushes his hand through his hair. I can see the sweat beading on his forehead, which makes me realize that I'm also sweating.

"We're running out of time, Negunn…"

"You're running out of time. That raxing stuff will get to you a lot sooner than it'll get to me." He crosses his arms over his chest and I pray to the stars for a comet or asteroid or whatever it was that blew apart the Paradise Voyager — one of the largest and most elite intra-Quadrant cruise ships ever built — to come here and land on top of Negunn's perfect rainbow head. "So what'll it be, Latanya? Is death really preferable to a lifetime with me?"

From the first time he insulted my Lemoran mother when I was a child, to the first time he petitioned the Court to have my father stripped of his title, to the first time he ruined the reputation of another Quadrant One prince who made me an offer...my answer has always been the same.

Yeffa. A thousand times yeffa.

I look at the glittery grey branches covered in glittery green leaves jutting out from the edge of the cliff in defiance of gravity. Thick charcoal vines drip from their boughs towards the raging ocean below, which is frothing and snarling up at us like the mouths of diseased beasts. My resolve sets. My mother, if she saw me now, would scream. My father would kill me.

I don't answer him. I just turn and run towards the edge of the cliff as if my life depended on it...because it might.

I'm three paces away from the cliff's edge when I hear thrashing. I look over my shoulder and lose my footing. I looked too late.

Negunn's full weight slams into my side and he takes me down to the soft, dewy undergrowth. Leaves, twigs, and branches in assorted shades of glittery browns, blues, greys and greens crunch underneath our collective weight. He smells great, like some expensive cologne. It makes me want to vomit all over him.

His breath even smells clean, like he just chewed bray leaves, when he leans down and says against my cheek, "I knew I'd get you under me eventually." And I hate him for it.

I thrash in his grip as he tries to contain my wrists. "Negunn!"

Taking both of my wrists in one of his much larger hands, he hauls me upright. His gaze skims the length of my shift. I had it on underneath the ballgown I'd been wearing earlier — a ballgown that's now being repurposed as magma fodder. He meets my gaze and smiles from up close and I can't help it.

All this anger and rage and frustration at how he's wasting my raxing time when I should be going to try to find my parents and the other survivors bubbles up into my face and bleeds into my mouth and expels itself as a wad of spit. The slobber slaps him right on the chin and Negunn looks so taken aback by it, I laugh at his reaction.

He releases me, shoving me to the right, up the path he'd been blocking before. I think this might be my chance for escape but the moment I pivot, he grabs a swatch of my bright white hair and yanks me back. His other hand finds my cheek in the form of a fist. He hits me once in the face and a second time in the stomach.

Pain splinters through me, but I somehow manage to keep my feet and stagger away. Delirious, I continue. I hear Negunn come after me but he curses a moment later. I slip and fall against a large tree trunk. My heart is beating in my head and my stomach is throbbing in my toes.

I blink open swelling eyelids and turn around to see something rather curious. I grin. Knee-high, dark purple flowers are opening up on the ground, puckering as if in anticipation of the magma and then eating it. But what's more interesting is that these flowers are big and

Negunn stepped into the center of one and it doesn't seem to want to release him.

Good note.

He's pulling on his leg, trying to free it before the magma comes. I hope he can't. I stagger away. "Don't you dare leave me like this! I'm your mate!"

"Psycho!" I shout over my shoulder. I don't stop running.

I follow the edge of the cliff for so long, I lose feeling in my feet. The foliage is rough and scratchy and I've got cuts up my legs, up to my knees. The stinging in my stomach and face reduce to a dull throb and I continue cursing Negunn under my breath until the single enormous sun in the sky changes tint from orange to yellow to a pale blue as it descends towards the frothy pink horizon. There's ocean as far as my eyes can see.

A few crazily-shaped islands stud the skyline, disrupting the pink water. Each one is composed of pale tan rock jutting straight up out of the water. Green covers the tops of the plateaus, some of which are relatively flat, while others seem more mountainous, like the island I'm on that has hills whose crests only become visible when when I peek up through gaps in the canopy of trees.

At points, I think I hear Negunn calling my name, hunting for me through the jungle. At other times, I come across more of those glittery gobbling flowers. I avoid those. I have to double back at two terrifying points when I hit more streams of mahogany magma, and then a third time when the jungle just gets too dense to pass through, until I eventually break through a small clearing where a bunch of trees have fallen…and I see why.

"Mom! Dad!" I shout at the wreckage of a dozen pods. Maybe even more. Metal odds and bobs and kintarr crystals lie shattered all over the forest floor but, as I begin picking through the wreckage, it's clear that the site has been abandoned for a while. I wonder where they fled…and what drove them out…

I try to find signs that one of the pods might have belonged to my mom or my dad, but they're all identical shells. They look like corkscrews with a central hull in the center large enough for one person and some supplies.

Pain shoots up my left leg. "Rax," I hiss. I lift my left foot and see a huge shard of pale pink kintarr jutting out of the sole of my foot. Produced primarily on Lemora, kintarr is both beautiful and tough and is our primary source of power on Quadrant One. And it's expensive. Perhaps, the most expensive substance in the known Quadrants.

My dad used to trade in kintarr and the part of me that used to help him out in his business grieves to see so much of it wasted here on the forest floor, soon to be consumed by magma. It's only be a matter of time.

I glance around, wondering what produces the magma, but I seem to have stumbled into a kind of depression and I can't see much of anything through the dense canopy up above and its rich web of tree branches dripping in vines and hanging moss, like the gowns of Quandrant One princesses whose pretty parasoles shield against the sun.

I shiver even though it's hotter than an oven out here with the one great sun punching as big as a fist in the face of the sky. I waver on my one good foot. My swollen right eye and cheek twitch and a bout of dizziness falls over me like a veil. I reach out and catch myself on the outer hull of the nearest pod, but it's sharp and digs into my palm. Rax.

"Okay, okay… Rest. Regroup, Latanya."

I hunker down into the blown open side of one of the pods, careful not to cut myself getting in. The seat hovers above my head and safety straps dangle down around my shoulders as I take a seat. They've all been cut. Hm. Someone escaped from here. Hope. I start pushing at the panels to release supplies, groaning as I stretch my legs out in front of me. The glass cut in fairly deep. It'll be hard to walk on.

"Luckily, all of these pods have med packs." I bang my fist on the large drawer marked with a circle with two dots inside. It springs open and I grab the grafting wand and a roll of waterproof bandaging.

I shove a tube of nutrition supplement into my mouth and concentrate on sucking on the sweet-tasting block instead of on how badly my hands are shaking as I extract the shard of kintarr from my foot. Tears well in my eyes and drip down my cheeks as I do, but I brush them back, body filling with warm relief as soon as I get the grafting wand turned on.

Small orange light dances between the tip of the wand and the sole of my foot as the device mends the deep tissue. By the time I've finished, all that's left is a dull throb and a scab. Still not great to walk on, but it'll do.

"It'll do."

I take the grafting wand to my other cuts, though it won't do any good for my eye. Finished, I let the wand thunk down against the metal interior of the hull while my head thunks back against the wall. It's cramped in here, dark, too. And outside, the sounds of things are getting louder. If it were thing singular, I'd suspect it's Negunn and prepare for war, but there are many things outside now and Negunn, I know, travels alone. Must be animals.

I haven't seen any animals so far, which frightens me given how many things I can hear now. Maybe they only come out during the lunar. I shove another nutrition pack into the corner of my mouth and slurp from the hydration tube as I start to look for a light source and something to defend myself with.

I nudge a drawer open that should have contained a spare bodysuit and a pair of boots. The bodysuit's gone, but the boots were left behind and shrink around my foot until they're nice and snug. Outside, somethings thrash violently through the brush.

"Rax." I bite my bottom lip and poke through cabinets and cupboards faster. The thrashing gets louder, punctuated now by thwacks and growls. Many of them. Freeing a space blanket jammed in the back of the drawer, I drag it quickly over the top of the shell before hunkering down and renewing my search for a weapon. The weapons cache has been totally emptied. While it may mean bad news for me, it also means that there were survivors. I will find them. I am not dying here.

Heat more violent than the thrashing outside thrashes through my veins while strength and determination steel my arms. I yank an exposed beam off of the back of the chair above my head. It doesn't come easily and by the time I get the warped metal free, the thrashing sound is nearly on me. Clearly, the blanket is providing zero cover. I look up, waiting for an animal to pop its ugly maw through the opening — or worse, for Negunn to — while my body burns, ready…

Sort of.

While I hold the beam in a death grip, I wonder absently if the seat it was attached to helped whoever was in here survive — my mom, my dad, maybe? Hopefully? Maybe it was even Prince Algerathon or Prince Wegerawe, two princes I expected to get an offer from on Paradise Voyager before Negunn got in the way.

My mouth is dry. The thrashing is louder. Separating itself from the thrashing is the sound of…of steps. Footsteps. Oh rax. Negunn…he must have tracked me here. Raxing suns, the bastard just doesn't quit!

I pull my feet underneath my ass, ignore the throbbing in my left foot and my right eye, and scrunch up into as compact a ball as possible. Every single muscle in my body is poised to spring. My hands are numb around the metal beam. It's gold, except for the jagged edges, which are black and silver, like they were burned. But there's no blood in here. They survived. Just like I'm going to. Maybe. Definitely. Hopefully.

I bite my bottom lip just as the blanket tears free and a face appears and it — rax. Well, it isn't Negunn and he looks far too surprised to see me to be a beast.

"Ermmm…" The word is mine, not his, and he jerks back momentarily before huffing out violently between his teeth — well, not exactly teeth. Tusks. Thick ivory tusks jut up from his bottom jaw, so long the sharpened tips press into his upper lip, going so far as to nearly frame his nose. Even without them, he'd still look every bit the predator, with his black slashes for eyes and huge, hulking frame. Atop layers and layers of muscle, his skin is a mottled green, dark and light all mixed together. I wonder if he isn't some form of Egama giant hybrid because I've never seen any other species with that coloring — or quite so massive — before. Then again, I know for a fact this isn't an Egama-controlled planet. And I also know that no Egama giants have blood red claws…

Trying not to focus too hard on the serrated blades sticking out of his hands that already look like they've been dipped in my blood, I take inventory of the rest of him and decide where exactly I might best run him through. Built like a raxing tree with a network of roots, he looks a bit too solid and dense for my flimsy metal but, rax it. I'm going to try anyway, because there's not a doubt in my mind that this…this orc, creature, ogre thing is deadly and I did not crash land on this inhospitable planet, survive and escape Negunn only to get eaten like a roast by this thing and his friends!

I shoot up onto my feet, the top of my head rising only as high as his pecs, and with a loud grunt, I strike for his abdomen. I fall short when he reaches out and captures the edge of my beam, which doesn't so much as scratch him, and easily takes it away from me.

Well, rax.

What to read next

Lord of Population (Population Book 1)
When Abel comes across one of the alien overlords, she loots his corpse, the good little scavenger she is. She doesn't expect his death to be erm, temporary. He hunts her down and gives her a choice. Accept his help... The catch? She's now his.

This is a sci-fi, fantasy, post-apocalyptic romance mashup with a guaranteed HEA and plenty of slow burn steam. Tropes include enemies-to-reluctant allies-to-lovers, found family, he falls first, he rescues her, she rescues him, she has a nightmare, "who did this to you", one bed

The Hunting Town (Twisted Fates Book 1)
Drugs, cartels, the mafia. Pain, greed, and revenge. These are what Plumeria brought with her when she took a new job tending bar in the fighting pits outside of town – fighting pits owned by five men, known as the Brothers. Knox wouldn't have put anything before his brothers – not even his own life – until he met Mer. But when her life is put at risk, he intervenes, dragging his entire family into her world.

This is a romantic suspense featuring two couples that both reach their HEA. The first couple are two cage fighters, the second a medical student turned exotic dancer and the grump who owns the club. Plenty of steam and mayhem await.

Dark City Omega (Berserker Kings Book 1)
There are three absolutes for any Omega who has the misfortune of finding herself in Paradise Hole:

The first - stay away from the cities.
The second - stay off the road.
The third - stay away from Alphas.

Echo knew the rules. She just never expected to be hunted by a lord among Alphas, by a Berserker himself, the savage of Dark City. But he's been on her scent for six weeks.

And now, he's found her.

Coming soon, this is an action-packed dark fantasy romance ripe with spice, magic, and battles and perfect for fans of diverse books, possessive heroes and strong lady leads. Tropes include omegaverse, enemies-to reluctant allies-to lovers, fated mates-ish, one sleeping mat, trek through the forest together, she's injured, he saves her, she saves him, grumpxgrump

All Books by Elizabeth

Berserker Kings - Enemies to lovers. With magic.
Dark City Omega, Book 1 (Echo and Adam)
more to come!

Population - Battles and Heroes that Bite.
Lord of Population, Book 1 (Abel and Kane)
Monster in the Oasis, Book 2 (Diego and Pia)
Immortal with Scars, Book 3 (Lahve and Candy)
more to come!

Twisted Fates - Mafia. Brotherhood. Murder.
The Hunting Town, Book 1 (Knox and Mer, Dixon and Sara)
The Hunted Rise, Book 2 (Aiden and Alina, Gavriil and Ify)
The Hunt, Book 3 (Anatoly and Candy, Charlie and Molly)

Xiveri Mates - Aliens. Heat. New Worlds.
Taken to Voraxia, Book 1 (Miari and Raku)
Taken to Nobu, Book 2 (Kiki and Va'Raku)
Exiled from Nobu, Book 2.5, a Novella (Lisbel and Jaxal)
Taken to Sasor, Book 3 (Mian and Neheyuu) *standalone
Taken to Heimo, Book 4 (Svera and Krisxox)
Taken to Kor, Book 5 (Deena and Rhork)
Taken to Lemora, Book 6 (Essmira and Raingar)
Taken by the Pikosa Warlord, Book 7 (Halima and Ero)
*standalone
Taken to Evernor, Book 8 (Nalia and Herannathon)
Taken to Sky, Book 9 (Ashmara and Jerrock)
Taken to Revatu, Book 10, A Novella (Latanya and Grizz)
*standalone

Collections

Xiveri Mates - Aliens. Heat. New Worlds.
Collection 1: Books 1-3 + Exiled from Nobu
More to come!

Audiobooks

Xiveri Mates - Aliens. Heat. New Worlds.
Taken to Voraxia, Book 1 (Miari and Raku)
Taken to Nobu, Book 2 (Kiki and Va'Raku)
Taken to Sasor, Book 3 (Mian and Neheyuu) *standalone
More to come!

French Language

Passion Xiveri : Unis Pour La Vie – Des extraterrestres. De la sensualité. De nouveaux mondes.
Capturée par le Roi de Voraxia, tome 1 (Miari et Raku)
Convoitée par le Seigneur de guerre de Nobu, tome 2 (Kiki et Va'Raku)
Kidnappée par le Métamorphe de Sasor, tome 3 (Mian et Neheyuu) *l'intrigue se situe hors du Quadrant 4*
D'autres livres seront bientôt publiés !